Triple Power Play 4

Obsessed Player's Club

Jessica Lyn

COPYRIGHT

Copyright © 2025 by Jessica Lyn

authorjessicalyn.com

All rights reserved. No part of this book may be reproduced in any form or by any electronic or mechanical means, including information storage and retrieval systems, without written permission from the author, except for the use of brief quotations in a book review.

This book was not created with AI. This is a work of fiction. Names, characters, businesses, places, events, and incidents are used in a fictitious manner and are a product of the author's imagination. Any resemblance to actual persons, living or dead, or actual events is purely coincidental.

This book series was originally published in September 2023 on Kindle Vella.

Edited by studioenp

Copyediting and Proofreading: The Fiction Fix

Cover design by Lori Jackson @lorilovesbooksjackson

Cover Photo by Michelle Lancaster @lanefotograf

Formatting by Prince Finnick @princefinnickreads

Warning: Please read!

First and foremost, your mental health is important.

This series is a dark romance, and although it's not as dark as others, it does contain themes of mental illness, including intrusive thoughts and ideations, past trauma, flashbacks, addiction, and substance use. Book four also contains graphic violence and kidnapping.

Please understand everyone's journey and experience with mental illness, trauma, addiction, and pregnancy are different.

This is a work of fiction.
The men are manipulative and over the top.
The sex is explicit.
The characters in this series are imperfect but no less deserving of love.
'Fixing' them is not within the plot.

Please do not read if that is not your thing.

Warning: Please read!

This series was originally published on Kindle Vella in September 2023. Current events and other similarities are purely coincidental.

Visit authorjessicalyn.com for a full list of content and trigger warnings.

*For those who dream of a villain to chase away their nightmares,
you have found your family.*

Chapter 1
Jackson

Ethan cradles my face, his eyes meeting mine. "I want this with you, but..." He glances away. "I'm not... For you, I can be soft, but if I do something you don't like, I'm worried it'll ruin everything."

He's concerned he'll be too rough and I'll have a flashback or get spooked. He's being overprotective, as usual.

And I leap from the cliff, hoping he doesn't let me free fall—or knock me out.

I fist his shirt, and his eyes widen, his lips parting slightly. I crash my mouth to his, and he freezes, but only for a second.

Holy fucking shit. I'm kissing Ethan.

Ethan's heart hammers under my fist clenching his shirt. His breath catches then washes over me in a shuddering exhale. He tangles his fingers in my hair and takes control of the kiss, and I let him.

I'd let him do anything. Probably.

Soft, pillowy lips move with mine, slowly exploring. We open our mouths, our tongues intertwining, and a jolt of raw electricity surges through me. My stomach plunges, and a heady rush of blood flows south with raging intensity.

I struggle to remain quiet, but when he deepens the kiss and growls—that throaty fucking growl—I'm done.

If it wasn't for the damn center console of his Porsche, I'd be all over him. I can't get close enough.

Mindful of the cut below his lip and the bruise on his chin, I cup his jaw and stroke the rough stubble with my thumb. I'm completely captivated, lost in every moan and sigh.

I savor his taste. It's uniquely his. Masculine—dark and strong like the coffee he drinks, tinged with a metallic tang of blood.

He breaks the kiss far too soon, his eyes half-lidded and pupils blown. "Fuck, Jax. What are you trying to do to me?"

"Everything," I whisper and find his lips once more. "You could choke me out, and I'd wake up and ask you to do it again. You won't hurt me. I know that. I trust you. Stop worrying."

I lean in for another kiss, and he grips my hair, stopping me.

"We can't do this here." His dimpled smile and lingering gaze suggest otherwise.

"We're in the underground parking lot of your apartment...and the windows are tinted." I trace his bottom lip with my tongue. "Please."

"My God. Control yourself. I know that's hard for you..."

That's not the only thing that's hard.

With a groan, he kisses me, teasing and languid, making me doubt I'm the only one losing control.

"...but we have to be careful," he mumbles against my lips.

"They might trade me. We'll be fine."

He withdraws, brows pinched in a scowl and jaw set. "Is that what you want?"

"If it means I get you." Hockey is the furthest thing from my mind, but I'll agree to anything if it brings his mouth back to me.

His head dips. "No," he rumbles before his teeth graze my neck. "You're mine. You're staying on *my* team."

"Yes, Coach." I full-on grin—a self-satisfied, lovesick, forbidden grin I can't hide.

I trace the defined contours of his chest and abs until I find the hem of his shirt and slide my hand inside. His skin is burning hot, and his muscles twitch and jump beneath my fingers.

His lips continue their trail down my throat, and I rest my head on the seat. I want him. I love him. It feels right—better than right, goddamn amazing. Why haven't we done this sooner?

He pauses at the curve of my shoulder. "I want to mark you so damn bad. You unleashed something in me with that fucking trade comment."

"Do it." My words are breathless, my heart pounding in anticipation. "I wanna look in the mirror and remember this moment." *Forever.*

When his mark fades, I'll instigate his possessiveness so he'll do it again and again. I'm addicted to him.

Without hesitation, he drags the neck of my shirt down and bites my collarbone, and I just about come in my pants. There's definitely a wet spot.

Pleasure and pain explode along my nerve endings. I suck air in through my teeth, hissing, then release it with a hoarse, desperate moan.

Fuck. Me. I have to be the luckiest bastard on the planet to have both him and Aurora—rough and gentle, yin and yang, my entire world.

When he's done, he traces the indentations with his

tongue then pulls back to inspect his work. "Okay, we have to go." He fixes my shirt.

An embarrassingly needy whine escapes my mouth. "What the hell am I supposed to do with this erection?"

He smirks. "Take a cold shower."

My brows shoot up. "With you?"

He chuckles and shakes his head. "You're going to be absolutely *obsessive* about this, aren't you?"

"Relentless, persistent, determined…but sure, we can go with obsessed. Whatever lets me touch you."

He playfully shoves my forehead. "Get out."

Chapter 2
Aurora

Reece pushes himself up in bed. "Now that we're finally alone, come here."

Hospital grip socks on my feet, I hobble to him, flinching each time a sore spot meets the floor. We're quite a pair.

He stretches toward me and grimaces with the effort. "I'm having them remove these damn wires and tubes. I can't help you, and it's pissing me off."

I sit on the edge of the mattress. "Don't you dare. I'm fine."

"Now I know you're fibbing. Lie with me and tell me about it."

"There's nothing to tell." I settle in next to him, and our fingers intertwine as if they haven't seen each other in weeks, lazily caressing. "You're the one who's hurt."

His chest rises and falls with exertion. His eyes are half open, his complexion pale. Still, he kisses my forehead and asks, "How are you feeling about those two being together?"

I scoff. "Nothing has changed. They're as close as ever, but it's a relief they're finally admitting it."

I've always felt guilty for not being strong enough for Jax

at his worst. He hurts when he hurts me, and I know it's difficult for him to control himself sometimes. Ethan can handle him and *maybe* control him. Jax needs that.

"Jesus, Ethan has his hands full with you two." Reece stifles a chuckle. "What if they skate off into the hockey sunset together?"

I smile softly. "Then it'll be you and me, Viking."

His eyes light up. "Always, princess."

The emotions of the last few days hit me hard. I roll onto my side and rest my head on his shoulder. "I could've lost you." Tears prickle my eyelids. "I felt so empty." I can barely get the words out, my body racking with sobs.

"Shh. I'd never leave, angel." He smooths my messy hair from my face. "I'd fight like hell to return to you. I dreamt of us the entire time I was under."

I release a shuddering exhale and swallow the tight lump in my throat. "What did you dream?"

He brushes his lips against mine. "That I love you."

The air catches in my lungs, butterflies fluttering in my stomach.

"That we were married with kids."

The butterflies die, sinking like a brick. "Do you want those things…with someone?"

Because one of those, obviously, won't be me.

"I want them with you," he says, low and hoarse.

I suck in a breath and brace myself. "And if you can't?"

He's quiet, and the longer he takes to answer, the louder my heart pounds. We've had this discussion before, or danced around it. I still doubt he'll settle for less than he deserves.

This differs from Ethan, who resisted kids and marriage. Who's as devoted to Jax as he is to me. Who was open to a threesome from the start.

Reece can have everything he desires and is worthy of, just not with me—but I'm selfishly attached to him.

"Then we keep dreaming." He kisses the tears from my cheek. "We live in our own world and write our own story."

Hope blossoms in my chest. "You sure?"

"You're all I thought about while bleeding out on that garage floor." His ocean-blue eyes turn glassy, brimming with emotion. "You have been the best part of my life."

"Don't say it like that." My lip trembles. "Like a goodbye. I won't survive."

"Stop it," he grits through his teeth, brows raised. "It's embarrassing enough for me to sit here in a gown, but if you make me bawl in front of the guys I command, I'll be ruined."

My shoulders slump. "Do you have to go back to work?"

His lips find mine. "Most likely."

"Seeing you in your black pants and T-shirt might give me flashbacks. No offense."

"I'll put on all my gear for you and we'll create better memories, I promise." The grin he throws me is deeply suggestive.

"Are you flirting with me, Viking?" I glide my fingers across the stubble on his jaw and thread them in his hair. "Who are you right now?"

"A man eager to get you in a bed."

Well, that's different.

I stare at him, my body unsure of how it wants to respond. I'm not feeling remotely sexy. I've lost track of how many days I've worn these clothes. Two? Three? There's a chance they were dirty when I threw them on. I wasn't exactly thinking straight.

And the hospital toothpaste might be chalk.

"Is that so?"

Again with the grin, this one teasing. "Yeah, you can't sleep here. You need to rest, eat, and shower."

"Wow." I stretch out the word. "Do I smell?"

"No... Okay, maybe a little." He laughs then winces. "Better than me, I'm sure."

I return to resting my head on his shoulder. "Deal with it. I'm not leaving until you do."

He suppresses a yawn. "That's what I'm afraid of, and tomorrow, you'll *definitely* smell."

"Shut up and go back to sleep, will ya?"

After a minute, he asks, "How long do you think Jax waited before he mauled Ethan?"

"Once he got in the car?"

His chest shakes with laughter, only to cease with a grunt. "Poor Ethan."

"Stop hurting yourself."

"Stop making me laugh."

Chapter 3
Ethan

I refuse to touch my erection in the shower. It's Antarctica in here, and it hasn't ebbed. It needs to quit. I have too many conflicting thoughts in my head.

Aurora. I haven't talked to her about me and Jax. It's wrong without her.

But she *is* with Reece... She's aware of our relationship. I could be tearing Jackson's clothes off, sinking my teeth into his skin instead of shivering with blue balls.

Fuck, I wouldn't know what to do if I *did* get him naked.

You have a dick; you'll figure it out.

I should stop this. We can't. He has been through too much.

Although *he* kissed *me*.

Joking about it is one thing, but actually *doing it?* I'm thirty-five. It's obscene to have a twenty-two-year-old girlfriend *and* a twenty-five-year-old boyfriend—who's also the captain of my hockey team. That's just insane.

Insane is also how I felt when I thought I'd lose him. The universe might as well rip my soul from my body. Losing him would leave a void that can't be filled. He's a pain in the ass, but I love him with every fiber of my being, the same as I do Aurora, and maybe have for a while.

Perspectives change in the heat of the moment. When the house was raided and he broke down, burying his face in my neck and gripping me as if I were his lifeline, something in me shifted. I knew with complete certainty that our attachment was deeper, that he was mine to protect, care for, and love.

Insane is how it felt to kiss him. Pure fucking insanity. As if I were free-falling from the sky without a parachute. As if all my wants, desires, and need for him, known and unknown, came rushing to the surface, hitting me all at once.

Love is insane. When I fell for Aurora, I was jittery, crazed, out of control. I fought it, and it did nothing but strain our relationship. I want to do better with Jax, but I also don't know *what* to do.

I envision him on his knees, staring up at me with those devilish green eyes as I forced him to take my cock down his throat.

My unrelenting dick jerks.

Nope.

No, I will not. I'm not going there.

I rest my head back against the tile and scrub my fingers through my hair. I'm taking forever in the shower, and I wonder if I'm subconsciously waiting for him. I quickly rinse and shut off the water.

I exit the bathroom, my ridiculous hard-on pressed to my stomach by the towel around my waist, and come to a halt. He's asleep in my bed, shirtless, his face buried in my pillow. I bet he sniffed it like a creeper too.

As long as he didn't jack off on my sheets.

That visual has my cock thickening further. I glance

down, giving it a scowl and a firm talking-to. *Goddammit, stop. The brat is asleep.*

My gaze scans the room for my phone. I find it on my dresser beside my belt and snatch it, eager to take a picture of him. *Now who's the creeper?*

Still, I snap the pic. He's too adorable not to.

Full lips parted, his chest rises and falls peacefully. I brush back the hair that's fallen in his face, allowing my knuckles to graze his forehead, then the stubble on his jaw. Fuck, I have it bad. This erection is never going away.

Taking a deep breath, I slip into a pair of boxers and climb in next to him. Anxiety roils in my stomach. I stare at the ceiling and run through everyone who's my responsibility.

The twins left with Charlie and another agent to return to the hospital. I sent Rocco a message yesterday, telling him to take whatever from my account to pay Desi and Dante and to ensure they have everything they needed. He responded by threatening to come to LA and insisting we move to New York.

The idea is tempting. If I wasn't coaching, I would.

Aurora is content with Reece, who's on a locked unit guarded by half his force. They're perfectly safe, and I have the twins taking them food and clothes.

As for my other team, I took a few days off, claiming we had a break-in—not a lie—and I won't return until tomorrow. We have two home games coming up, and for the first time, I'm not excited to coach. But I can't let personal issues ruin the season for an entire organization.

An arm wraps around my torso, and Jax rests his head on my shoulder. "I can hear you thinking." His knee comes over me and brushes my relentless hard-on. "You want me to take care of that?"

I don't have to look at him to know he's grinning.

My breath picks up. "No..." Doubt sets in. "Is this not new for you?" How did he jump into this easily?

This is Jackson. Why am I even questioning it? He's impulsive and persistent when he wants something.

And now he wants *me*. Fuck.

"Everything with the three of us is new." He props up on his elbow.

I turn toward him, doing the same. "Is that why you like it?"

He trails his fingers over my bare stomach. The muscles tighten and twitch at his touch.

"I love it. Every part. From the moment you snuck into our bed in New York, I couldn't wait for more."

My lips twist with unease as I trace my bite mark on his collarbone. "Is it just a fascination for you?"

His hand settles on my waist. "It's not a phase, if that's what you're asking. I've always been this way."

"What way?"

He draws circles on my pebbled skin and contemplates his answer. "Disinterested in people unless I was emotionally connected to them, trusted them. Open-minded about who that might be."

"Like Grant?" My voice comes across harsher than intended.

He smiles, picking up on my absurd jealousy. "Just because only a few people make it in doesn't mean I'm attracted to them all. I'm not interested in Grant—he's a self-proclaimed slut. That's fine, but we're not the same."

I can't help but chuckle at his seriousness. No, Jackson could never fathom engaging in sex without some level of emotional attachment. "I was a slut once. It happens."

His smile fades. "Please don't tell me that. New York doesn't need another murderer."

I laugh and nudge his shoulder. "Shut up."

He lands on his back dramatically and rolls onto his other side, tucking the pillow under his head. "I can't look at you right now."

My chest vibrates with amusement. I lie beside him, wrap an arm around him, and pull him close. He smells of my bodywash—woodsy or pine needles or some crap. He must have taken a quick shower in the other bathroom. His hair isn't wet. He probably refused to use my cheap shampoo, and my lips spread into a smile.

"You're such a brat." I give in to temptation and kiss the curve of his neck.

His hips shift. "Don't stop," he whispers.

I picture my hand clasping his throat, fingertips pressed into his jaw, holding him to me as I make him come. What noises would he make for me? Would he beg?

Jesus, I need to stop.

"What if you get bored?" I ask, a little too breathless.

The last thing I want is to become utterly enthralled, only for him to move on to his next obsession.

Who am I kidding? I'm already there.

"I won't get bored." He weaves his fingers through mine and brings them to his heart.

"How do you know?" I nuzzle his hair. He definitely didn't use my shampoo. The scent is purely him—coconut and citrus, reminiscent of summer and sunshine.

"Sometimes, I have these voices in my head—not real voices," he clarifies when I go still. "Obsessive thoughts, I guess. For a while, one of them has been chanting, *Ethan, Ethan, Ethan, Ethan, Ethan,*" he says like a rapid heartbeat. "I hear Aurora's name, but it's, *Auuuroooraaaa,*" he singsongs. "It's dreamy, sleepy sex. It's a lazy, sunny day at the beach, surfing and catching waves. She's the light I can't live without. But you..." He sighs softly and squeezes my fingers. "You're the craving in the dark. You're cocaine in my veins, a compulsion driving me mad. I have to have it. I want to know everything. I fear I'll lose you. I want to breathe you in until you're a part of me and can't escape. You'll never go away; I won't let you."

It's the most Jackson answer I've ever heard, and even though he's completely fucking insane, I grin. "Only you could make falling in love sound like a stalker kidnapping his victim and have it be totally desirable."

Chapter 4
Reece

I peel the bandage from my skin, cursing when the tape rips out my chest hair. "Motherfucker."

"That's it, Viking. I'm coming in!" Aurora yells from outside the bathroom door.

"Don't you dare."

Two weeks have passed since I was shot, and they've been painful—agonizing.

I left the hospital a week ago and have been recuperating at Ethan's apartment with Aurora. She was reluctant to leave when the guys were away for a few games. They weren't happy, but they agreed to let her stay with the twins and Charlie here.

It's been a whirlwind. In a combined effort with the FBI, HSI, and ATF, twenty-three properties were raided in what the news is calling Black Friday, in reference to our SWAT-style approach and uniforms. I don't have all the details—I suspect that's intentional—but the evidence has resulted in over fifty arrests, primarily for sex crimes.

Jax had a few peaceful days before the media storm hit. Luckily for him, his father was never charged with anything. There's only intense speculation, given the LAPD's corruption, our presence at Kyle's home, and that Hugo, Kyle's ex-partner, is now the center of the investigation—even dead.

Hugo's gruesome death didn't seem to faze Jackson. He only requested we not disclose details of the case, or his abuse, to Aurora.

Distracting her isn't difficult, since she insists on giving me all her attention. And it's not only her. Charlie had the nerve to call my sisters when I went into surgery, and now they won't quit texting. Then, there's the nurse Jax hired for no reason, and let's not forget Ethan, who checks in ten times a day.

I hate being fussed over. I can't stand it. I'm no good at accepting help. I'd rather suffer in silence than be pampered.

Which is why I'm locked in the guest bathroom, struggling to change my own bandages.

I reach over my shoulder and tug on the gauze affixed to my skin. The door handle rattles, and I shake my head at Aurora's persistence.

A strip of tape comes loose, and I yank at it, wincing as it catches my wound. "Fuck." I drop my arm to my side, already exhausted.

The door pops open, and she grins triumphantly.

I glare at her in the mirror. "How the hell did you get in?"

She holds up a bent credit card. "You learn a few tricks when you grow up in the Valley."

"You did not learn to shimmy locks growing up. I doubt you even left your house."

"Okay, it's from losing my key when I lived with Emily. I wasn't on the lease, so…" She glances at the incision on my upper arm and grimaces. "It's looking better," she lies and steps forward. "Let me help you with the rest."

I turn away from her. "The nurse will help me." It's not

true. The nurse left my stubborn ass after I refused all treatment.

She cocks her head. "Seriously, Reece? Are you intentionally provoking my jealousy?"

I smirk, but it's half-hearted. "Tinker Bell, you can go, okay? I'm taking a shower once I remove these damn bandages."

"Fine. I'll shower with you."

"No, you will not."

"Why?" Her flirtatious tone shifts to disappointment and frustration.

"I'm not about to be injured and unable to use one arm the first time we're naked together."

"I'm six months pregnant by a six-foot-five-inch former defensive hockey player. I look like I swallowed a beach ball."

"No, you do not." I chuckle at her dramatics. "Maybe a basketball."

"See? We're even." She moves closer and extends her hand. "I'll remove these bandages and help you wash."

I bat her arm away. "Go, Aurora. I mean it."

The semi-playful atmosphere comes to an abrupt and harsh end.

She draws a steadying breath and releases it slowly. "How did you picture us married if you won't let me help you? Or shower with you? Or sleep with you? You won't even tell me when you're hungry. We're going to your sister's wedding. Who will I be to you?"

"You don't have to go." Hell, *I* don't want to go.

Her jaw tightens and her voice rises. "I want to go. What are you not getting? I want to be with you. I want to care for you. Now, answer the question."

I drag my fingers through my hair while I contemplate a response. "It's not you. It's them. They won't understand this arrangement, and it's not worth the hassle." Once the words escape my mouth, I realize how bad they sound. "That's not—I didn't mean it like that. You're worth it."

Her eyes glisten, and she heads for the door. "I'll leave you alone."

I scramble for something to say. "When I picture us married, I picture caring for *you*, not you waiting on me hand and foot."

"And I picture loving you freely." The door slams shut.

I manage to remove the gauze and shower, and then I decide to let the incisions air out.

Yeah, that's what I'm doing. It's definitely not because I couldn't get the bandage on my shoulder to stay properly, or because I threw the roll of medical tape across the room.

One-handed, I stumble into a pair of boxers and shorts. I yank a clean white T-shirt over my head, wrestle my useless arm through the sleeve, and then wrestle some more with the flimsy sling. I'm reminded I could have chosen a ten-thousand-dollar bionic arm brace and made this recovery a hell of a lot easier on myself, but I stubbornly refused.

When I leave the bathroom, I'm overworked, overtired, and overstimulated, the cotton grating against my hypersensitive skin.

Still, I search for Aurora, expecting her to be reading on the couch or napping in Ethan's room. She tried to tell me about her newest book, but I couldn't keep my eyes open—something about a psychopath who collects the hearts of his girl's enemies and stores them in glass jars.

That's an idea. We have three of Hugo's guys in lock-up. Maybe cutting out their hearts will improve my piss-poor mood.

Instead of Aurora, I find Charlie making an espresso using the fancy new machine Jax bought. God forbid his boyfriend use a twenty-dollar drip coffeemaker.

"She's not here," my partner says before I ask.

"What do you mean she's not here? Where the hell would she go?"

"The twins took her to the beach house." He brings the tiny mug to his lips—pinky sticking out slightly—takes a sip, and sighs longingly.

I attempt to shake off the irritability, reminding myself I wanted to be alone. But now that I am, I only feel worse. "Why? And aren't you supposed to be watching them?"

He tilts his head back with a dramatic groan. "They're so annoying. One never shuts up, and the other glares at me with murderous intentions. Which wouldn't be so terrifying if I hadn't *witnessed* him murder someone."

"You've seen me kill plenty of people." I open the fridge, grab a water bottle, and stare at the cap before using my teeth to twist it. I squeeze too hard, and the liquid spills down my chin and fingers.

Charlie pretends not to notice, but his eyes are grinning. "Yeah, but you didn't enjoy it. I heard Dante growl, 'Wrong house, wrong night, motherfucker'," he mocks, his voice dropping to lethal levels. "Then, *pop*! He shot the guy in the forehead with *my* gun."

He's oddly excited and animated for someone who claims to be annoyed.

"You wiped the security footage, right?"

"Yes, of course." He waves me off. "I've never seen him smile, not even in New York—"

"Wait." I scrunch my brows. "When did you see him in New York?"

"Surveillance." His face twists, as if that's obvious, as if he wasn't supposed to be watching Aurora and Jax. He continues to ramble while opening a bag of dark-roasted beans. "But I swear on the Jedi Code, I saw his teeth sparkling in the pitch-black while he was breaking necks and taking names."

He abandons the coffee and busts into a karate move, apparently mimicking Dante, and I glance around the room, wondering if I'm being pranked. Who is this person? What meds am I on?

My gaze gravitates to the miniature cups stacked on the espresso machine and lining the sink. "Exactly how many of those have you had?"

He dumps the bag into the hopper, the smell perking up my senses.

"Only five. They're small."

I release a long breath and pray for patience. "Why'd Aurora go to the beach house?"

"Probably because you're an asshole."

"Thanks," I mumble before I chug the water.

"No joke. I've been through this with you. You're a good dude. You'd take a bullet for anyone on the team—shit, for any random person walking the street—but you're terrible at self-care. You'd smack any of us for acting the way you are."

I crush the empty bottle in my hand to ease my frustration. "I'm fucking tired."

He faces me, shoulders squared. "Then go to bed. Have an espresso. We're all tired. I'm tired of people—period. I'd much rather be trailing perps than playing chauffeur and answering questions like I'm fucking Google."

"Then get another agent to do it."

He ignores me. "Aurora *has* to be tired. She's pregnant and taking care of your dumb ass, all while making sure we're fed and not bored. She went through something traumatic too. She could be huddled in a corner crying, but she's not. She's staying busy."

Agitation swarms in my chest. "Why do you think I'm miserable?"

He scoffs. "Feeling sorry for yourself won't fix a damn thing."

A beat of silence. I want to argue with him, but he's not wrong. I have to push through this hell. Embrace the suck.

"Fine," I huff. "What is she doing at the beach house?"

"Meeting a contractor and bringing our team pizza."

"They can order their own pizza."

"She's being *nice*. You remember what nice is, right? Besides, they're cleaning the place up."

Again, I'm struck with confusion. "Why?"

He holds my gaze. "Because Aurora is family to you."

I'm at a loss for words, struggling to fight the guilt. Fuck, I need to get over there. I need to do *something*.

"And your sister already knows about Aurora. You didn't think she'd demand to know the person you're bringing to her wedding?"

A jolt of adrenaline courses through me, and my gut churns. "You told her?"

"Bennett, our commander, has had how many partners? Four? Five? Yet we welcome each one with jazz hands and pom-poms, because this job is lonely. Good for her for trying. I didn't recognize it at first, but it's clear you love Aurora, and we're going to rally around you whether you like it or not. Fuck your parents if they can't accept her...and Jax...and Ethan." He throws his hands up and shrugs. "Y'all could be fantasizing about each other, but instead, you're living it out. Who cares?"

"I'm not fantasizing about anyone except Aurora."

He turns on the coffee grinder, drowning me out, and I toss the water bottle and grab another.

When he's through making his sixth shot of caffeine, I ask, "What did my sister say?"

"She didn't believe me. She said there's no chance her broody brother is dating a model, especially one married to Jackson O'Reilly."

My lips curve into a smile, and I can't help but chuckle. "Wow, great to know she has faith in me."

"She's going to shit her pants when y'all show up." He shoots me a side-eye. "By the way, your shoulder is bleeding. It'll be a bitch when the blood dries and you rip off that shirt."

"Shut up and make me an espresso. I need you to drive me to Santa Monica."

"Awesome," he deadpans. "Just what I want to do."

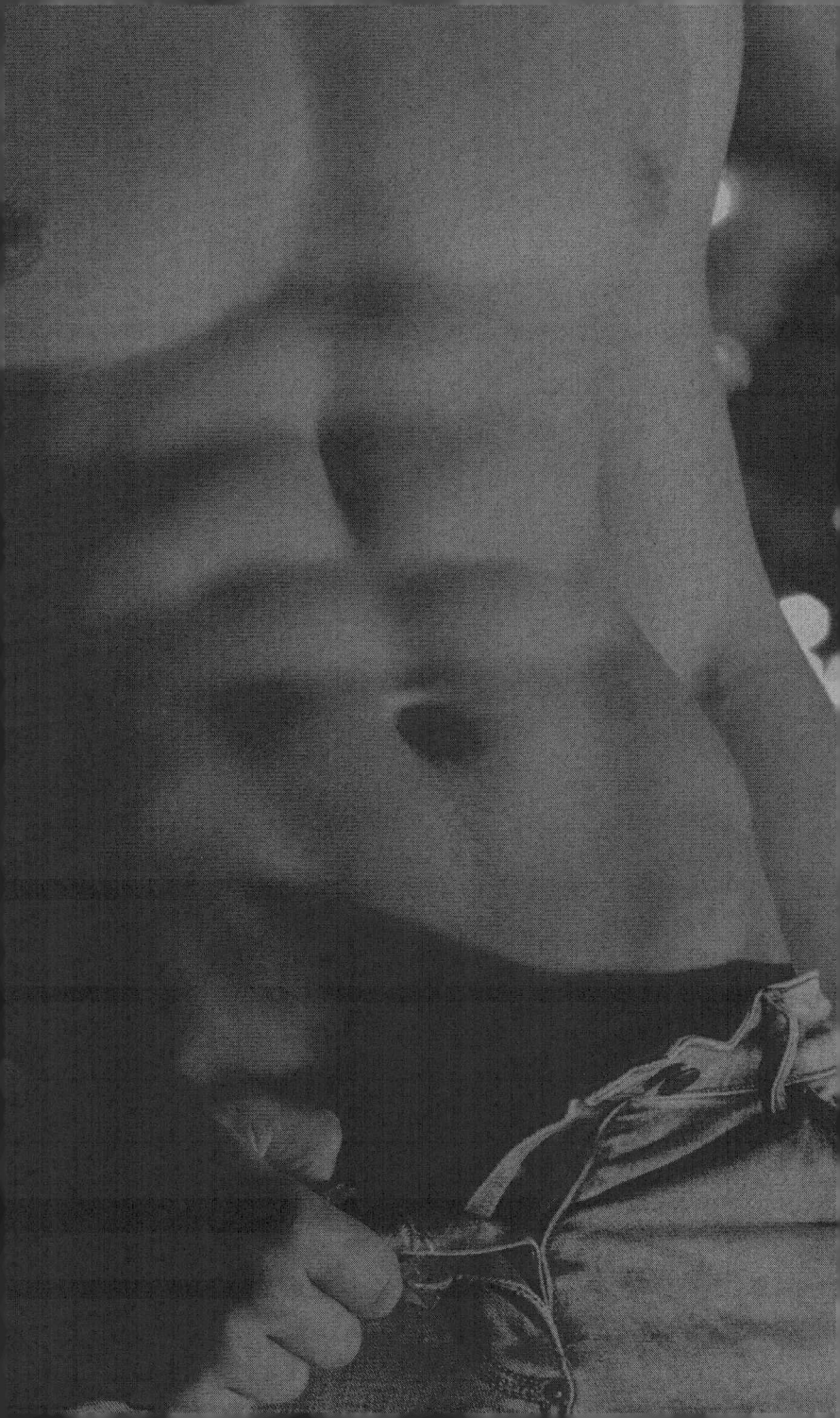

Chapter 5
Jackson

"Hey, you okay?"

Lost in my thoughts, I utter a noncommittal sound.

"Look at me, baby." Ethan lifts my chin, brows pinched in concern. "Are you having a difficult time?"

Sucking on a Jolly Rancher, I sit on the windowsill of our hotel room and peer out over Denver. It's snowing, white flurries dancing in the yellow glow of the city lights. It's pretty from afar, where I'm not freezing my balls off.

"A little." I gently brush my knuckles over the fading bruises on his chin. "But Aurora's at the beach house, so I can see her."

"You mean, stalk her?" He smiles, lighting up his eyes. "What's she doing?"

My hands find their way to his waist. He's powerfully built, solid and thick, while I'm lean and cut. I yearn to touch him, to memorize every contour and muscle, but I hold back, letting him lead.

"The contractor came over to assess the damage. Anything you want changed while he's drawing up plans?"

"We should think about the beach access. Is it worth the risk to our safety?"

I untuck his shirt. "Apart from building a ten-foot wall, nowhere is one hundred percent safe. The security system alerted when someone entered the property. I have an idea, though. Anything else?"

His fingers thread through the back of my hair. "No, it's perfect. You did an amazing job. I'm glad Aurora chose to stay."

"Me too. I'm having the pool house remodeled. It'll eat up some of the yard, but I'm contemplating asking Charlie if he's interested in working surveillance. He's up all night and attached to Reece, and right now, we don't have anyone. I'm sure the twins will want to return to New York soon."

"Okay, that's something we can discuss. Is that why you missed dinner? Are you worried?" He bends down and presses his lips to mine. "Fuck, I've wanted to do that all day."

He lingers, and I'm tempted to deepen the kiss, but it's our first night on the road together, and I don't want to push it.

We break apart, and I reach up to loosen the knot of his tie. "I was giving you space. I didn't want you to feel uncomfortable when I stared at you the entire time."

Truth be told, yes, I'm worried. Not only about our safety, but about *us*. All of us. I want to be home, ensuring our relationship is solid and everyone is happy.

He scoffs, removes the tie, and tosses it on the chair. "Grant was asking for you."

"Did you tell him where I was?"

I begin with the top button of his plain white dress shirt. I should order him clothes. He'll hate it, but I'll do it anyway. I've already switched out his hair products but left his soap because it smells like him.

"No. Why would I do that?" The corner of his mouth twitches into a slight smirk.

I work my way down his shirt, anticipation building with each button. "Because you want me to be happy and have friends."

"No, I don't. I want you in my room, waiting for me. It's much better than worrying about what trouble you're causing."

Once his shirt is open, I slip it over his broad shoulders. "I'm trying to cause trouble now, if you'll let me."

He shrugs it off and throws it with the tie. "Promise?"

"What has gotten into you?" I smile and lift the hem of his undershirt. I glide my palms over his heated skin, and goosebumps rise along my arms.

He has let me touch him *some* over the past week; not much, mostly cuddling and brief kisses. With hockey, the case, Reece being in the hospital, and a crowded house, we've had little time, energy, or privacy.

His two-bedroom apartment is relatively small, another reason I'm rushing to finish the beach house. He's also hesitant regarding Aurora—although she knows about us and is okay with it—and she's been preoccupied and exhausted.

He yanks the shirt over his head and drops it to the floor. Drawn to him, I trace the lines of his well-defined chest and abs.

I'm starving for him, practically begging—I would beg if he wanted me to.

He returns to running his fingers through my hair. "I missed you today. Meetings without you are boring, and when we are together, you're a magnetic force, my body always aware of your presence. It's a fight to ignore, and I'm prickly."

My heart flutters with excitement and nerves. I kiss his

bare stomach to hide my stupid grin. "Prickly, huh? Is that what you call it?"

He fists my hair and tilts my head back. "I can go to the gym if you'd like."

"Absolutely not."

His intense gray eyes bore into mine, and he brushes his thumb over my bottom lip. "What do you want?"

Undressing him had my cock thickening, but it's that deep rumble that gets me achingly hard. "Whatever you'll give me." I'll do anything, *take* anything.

His caress moves to my jawline. "Are you sure?"

"Yes. I haven't changed my mind. I'll never change my mind. Now, can I undo your belt?"

He releases me, and I take that as permission. With a tug, I unbuckle it, the click of the metal the only sound in the room.

"I like you undressing me. We may need to do this every night."

"Promise?" I ask, echoing him.

***

Ethan

My body vibrates with pent-up agitation. Aurora is home, and although she's well protected, it weighs on me. On the road, Jax avoids me. He does it for my benefit. If I let him, he'd sit next to me with his head on my shoulder, his hands all over me.

And I'd love it—in private.

Instead, he sits with Grant and Killian, the three of them whispering. I know because I'm acutely aware of Jax. If he's in my vicinity, my body senses him—my *soul* senses him—wanting nothing more than to touch him. I'm irritated when

I can't, irritated with myself for being distracted when he's close and twice as irritated when he's not.

I'm prickly. No other description fits.

Robert, the owner of the Huskies, rejected Jackson's trade offer, and I'm doing everything in my power to prevent them from having reason to separate us.

But I also don't want to screw this up with Jax.

The button of my pants comes loose, and he glances up to gauge my reaction.

I brush his hair from his forehead and thread my fingers through the top. "We have to keep this between us," I mumble, ashamed to even say it. "Around the team."

His hands run up my sides, and I shudder, my breath catching in my throat. He trails open-mouthed kisses along my waistband, and my stomach flip-flops.

"How about when you walk inside this room, you forget about what's outside it? It's just you and me."

"I care about how this will affect you. Remember PR Patty? Remember your jealousy?"

"Being affectionate in private helps me obtain my daily dose of Ethan." He gives me that devilish smile, a slow, sly curve of his lips. "I'll be good, I promise."

He's a damn liar.

He lowers my zipper, easing some of the pressure on my aching erection, and I want more than anything to believe him.

I'm wearing black boxer briefs. There's no hiding the giant bulge in front of his face, and I know the moment he sees how hard I am for him. He sucks his bottom lip into his mouth, biting it to suppress his grin.

My traitorous cock jerks. "I wanna bite that lip."

He traces his finger over the outline of my length, and the searing heat of his touch is undeniable. I feel it in every cell of my body, spreading like wildfire.

"You're killing me, Jax. Take me out."

He full-on grins, tugs my boxers down, and wraps his fingers around my shaft without hesitation. "What can I do?"

Fuck if I know. I can't believe this is actually happening. I'm barely able to remember my name at the moment. *Anything?* "What do you want to do?"

"Make you come. Repeatedly."

Those raspy words alone might do it.

Precum beads at the tip of my cock. His tongue darts out, licking along the slit and tasting me.

Fuck me. I'm going to last an embarrassingly short amount of time.

I collar the back of his neck then reconsider. Without a word, he snatches my hand and returns it.

He licks from base to head, following a bulging vein. My cock throbs, and it takes all my willpower to remain still.

"Fuck, baby boy." The words slip from my mouth, and I immediately regret them. I run my fingers through his hair. "Shit, sorry."

"You can say it. I like it."

He flicks the sensitive underside with his tongue, and sparks of pleasure shoot straight to my balls.

"You sure?" I ask, somewhere between a grunt and a groan.

He reaches down and fists his thick length over his joggers. "Yep."

I'm staring at his erection, wondering what the hell I'm going to do with *that*, when he grabs my waist and wraps his lips around the head of my cock.

"Fuck." That's all I can manage. My mind is blank, overcome with the pleasure of it being him.

Him sucking my cock. *Jax*.

He draws me in deep, and my restraint unravels.

One hand in his hair, the other clasping his nape, I punch my hips forward. "Your mouth feels so fucking good."

His pupils blown wide, he groans, and I feel it everywhere, from my dick to my fingertips.

I tense my muscles to stop from losing control, but I can't stop my mouth. "You like that? You want me to fuck your throat, is that it?"

Even as I say it, I'm not sure I can do it. I'm not sure I can be rough with him.

He loosens his jaw, permitting me to take what I need, and icy flames crackle along my skin.

My grip on his hair tightens, I flex my hips, and he gags, the muscles of his throat squeezing me.

"That's it, baby. Fuck. You're doing so well." He feels incredible. Still, I hold back, not wanting to scare him.

He doesn't let me though. He clutches my hip, takes me deep, and strokes my shaft in tandem with his mouth.

I can't look away. I'm mesmerized by those perfect pink lips. "Your mouth wrapped around my cock has got to be one of the most beautiful things I've ever seen."

He doubles down, sucking me harder, his cheeks hollowing. His hand moves from my hip to massage my balls, and I break.

I thrust unrestrained, my cock hits the back of his throat, and I jerk in his mouth.

"Oh, fuck." My orgasm hits hard and fast. "I'm gonna come, baby boy… Fuck…be good. Don't swallow." My words are fractured and strained, my body engulfed in flames.

The entire time I'm coming, his gaze never leaves mine. He moans right along with me, my ecstasy mirrored in his eyes.

I'm feral for him. I yank him to his feet, hold out my hand, and demand, "Spit."

He unloads cum and saliva into my palm and then licks his lips.

"Good boy." I rip down his joggers and boxers far enough to get my wet fist wrapped around his cock.

I devour his mouth, backing him up against the window. He tastes sweet and salty—cherry Jolly Ranchers and cum, a mix of him and me. "You taste so fucking good with my cum on your tongue."

His hands roam my body and tangle in my hair, our kiss punctuated by his soft moans. He flexes his hips, chasing his orgasm. I bite his swollen bottom lip then capture his mouth once more, our tongues intertwining, while I stroke his cum-covered cock.

"You mean the world to me, you know that?" I say between kisses. "You and Aurora, I couldn't live without you."

"Fuck." He tilts his head back against the glass, the snow dancing in the city lights behind him. "You're gonna make me come."

I pump my fist faster and sink my teeth into the curve of his neck. He comes with a strangled, throaty moan of my name and coats my fingers with his hot release.

"So fucking good." I slip under his T-shirt and rub my hand over his stomach.

His lips curl into a dreamy smile. "Are you marking me in every way possible?"

"Maybe," I mumble, unable to stop kissing him.

I draw a finger over his skin—a line, a curve, another curve, a swoop.

His smile grows. "Did you just write 'I love you' in cum on my stomach?"

"I might have."

"That's fucking hot. Who knew you were so romantic, Coach?"

Chapter 6
Aurora

My Tiffany-blue velvet couch is covered in blood spatter and bullet holes. I text Jax a picture with a crying emoji. He sends me a promise to order another one, along with a selfie of him in front of a snowy window, his nose scrunched and his lip curled. He's so handsome, even when perturbed.

> I miss you. 😊

MY HUSBAND
> Miss you too. You're doing too much. Lie down.

I prop the broom against the wall and raise my middle finger, spinning in a circle to ensure he sees it. I have no idea where he hides these cameras. I tuck my phone into my hoodie pocket and return to sweeping up the shattered glass. It's never-ending, like glitter—glass fragments lie beneath, within, and around the furniture, both upstairs and downstairs.

Reece's team boarded up the windows and secured the

kicked-in back door. A crime scene specialist came yesterday and removed what blood and gore they could. The couch, unfortunately, is unsalvageable.

They're only material objects, I remind myself. They can be replaced—or not. Either way, they don't matter. What matters is we're all alive. Our wounds will heal eventually.

My phone buzzes, and I pause once again.

MY HUSBAND
I saw that!

Good. 🤢

MY HUSBAND
Go rest! Now that the biohazard team is finished, I'll hire a cleaning crew.

Staying busy keeps my mind off everything.

MY HUSBAND
Nothing for you to worry about. It's over. I promise.

If only my brain got the memo. Whenever I'm not occupied, I relive the night over in my head, searching for... mistakes? Reasoning? Solace? It hasn't found it yet, whatever 'it' is.

A familiar, heavy thud of footsteps on the stairs sends me scrambling to find a hiding place. I drop the broom and dart for the yoga studio, which leads to the terrace. I'd rather not receive a scolding from Reece for leaving the apartment while he's already grumpy.

"Don't you dare run." His deep voice booms down the hall, his words sharp. "You won't get your surprise if I have to chase you."

Curiosity piqued, I step around the corner, meeting him at the bottom of the stairs. "What surprise?"

Too quick for me to react, he bends down and scoops me up with one arm under my ass and thighs. "You'll see." He adjusts me, careful of my stomach. "Hold on."

"Reece!" I press into his uninjured side and hug his neck. "You shouldn't be carrying me!"

"And you shouldn't be taking off without me. I swear, you do this shit on purpose."

I attempt to stretch my feet to the floor. "Put me down! You're hurt."

Our faces only inches apart, he shoots me an icy glare, daring me to keep it up.

His usual calm and patient demeanor has been replaced with simmering agitation. I've never known him to be this irritable. It's hot, minus the dark circles under his eyes and pale complexion.

Without missing a step, he carries me up the stairs and takes a right toward my room. "Are your feet sore?"

I reply, "No," a little too quickly.

He gives me a side-eye. "Liar."

We enter my bedroom suite to the soothing scent of lavender and mint. He kicks the door shut behind us, briefly glancing around, then heads to my bathroom.

"Worried?" I wonder if his mind is also in the woods.

He sets me down in front of the enormous tub. "Nope, I already cleared the house. Force of habit. Are you worried?"

"My brain is. It won't stop replaying the break-in."

He cups the back of my neck and kisses my forehead. "That's normal. It'll fade as we renovate and replace the bad memories with happier ones."

He crouches, and the bathtub snatches my attention.

The dimly lit room is illuminated by a small LED flashlight in a cup beside the faucet, most likely from his gear. Steam fogs the window overlooking the ocean, and the jetted tub overflows with bubbles.

"You don't have candles," he points out, untying my shoes.

"The smell is overpowering." I perch on the edge of the tile and reach down to stop him. "I can do that."

He shoos me away. "I know," he answers both my statements, loosening my laces and pulling off my sneakers with one hand.

When he goes to remove my socks, I retract my foot. "I'm sweaty."

Ignoring me, he hooks the tops of my socks with his finger and swiftly removes them. He lifts my feet to inspect the cuts on my soles, scowls, and stands. "Get in," he demands, all gruff and annoyed.

He turns to go, and I let out a pouty whine. How dare he set this up and leave?

"So dramatic, princess. I won't be long." He's out the door without a glance back.

There's a higher chance of it snowing on the beach in Santa Monica than Reece getting in this bath with me, but, hey, a girl can dream. He might sit in here with me though.

I slip out of my clothes and peek in the mirror, but the glass is fogged. I throw my hair in a messy bun, hoping I'm not a total wreck, then lower myself into the steamy water. My tense muscles ease, and I release a heavy sigh.

Moments later, Reece returns, carrying a stack of books. My stomach sinks. He's going to hand me a book and walk out, avoiding my naked body like the plague. Weeks ago, I would've stood and enticed him with my figure, but I doubt six months pregnant is all that alluring.

He drops the books on the tile and twirls his finger. "Turn around and close your eyes."

I stare up at him with furrowed brows.

He cocks his head. "You want me to join you? The bath isn't your only surprise."

I spin so fast, the water sloshes.

Reece

I lay a towel beside Aurora's books for her to dry her hands before reading then take off my sling, shirt, shorts, and boxers. My hard cock bobs between my legs, anticipation racing through my heated veins. I step over the side of the tub, sink into the water opposite her, and rest my forearm on the tiled edge.

My arm isn't immobile, but movement is painful, and I'm supposed to keep it in a sling for four weeks. The longest four weeks of my life. Then, there's physical therapy, which I'm capable of doing myself.

She releases an audible exhale. "Can I turn around now?"

"You have zero patience." I rake my fingers through my hair and remember I still need it cut. It's shaggy on top and falling into my eyes. "Go ahead."

The tub is massive—clearly, Jax was planning on the three of them bathing together—and she easily twists to face me.

Her gaze traces the contours of my upper body, her eyes sparkling with excitement. "Can I sit with you?"

She'll ask a million questions when she sees me up close. *What's this tattoo? What does it mean? What's this scar? How did that happen?* And I'm not in the mood to explain every injury and memory I obtained in the military.

There's one question I know she won't be able to contain, but I try anyway. "Yes—as long as you don't ask any more questions."

She raises a brow. "Can I kiss you?"

"That's a question."

She mimics zipping her lips and throwing away the key.

"Pick a book," I tell her.

She dries her hands and chooses a book then nestles

between my thighs and relaxes into my chest. Bubbles cover her body, only the swells of her breasts visible, until she reaches up to kiss me, offering a glimpse of full, glistening tits and peaked nipples.

My dick twitches. Her touch alone might make me come. This is the most action I've had since going on random Tinder dates before meeting her, which now feels repulsive to even think about.

I cradle the back of her head, deepen the kiss, and forget all about my time before her. Our tongues tangle, and she moans softly, rising on her knees to straddle me.

Abruptly, I break the kiss. "Read." The word comes out raspy, not at all stern.

She releases a frustrated sigh, settles into my chest, and opens the book.

I hadn't noticed until now, but she chose the smallest paperback. She holds it open with one hand while her other hand drifts to my inner thigh, caressing and teasing.

A shiver runs down my spine, my cock a steel bar between my legs. "You're devious, you know that?"

I trail kisses over the curve of her neck, cup her breasts, and tweak her nipples. She whimpers and grinds her ass against me.

My dick throbs, and I'm too preoccupied salivating over her tits to catch her hand reaching between us to fist my shaft.

An involuntary "Fuck" slips from my lips.

She strokes my length, her palm grazes my Jacob's ladder piercings, and she freezes, nearly dropping the book into the water.

Here it comes, in five, four, three, two—

She tosses the book to the floor and spins around, her mouth agape. "You're pierced? Who did you get that for?"

I shake my head, a deep laugh bursting from my chest. "I

knew without a shadow of a doubt that'd be your response." Encircling my uninjured arm about her waist, I guide her onto my lap hoping to distract her with my cock—in a more pleasurable way that doesn't have her scowling at me. "No questions, remember?"

"Tell me," she insists, jaw tight and lips pouty. "You're seven years older than me. I know hardly anything about you. You could've been married or engaged for all I know."

"I haven't." My gaze is unwavering. "Like all my piercings and tattoos, it was because I wanted to. For the challenge, for the pain. Not for anyone else."

She hangs her head and traces her thumb over the tiny bar in my nipple. She's either mulling it over or sulking. Sometimes, I forget she's only twenty-two…and sheltered… and spoiled.

"If you're worried I've been in a serious, long-term relationship, you can stop. I haven't. You're the only one." I flex my hips, and the bars on the underside glide through her slit. Fuck, she feels amazing, and I do it again, bumping over her clit. "We could fight about it, or you could sit on my cock, but I don't have the energy for both."

Her head snaps up, her expression shocked but her smile salacious. "I'd choose to sit on your cock any day."

One hand on my shoulder, she lifts to line us up. I restrain her, tightening my arm around her waist.

"We can't have sex in the bath." Unable to stop, I suck her nipple into my mouth.

She gasps and rocks her hips, her pussy sliding back and forth over my piercings. "You're such a buzzkill."

I draw her other nipple into my mouth then take turns biting each one. "Your bed or mine?"

Her fingers weave into my hair. "Mine. It's closer."

I can't resist grinning. Her husband will love that.

Chapter 7
Reece

Once my back hits the mattress, Aurora straddles me. She removes her hair tie, and dark waves cascade over her shoulders. Twilight descends, the setting sun casting a hazy glow that silhouettes her and highlights her curvy figure.

Head bowed, she traces her finger over my erection, base to tip. She teases the ring at the crown, and my cock jerks, leaking precum.

With my arm bent above me, I clutch the pillow to prevent my hips from flexing. "Stop staring at my dick." My husky voice breaks the silence, and I swallow to wet my dry throat. "You have two others."

Eyes wide and transfixed, she shakes her head lazily, as if in a daze. "Not like this, I don't."

"Jesus, the shit you say." A chuckle vibrates my chest, and my face flushes—fuck, my entire body flushes.

"You have..." she touches each piercing, "six."

I smile, amused by her astonishment. "Yes, princess. I'm aware."

She flicks the tiny ring at the base just above my balls, and her gaze darts to mine to appraise my reaction. "It doesn't hurt you? If they pull?"

"You won't hurt me. Here, give me your hand." I curl her fingers around my shaft and jerk roughly, stroking each piercing. "See?" I rasp, the word strained.

I remove my grip, and the sight of her small hand encircling me has my hips jolting, thrusting into her fist.

More precum flows, slicking her grasp, and she goes harder, faster.

Desperation swims through my veins, my abs tense, and I pulse in her palm. "Fuck. If you don't ride me, I'm going to come all over your fingers—and I *really* wanna come inside you and make you mine."

***

Aurora

Reece is all man—muscles, tattoos, scars, bruises, and bandages—looking like he walked off the set of an action film. He's tall, his long legs stretching to the foot of the bed. His tone is throaty, words blunt. His hair is overgrown, curling at the ends, and a few weeks' worth of stubble roughens his jawline. His eyes, a midnight blue in the dim light, are half-lidded and lustful, an aphrodisiac that shoots straight to my core.

His large hand finds my hip and guides me over him. I rise on my knees, my heart thundering with anticipation, and align myself. The recent memory of his piercings teasing my clit sends a thrill through me, and the thought of them inside me has a surge of wetness dampening my slit.

Palm on his chest, I lower myself onto him, agonizingly slow, relishing in the sensation of him filling me.

His fingertips dig into the muscle of my ass. I glance up,

and his gaze is fixed on where he enters me, his brows pinched, his jaw clenched.

"You're killing me, princess." His grip tightens. "We can do soft and slow later. Right now, I need to fuck and fill you." He lifts his hips and plunges into me.

I gasp and cry out. It's intense. The stretch. The piercings. I feel every inch of him, every barbell and ring.

"Holy fuck, *fuck*." His dark gaze connects with mine, mouth open and chest heaving. "Goddamn, you're tight. Don't move. You'll adjust. I'll go slower. Fuck."

He pulses inside me, and I drop my weight to take him fully. I can't remain still—he feels too good.

I whimper and writhe, desperately in need of friction. "Reece, please."

He lets out a rough groan and circles my clit with his thumb. "Better?"

"Yes, please move." I rock my hips, and another wave of wetness coats him.

He clasps my nape and drags me down for a hungry, frantic kiss. Our tongues intertwine, and he buries his cock in one, smooth stroke, his piercings hitting every erotic spot imaginable. A needy moan slips from my throat, and I squeeze around him.

"Fuck," he exhales. "There's no going back. You know that, right?"

"Yes," I whimper, mindless to the pleasure of him so deep inside me.

"You'd better tell me now if you're not all in." He fucks me from below, pulling out halfway before driving into me and grinding his pelvis against my clit. "Because I am, and after I fill you, there's no getting rid of me."

"I am—I want you." I fist the sheets beside his head to keep my weight off his injured shoulder and meet him thrust for thrust.

His mouth is everywhere he can reach—my jaw, my throat, my tits, his teeth grazing my nipples. Over and over, those barbells hit just the right spot, and my body breaks out in a flash of heat, my legs trembling around his waist.

"You gonna come on my cock, angel?"

"Yes," I moan, unable to manage anything more.

"Thank fuck." He slams into me, his hips slapping my ass, his length filling me to the brim.

The fullness…the pressure…the piercings… I can't take any more and shatter with a cry of his name.

His cock thickens, stretching me farther, and I gush, clenching him tight. He hisses and pounds into me, his rhythm desperate and relentless. He jerks inside me and comes with a primal growl.

I collapse onto the mattress beside him, drifting in a pleasure haze, every nerve ending alive and humming.

"Te amo." He peppers my face with kisses and brushes his fingers through my hair. "I can't wait to fuck you properly."

My eyes flutter shut, breath uneven, pulse still hammering. "Sir, I'm not sure I'd survive if you did."

Chapter 8
Charlie

The security feed picks up movement in the backyard, and my video game freezes. I mutter a curse. I was seconds from wiping out an enemy.

The split-screen shows Desi and Dante emerging from the pool house—Desi with a towel over his shoulder, Dante with an unlit cigarette dangling from his lips.

I return to the game, closing the split-screen, but I keep glancing at the main security feed, watching them. Desi is in swim trunks, shirtless, while Dante is in faded black jeans, threadbare at the knees, and a black band tee.

My focus flits between Desi's athletic physique diving into the water and Dante lighting up as he straddles a lounger. I shouldn't be gawking at them, but they're fascinating—scientifically, of course—identical twins, mirroring DNA, exact replicas, but possessing uniquely separate personalities.

Dante, despite being the same age, is the protective older brother and leader. He's serious and conscientious. Desmond has the goofy, happy-go-lucky vibe of a younger sibling.

The night of the attack, Dante ordered Desi to remain

upstairs while he took care of the first intruders downstairs. His goal was to keep his brother—and Aurora—safe, although Desi is equally capable.

It makes me wonder why, if they're the same, Dante is so protective and Desi is so dependent on him. Has it always been that way? Or did something happen? Nature versus nurture—my inquisitive brain wants to know, for research purposes. Perhaps they're just fiercely loyal and perfectly complement one another.

Desi floats on his back and gazes up at the stars. Secretly, I check out his wet body glistening in the pool lights. He's muscular but not beefy, over six feet tall, with dark hair and onyx eyes. It's a struggle every time I see him—or *them*. I want to stare until my bizarre infatuation is sated. Instead, I avoid them.

My character is filled with bullets, snatching my attention. I release a stream of expletives and pulverize the controller buttons. Serves me right for ogling.

I engross myself in the game, repositioning my team. When I check the security feed next, the patio is empty. I dismiss it, but a pang of regret hits me. I wish I were bold enough to join them in the pool without requiring an explicit invitation. Even if I got one, though, I wouldn't go.

First, I'd need shorts that fit. Nobody here is my size. Then, I'd have to take my shirt off, exposing my burns to their curious gazes. *Like you stare at them?* True but different. They're physically attractive; I'm mediocre at best and scarred.

Desi's gamertag appears onscreen, joining my team—something he's done countless times over the past two weeks. Today, they moved into the pool house to be close to Aurora while Ethan and Jax are traveling. Before now, they were staying at Jackson's downtown penthouse, and I was with Reece at Ethan's apartment.

"*Piccino*," Desi's deep voice, a purr against the crack of gunfire and the metallic clink of reloading, filters through my headset.

My brows knit together. I'm alone online because I don't enjoy listening to the yelling, but he can't be talking to me.

"*Piccino*," he drawls once more.

Piccino? What does that even mean? "Are you talking to me?" The controller vibrates in my hand, a sniper trying to take me down.

"*Who else would I be talking to?*" He chuckles, low and breathy, almost playful.

The sharpshooter drops from the rooftop with a satisfying thunk, thanks to Desi.

"Ah…your scary brother?"

His chuckle becomes a full-blown laugh. "*Definitely not.*"

Heavy silence falls between us, broken only by artillery fire and the frantic clicking of buttons as we coordinate to eliminate the next unit.

"*Question for you.*" His words are hesitant and uncertain, unlike his usual bold confidence. "*Do you have a thing for Reece?*"

Irritation swarms in my gut, and I snap, "Do you have a thing for Ethan?" It wouldn't be the first time I've been teased about my relationship with my partner.

"*Wow,*" he draws out. "*Defensive much? We're blood. Not the same.*"

"Both questions are equally stupid." All the noise and action add to my agitation, and I can't concentrate. I get killed repeatedly. "You barely know him."

"*Ethan's father took the fall for the family. We wouldn't be alive if it wasn't for Enzo.*"

"Likewise, Reece saved my life."

My last therapist concluded Reece was an unhealthy security blanket. She said I was attached to the safety he presented, enabling my avoidance and isolation. She suggested I make a clean break and live independently. I hacked her computer, deleted my patient files, and never returned.

"That doesn't mean you don't have a thing for him."

I roll my eyes, although he can't see it. "I don't. Besides, what's it matter?"

"I was going to invite you over."

My heart rate skyrockets, but I haven't a clue why. My mind is drawing a blank. "For what?"

Neither of us moves onscreen, the game forgotten.

"I've seen you staring at me."

His voice is deeper, flirtatious, and I feel hot all over, my palms sweaty.

"What about Dante?" What am I asking and why am I whispering?

"What about him? You don't stare at him."

"Because I'm afraid he'll murder me. You're carbon copies. If I find one of you attractive, it's impossible not to find the other attractive. It's a scientific fact."

"You're the weirdest person I know." He chuckles. It's affectionate, not cruel, but still...

Perhaps that therapist was right. I need to live my own life, tonight, underground, far from LA. "Okay, well, goodnight."

Before I remove my headset and disappear, never to be seen again, he says, *"Piccino, come over to the pool house, or we're coming to get you. Your choice."*

Chapter 9
Dante

The day my twin finds love is the day I no longer exist. That sounds dramatic, but he's my other half, and I don't foresee a worthwhile life without him. Luckily, most people are shit and don't deserve to glance his way.

A few years ago, Desi fell hard for a girl we met while working security at a club. I hated her, saw right through her lies and phony act. Late one night, we caught her in the back office, screwing the manager. She used Desi, was climbing her way to the top—or so she thought. Little did she know, our family owned the entire building, including the club.

I wanted to murder them both. My twin only wanted to escape. He got drunk and passed out in my room after playing video games for hours. He laughed through his pain, but I felt it, sharp and agonizing, every time I looked at him.

While he was out cold, I killed them anyhow; drove a knife through their rib cages and dumped their bodies in the Adirondack mountains. He never asked where they were or why they hadn't returned to work. He knew.

Desi is too pure for this world. He smiles at strangers and

engages them in conversation if they appear sad. He calls our mom almost daily. No matter how rough it gets, he loves life.

He has no filter; he says whatever is on his mind. He flirts with everybody, and I mean *everybody*. He enjoys sex, but he no longer dates or becomes attached.

And he has *never* called anyone 'piccino,' a term of endearment meaning 'little one' that our grandma gave us before she switched to 'polpetto,' or 'meatball,' which was more fitting.

Twenty-six-year-old Lucas Parker-Mercer, aka Charlie, is just the type who'd capture my brother's interest: an awkward, wounded, dependent, genius-hero who struggles socially, resists change, and desperately needs a friend. In Desi's eyes, he's *safe*.

"This is not a good idea, Des."

Dressed in nothing but a pair of basketball shorts, he places the controller and headset on the glass coffee table. "He likes you too."

My expression contorts, and my brows pinch. "No, he doesn't."

He grins, that familiar grin that grants him whatever he desires, the one that makes it hard to believe we're twins. "Yes, he does. He asked about you. He said he was attracted to us equally."

That blows my mind. I was certain Charlie wanted me in a max-level prison. He side-eyes me as if I'm a snarling wolf poised to attack. His interest can only be physical. "So…?"

"So," my other half drags out. "We've shared people before. Right?"

"Women. For one night." *And I didn't exactly love it.* "Not a man who's practically family and works for Homeland Security."

I walk into the adjoining kitchen and open the fridge, only to remember we don't have any alcohol to get me through this, and I slam it shut. Ethan made the rules for staying here very clear: no drugs or alcohol, no smoking indoors, and no bringing anyone home, particularly women. I think he expected us to throw a rager and fill the pool with liquor and naked chicks.

He's only ten years older than us, but Ethan reminds me of our dad—not much for words, but when he speaks, you'd better listen. And both of them are ridiculously protective.

Desi meets me in the kitchen. Resting his elbows on the island, he tilts his head in slight annoyance. "He works for Homeland Security because he's brilliant."

"No. He works for Homeland Security because Reece does. He *chose* to be on his team. Another reason he's a terrible idea."

I don't want anyone breaking my brother's heart, especially someone I can't easily get rid of.

He smirks and his eyes light up. "The more you worry about a person, the more I know you like them."

I lower my gaze and shake my head. There's no fooling my twin. "No."

"Oh yeah? You don't run background checks on one-night stands. Tell me what you found. Does he pass your strict approval?"

"Des—"

"Give me a summary at least. Before he gets here."

I release a defeated sigh, knowing he won't give up, and lean against the counter. "Lucas Parker-Mercer. Age twenty-six. Adopted. Has two moms, hence the two last names. Went by Parker prior to the military. Has a handful of foster siblings. Near-genius IQ. Forced to work for the government at eighteen after repeatedly hacking into the Pentagon for the challenge and attempting to erase student loan debt. Injured in combat and developed agoraphobia. Discharged from the military around four years ago. Offered a job with the CIA but accepted a lesser position with Homeland Security to be on Reece's team," my gaze connects with deep-brown eyes that mirror mine, "who he'll never leave. Which means, unless they all move to New York, this is only temporary."

Desi rests his chin on his fist, closes his eyes, and swoons dramatically. "He sounds sweet. Perfect for us. Ma will love him. Let's drag him over here and make him a twin sandwich."

A fire ignites within me, and my blood heats. This cannot be happening. "Are you listening to me at all?"

Standing to his full height, he dismisses me with a wave and turns to leave. "Reece is becoming more involved with Aurora. Parker will be the perfect house husband."

I grab him by the collar just as he reaches the door. "No, Des!"

There's a knock. He peers at me over his shoulder, a diabolical grin on his face. "You're going to love him."

This is why I smoke.

Chapter 10
Desmond

I swing the door open, and Charlie's soft, green-eyed gaze fixates on my bare chest. I could've worn a shirt, but where's the fun in that? I lean against the doorway and hook my thumb in the waistband of my shorts.

"Hello, piccino."

He gulps, his gaze slowly meeting mine, and raises his hand. "Hi."

I smile, finding his social awkwardness absolutely adorable. I'd be lying if I said I wasn't smitten, and his history only strengthens my determination to have him.

I knew he was special.

My twin realizes it too. He's just stubborn and emotionally cold. He shows his love through loyalty and protection, as does Charlie.

They're also both intelligent, experienced with weapons, and dislike people. The only difference is Charlie comes in a smaller, gentler package, which my brother appreciates.

Me? I'm not picky. Fun is fun is fun, you know?

Tonight, Agent Mercer is dressed in skinny khakis, a cream sweater, and white tennis shoes, looking all posh and preppy. His brown hair is short on the sides and messy on top, falling into his eyes like a shield. He's delicious; I could eat him up.

He's perfect—for both of us—but Dante won't chase anyone, especially someone he thinks I want.

Charlie catches me gawking and blushes. He glances behind me then drops his gaze, and I'll bet anything my brother is scowling.

"You gonna let him in or stare at him all night?" my twin grumbles.

I peer over my shoulder. "You gonna stop mean-mugging, or should we go for a walk on the beach, Tay?"

He narrows his eyes at my use of his nickname—one I've used since childhood, when I struggled with speech and couldn't pronounce his full name.

Our locked gaze becomes intense. I want Charlie. *He* wants Charlie. He just needs a push, and for me, he's selfless. He'll give me what I want, and vice versa, and my wish is for us to share, because he'd enjoy it if he let his guard down.

"We'll play *COD*," I offer.

I've studied Charlie for the past two weeks. His moods range from enthusiastic interest to anxious rambling to quiet distrust. I asked his favorite video game, and he launched into a thirty-minute monologue about *COD*. It took me a few days, but the pool house now has a sweet gaming setup. It's not as fancy as the one in the security room, but it's sure to tempt the little nerd into spending time with me.

If that fails, I'll take it apart and pretend I need him to fix it.

My deception must be written all over my face, because my twin shakes his head and mutters, "You're obsessed."

"It's a great game." I grin and step back to let Charlie inside.

He toes off his shoes, revealing pink polka-dot socks, his

observant gaze darting around the open space. The studio is well-appointed—high ceilings, stained concrete floors, and expansive windows overlooking the moonlit pool. A sleek, modern kitchen on one side, leather seating surrounding a dual stone fireplace in the middle, and a plush king bed and full bath on the other.

The only time we slept here, Dante took the couch and I took the bed. Tonight will be interesting, provided I can get our gamer geek to stay.

I plop down on the couch and grab two controllers. When he's close enough, I wrap an arm around Charlie's waist and pull him onto my lap. "Do you prefer Charlie or Parker?"

***

Charlie

I stiffen. Lava erupts in the pit of my stomach and rushes through my veins. I've never been in a man's lap. Ever. Nor have I been with someone as powerful as Desmond Rossi.

I'm an average-sized guy. Although few, the men I've dated have been my size. I may be small compared to the twins, but I'm not tiny. Am I? They make me feel tiny and something else I can't quite put my finger on. Safe?

Desi's hand flattens over my abdomen. He guides me back against his chest and hands me a controller. "You're okay, piccino. Get comfortable."

There's that word again.

My fingers tremble. Why did I come here? Is this what I wanted? It must be because my body relaxes into his, even though I can't seem to catch my breath.

Reece is next door. Nothing will happen. They wouldn't dare harm you.

Dante drops beside us and stares at me expectantly, those dark eyes straight out of a nightmare—not mine, but someone's—and I recall being asked a question.

"Wh-what?"

"They call you Charlie. Do you prefer Parker?" Dante asks, rough and smoky.

My lips part and my brows furrow. "How do you know that?"

He tilts his head, much like a wild animal assessing his prey. "You've done your homework, I'm sure."

"On you?" I blink, my mind reeling. "Yes, it's my job."

"Then you're aware I'm capable of doing the same."

A tense sigh escapes me, followed by a curt nod. "Right. Of course. Um…" What do I prefer? I don't even know. Parker was my birth name, and Charlie was given to me. I wear it as a badge of honor, a representation of survival, but it also weighs heavily with survivor's guilt.

Perhaps that therapist was right and I *have* lost my identity.

"You don't have to decide now." Nuzzling my neck, Desi launches the game.

He smells faintly of sea salt and strongly of bad choices. His thighs are rock-hard beneath me, and I'm acutely aware of *other* parts of him.

His stubble scrapes my skin, and my nipples tighten. My hips shift. Only my anxiety and his brother's penetrating judgment are keeping me from getting an embarrassing erection.

When it's my turn to set up my character, he slips under my sweater. I freeze, sucking in my stomach, and snatch his wrist.

He doesn't continue, but he also doesn't remove his hand. "I'm going to feel you, see you, at some point."

Nausea churns my gut. My insecurities war with my

body. I long to be touched, desired, but I may never leave my room if rejected. "Why?"

"Why not?"

Chapter 11
Dante

My brother is impulsive, and I have zero patience. "What's wrong with your stomach?"

Engrossed in the game, Charlie answers, "I was burned in a bombing…in the military." A flush creeps up his neck, and he swallows hard, but he remains focused on the flatscreen.

My gaze is drawn to where Des' arm is wrapped around Charlie's waist, caressing his side with his thumb. A sliver of taut, discolored skin shows, but it's nothing hideous and certainly nothing to be ashamed of.

My brother likes him—too much. I'll admit he's attractive, and his skittish behavior arouses my protective instincts, but he's not for us. No way we're getting involved with a federal agent. He's devoted to Reece, and when we return to New York, he'll remain with Reece.

Still, he sits rigid in my twin's lap, shoulders curled forward and jaw tense. His nervous energy is palpable, and it bothers me. "Put him between us, Des. Let him relax."

Desi narrows his eyes in warning then releases him. Charlie scoots closer, casting a suspicious glance in my direction.

I'm not much of a toucher or hugger. I learned to comfort my brother as a kid, but I've never felt the urge to do so with anyone else. Until now.

No one speaks; only the chaotic sounds of virtual shooting and controllers clicking fill the room. I try to concentrate on the game, but the more awkward it grows between us, the more irritated I become. If I wasn't here, they'd be dry humping each other already. I consider leaving, but the thought grates on me, aggravating me further.

I want him—I do. In an alternate universe, one in which Charlie wasn't a federal agent and I wasn't consumed with worry and responsibility, I'd be as eager as Des to explore this attraction.

What's the worst that could happen? My brother becomes attached and wants to stay in LA? I guess we'll stay in LA, or maybe split our time, as long as we're not bringing an agent home.

And if Charlie decides he's not interested, leaves, and my twin is heartbroken? I'll find Charlie and haul his ass back here.

Maybe one night won't hurt.

I clasp Charlie's nape, and he jumps, snapping his head around to stare at me wide-eyed.

"What about Lucas?" I weave my fingers through his soft, shaggy hair. "You shouldn't have to carry the burden of your past. The scars are already on your body."

The controller falls from his hands. "I...I was named after Luke Skywalker." His speech is rapid, his voice higher pitched.

I wonder if he's having some sort of fit until Desi hides a chuckle behind his fist, and I realize I'm making Charlie more nervous. How can a person be so composed in emergencies yet socially anxious?

"Oh...that's nice."

It comes out forced, and my brother laughs harder, his face turning red and his eyes watering. I'm as bad as the man between us and completely fucking this up.

Charlie grins, perhaps also finding my struggle amusing. "I like Lucas."

I return his smile, the sensation unfamiliar, and his gaze drops to my lips.

My dick stirs, and my tone lowers. "You want to kiss me, Lucas?"

"Y-yes," he says without hesitation.

Cupping the back of his head, I lean in slowly, giving him the chance to change his mind. He doesn't, and when our mouths meet, he releases the sweetest groan—as if he's been waiting forever to be genuinely touched. Fuck, I know that feeling.

I swallow it down, deepening the kiss. His lips are soft and gentle. Our tongues intertwine, his hand moving to the back of my neck, gripping me, and my heart beats a violent rhythm.

The urge to have him in my lap, his body against mine, my mouth on his skin, is fierce. Before I take it too far, I break the kiss but don't release him. I'm not sure I can at this point.

My gaze finds my twin. "What's next, brother?"

The smug grin plastered on his face tells me he knew what he was doing when he invited Lucas over, knew I'd want him.

Des snatches Lucas' controller and tosses it on the coffee table then shuts off the TV. Only the shimmering reflection of the pool dancing on the ceiling remains.

"My turn." With desperation, Desi devours Lucas, their kiss punctuated by soft moans.

I'm hard and aching. Lucas wants us both; we want him. Desi was right—he's perfect.

Just tonight, or maybe a few nights, I tell myself, knowing it's a lie, knowing this could be something more.

Desi pulls back and grabs the hem of Lucas' sweater. "Can I take this off?"

He hesitates, and, not ready for this to end, I nod toward the other side of the studio. "Let's move this to the bed."

He'll be less exposed and more comfortable under the covers.

***

<u>Lucas</u>
(<u>AKA Charlie)</u>

My lungs are sore; I can't catch my breath. Only in my wildest dreams did I picture the three of us together. I'm still clutching Dante's nape like a lifeline when he lifts and sets me on my feet as if I weigh nothing at all.

They waste no time stripping, clothes strewn from the couch to the bed.

I'm a little slower, unable to take my eyes off them. They're absolutely stunning—defined muscles flexing as they move, tattoos I want to study and draw.

Out of habit, I face away, removing everything down to my boxer briefs.

Strong arms wrap around me from behind, initially startling me.

"Fuck, you're beautiful. Your ass is utter perfection." Desi rolls his hips, his impressive length grinding between my cheeks, and trails kisses over my shoulder. "I can't remember the last time I was this fucking hard."

He runs his hands over my chest and stomach with no reluctance or revulsion then slips into my boxers, palming my erection. His strokes are unhurried, his lips worshiping my skin. I tip my head back onto his shoulder and allow myself to feel. No doubts. No anxieties. No insecurities. Just the bliss of this moment.

"Des. Share," interrupts Dante's gruff voice.

"Yes, Tay Tay," his twin calls out, releasing me.

Kicking off my boxers, I join Dante in bed, Desi climbing in after. It's pure pleasure, both of them kissing and caressing me. I've been with men and women, but nothing compares to this. I doubt any sexual experience ever will.

I'm steadily leaking precum onto Dante's fingers as he jerks me off, and I do the same to him. Des massages my balls, and the dual sensation has me lightheaded, floating in a cloud of ecstasy.

My cock pulses, and I moan into Dante's mouth, pushing back against Des. "I need to come."

"Can I suck you or fuck you?" Des asks, husky and rough.

A chill runs down my spine, and goosebumps erupt along my feverish skin. I already know what I'm choosing. I'll regret it if I don't. "I want you inside me while I suck Dante."

"Fuuuuuck," they both curse.

Chapter 12
Desmond

I scramble from the bed in search of my bag, finding it by the door. Front pocket. Lube and condom. Got it.

This might be the most incredible night of my life. My twin typically takes several rounds of shots and relentless badgering to go out with someone, let alone sleep with them. He's stuck in his head. Not exactly fun, or the best wingman, but he goes along for my sake.

Before now, I assumed he disliked kissing, but perhaps he disliked the other person and wasn't willing to force it.

Tonight, his affections are undoubtedly authentic. You can't fake passion, tenderness, or possessiveness. He genuinely likes Agent Mercer, and I knew he would.

I palm my angry erection, stroking lazily, and consider the best way to do this. I need everyone to be comfortable, able to focus on having a mind-blowing orgasm, like I'm about to. The position they're in now won't work—sideways head is annoying, I know that much.

As if reading my thoughts, my brother props himself up against the pillows and headboard. Lucas climbs between his legs, but before he can lie down on the mattress, Dante pulls him in for a brief kiss.

"You okay with this?"

"Yes," he answers, quiet but confident.

We're about six-three. Lucas is average height—maybe five-nine—and skinny, like he has never lifted a weight in his life. He's probably a hell of a runner. He has those runner's legs and ass, those toned abs.

My twin threads his fingers through Lucas' wild hair. "Have you done this before?"

Another, more confident, "Yes."

"Not exactly what I wanted to hear," Dante grumbles.

I smile at his jealousy. He was worried about *me* becoming attached—ha! He needs to worry about himself.

"Not with two people, if that's what you're asking," Lucas clarifies.

"Hmm...a little better." Dante pecks his lips. "I wanna make sure we don't hurt you."

"You won't. I...I prepped before I came over."

My dick jerks in response.

Dante's brows shoot skyward. "In case Desi wanted to fuck you?"

"Y-yes...is that bad?"

He shakes his head, a rare smile on his grumpy mug. "Not at all. It's fucking hot, but next time, we'll do it for you." He fists Lucas' hair. "Get down there and suck my cock. Show my twin that pretty ass of yours."

Chest to the mattress, bubble butt in the air, our shy nerd obeys.

Dante breathes out, "Ummph...damn," and I take that as my cue.

I crawl up, kneeling behind Lucas and flipping the top on the lube. Even though he said he prepped, I use a generous amount when circling his rim. I work in one finger, then two, then three, to the sounds of his muffled whimpers.

Goddamn, I'll be hearing those whimpers in my dreams.

Slowly, I fuck him with my fingers, kissing and biting his ass. I sink my teeth into the muscle hard enough to leave a mark. If he is screwing someone else—a lethal situation that better end tonight—I want that soon-to-be-missing person to know he's mine.

I wonder if he'll let me tattoo my name on him: *Property of Desmond Rossi.* It'd hold significant meaning in New York, not so much in LA. We'll have to move.

Lucas squeezes around my fingers, breaking me from my possessive thoughts, and pushes back against me. I interpret that as a silent indication he wants me to fill him.

Thank fuck, because I'm steadily leaking precum and dying to get inside him. I tear open the condom and roll it on, hoping to ditch them next time. I want to feel him raw, load his ass with my cum. My dick kicks in agreement as I line us up.

"Hurry up, Des. I'm not gonna last long. His mouth is fucking phenomenal."

My twin's strained words and Lucas' erotic moans send zaps of pleasure straight to my balls, drawing them up tight.

I seize his hips and slide into him in one smooth, firm stroke. To say he feels like home would be cheesy, but… "Jesus, fuck, your ass just swallowed my soul."

Dante releases a babble of expletives, but my gaze remains glued to the sight of Lucas stretched around my girth. It's hypnotizing. Addicting. "All mine." *Ours?* I don't know; my head is on cloud nine.

I pull back until only the crown of my cock is squeezed by him and punch forward, driving all the way in. He cries out, gripping me like a vise and milking me. Fucking heaven.

The three of us turn feral, falling into a mad rhythm of

desperate moans and slapping skin. I fuck Lucas hard and deep while his head bobs, blowing my twin. Nothing could be more perfect.

My heart hammers, muscles coiled tight, and my breath hitches in my throat. Wildfire consumes my body. I won't last long. "Come with me, piccino. Make yourself come."

I piston in and out of his ass while he jerks himself furiously. He lets out a strangled cry, pulsing around me as he comes, and I'm a goner.

"Fucking...fuck." I slam into him, jolting and cursing this condom for ruining my best orgasm. We'll have to try again. Tomorrow morning. If he lets me.

The momentum of my final thrusts causes Lucas to choke on my brother, and Dante growls.

"I'm gonna come, baby. Keep sucking my cock... So fucking good..." His words trail off with a rumbling groan.

I gasp for breath and shudder with aftershocks. "Do I propose now or...?"

Chapter 13
Ethan

I wake with Jackson nuzzled against my side, his leg between mine, his hand resting below my collarbone. I'd fallen asleep last night playing with his hair while he talked about Aurora and how he believes she and Reece are fighting, how he thinks Reece is struggling.

I get it. Reece and I share certain similarities. We both believe a man's role is to protect and provide, and right now, he's injured, reliant on others. I'd hate it too.

I'm not worried about Reece. He'll manage, he always does. Even if he's struggling, he'll look after our girl, and he'll let me know if he can't. Plus, I have the twins. They'll safeguard what's mine as if it were their own, and they're damn good at it.

I'm more worried about the man lying on my chest.

Jesus, I never thought those words would enter my consciousness.

I turn my head and inhale the scent of coconut and citrus. I run my fingers through Jackson's soft hair, and a highlight reel of him sucking me off last night replays in my mind.

The way he stared up at me, pleading eyes brimming with

desperate hunger, as if he wanted to devour every part of me—body, heart, and soul.

The image alone stirs something deep within me.

He's addictive and unpredictable. I thought being in love with Aurora was scary—Jax is ten times worse. I can't control him. *He* can't control himself. When he's depressed or on the edge, or when he puts himself in danger to protect us…

Losing him would kill me. If anyone could bring me straight to my knees, it'd be him.

Insecurities invade my mind, and my stomach knots. I don't think I can give him everything he's willing to give me—not that I didn't love every second of last night, because I did.

Nor do I regret it.

Well, most of it.

I regret some shit I let slip. I worry it'll be awkward between us. I fear he's in a fragile state, and when things settle, he'll realize he doesn't enjoy being dominated by me. Or anything sexual with me, for that matter.

Then, there's the team and management. I can't show him the affection and commitment he deserves. I already have to restrain myself publicly with Aurora. Now Jax too, but more so.

Guilt has my breath quickening. What if he grows to resent being a secret? Resents me? I'm only setting him up for destruction, setting us up for failure.

"Stop panicking." His raspy, sleep-filled tone interrupts my downward spiral. He kisses my aching chest, his hand over my racing heart. "I loved everything." Another kiss, lower. "I won't tell a soul." His lips drift to my stomach. "I love you. I love being with you."

He dips under the covers, and, once again, my brain battles with my body.

For the moment, my brain triumphs. "Jax."

He palms my erection over the boxers I put on after showering last night.

"Jax." I raise my voice.

He ignores me and kisses the head of my cock, an open-mouthed kiss that soaks my boxers, and I jerk, my body begging for more.

"Jax," I growl and yank his hair.

"What?" He throws the blanket back. "I want it," he whines.

I lift my brows. "Come here."

His eyes glint with mischief. "No. I'm busy."

"Get up here."

"No." His stare is an unwavering challenge, a dare.

And I'm so close to caving.

When I say nothing more, he pulls down the waistband of my boxers and runs his tongue up my length, still holding eye contact, still testing me.

I'm tempted to let him have it then punish him by choking him with my dick. "You want me to take control? Is that it?"

"I want you satisfied."

Confused, I scowl. "I am satisfied."

He crawls up my body, his cock brushing mine. "No, I want you to be truly satisfied. I want you to come to our hotel room, knowing you have the power to take what you want. No holding back."

No holding back. Privately.

I trace my thumb over his perfect lips. "I don't want to hurt you, and I don't want to lose you." I can't look him in the eyes. "I…I don't think I can give you everything you give me."

When I risk a glance, his head is cocked, his expression something I'd expect on my own face—irked. He falls to his side, propping up on his elbow, and I miss the weight of him immediately.

He releases an exasperated sigh. "This is really bothering you?"

I clear my throat, garnering the courage to continue. "I almost lost you. I refuse to feel that way again."

"You won't lose me. We live together, share the same girl, and sleep in the same bed. People know. We're just not making it obvious." He twirls his finger through my chest hair. "And I'm okay with whatever you give me. I told you that."

"You all but demanded a public commitment."

"I wanted proof. I needed somewhere to express the feelings I had for you when hugging wasn't enough. I have that now. You've given me that."

"Promise?" I ask, although I don't believe him. "You're not going to get all obsessive and jealous and clingy?"

He glances at the ceiling and taps his lip. "Can we get a yacht?"

He's deflecting, and I shake my head. "You don't need a yacht."

"An endless vacation of sex." He gestures with a wave. "Just think about all—"

I shut him up with my mouth and tongue. His body returns to mine. He rolls his hips, grinding our erections together, and an icy-hot sensation skitters across my skin.

He breaks away, placing gentle kisses along my jawline. "I want you. I'll do whatever you say. Now, can you stop ruining my playtime with useless worries? I need my daily dose of Ethan."

My lips spread into an unrestrained grin, and I forget all about the dark side of Jackson O'Reilly. "You just had me."

"I want you again…" His teeth graze my throat, leaving goosebumps in their wake. "And again tonight."

"We'll be on a plane."

"Sounds hot. We should get a private jet too. Then I can have you whenever I want."

Fuck me. He's going to be my undoing. "You're insatiable."

***

Jackson

I was going to take off. I injured him. I put everyone in danger. Reece was shot because of me. Yet, Ethan *still* worries about hurting or losing me. Me? When he's the one who should be disgusted and toss me aside.

For that reason alone, I'll worship him and his impressive body as long as he lets me. I don't care if he doesn't repay the favor in the same way. Getting him off is a huge fucking turn-on.

My knees hug his waist, my weight on my forearms, my fingers in his messy hair, and I kiss him. His lips are full, softer than imagined, but his kiss is fierce, possessive. Add the scratch of his beard, and it's intoxicating. Purely Ethan.

His hands explore me, tracing the contours of my muscles, ribs, and spine. His touch is electrifying. My hips flex, and I thrust my erection along his.

He palms my ass and grinds into me then tugs at my boxers. "Take these off. I want to feel you bare."

This is something out of a wet dream, and I'm rock-hard and leaking before I'm even naked.

We both strip, our lips meeting in a chaotic tangle of teeth and tongue. We're two people consumed by love and lust, lost in the fever of wanting one another.

I slide against him, slick with precum, and my breath hitches. I'm not small by any means, but he's bigger—not by a lot, only proportional to the rest of him, and my dick is curved upward. He's perfection.

He releases a drawn-out, rumbling groan that vibrates in his chest. "Fuck, you feel good. You're dripping all over me."

I'm incapable of speech. In fact, if he keeps talking dirty, I might blow.

He snakes his arm between our bodies and wraps his hand around us both. His fingers and his cock glide along mine, and my legs tremble. My lips part. Apparently, I'm unable to kiss as well.

"Can you come like this, baby?" He strokes our lengths, firm and rough.

"Yes," I moan and throb in his tight grip.

"Will you still give me that beautiful mouth of yours? Let me come down your throat."

His praise lights up my veins, and my muscles tense with the need for more—more of his words, more friction, more of him and me.

I roll my hips and meet his strokes. "Hell yeah."

He does the same, thrusting against me with a rhythm that sends jolts of ecstasy through me, and more wetness slicks between us. Pleasure fogs my mind and leaves me dizzy.

His fingers thread into my hair and tighten. "I fucking love the feel of you. Fuck my fist, baby boy. Come all over my cock before you suck it." He yanks my head back and sinks his teeth into my collarbone.

"Oh...*fuck*." My balls hug my shaft, my vision darkens, and every muscle in my body twitches. I clutch the sheets and lose my breath, jerking in his hand and shooting cum all over his stomach, fingers, and dick.

Eager to please him and still high and tingling from the orgasm, I trail kisses down his chest and abs, tasting myself on his skin.

His stiff cock is covered in my release, and I take a minute to lick it up, my eyes finding his.

Impatient, he fists my hair. "Be a good boy and suck it. Make me come."

I pull him into my mouth as far as I can. He flexes his hips gently, still hesitating, and bumps the back of my throat. I want him to use me, fuck my mouth, and lose restraint. Being rough and taking power is his love language, his way of showing ownership.

Anything less is indifference.

When his cock is in my mouth, my head is quiet. I'm focused on pleasing him. My anxieties disappear. I'm fulfilled. Every gasp, every moan, every thrust of his hips, every tug of my hair is my reward—I only need to get him there.

He swells, stretching my lips farther, and I withdraw slowly, increasing suction as I go. Aurora does this, and it drives me mad.

"Jax," he warns.

I glare up at him. "What do you call me when your cock is in my mouth?"

His expression is priceless. It shifts from shock to slight humor to *absolutely fucking not*. There's no way in hell he'll allow me to dominate him, and I'm looking forward to the retribution.

His tone becomes vicious. "Then put it in your fucking mouth, brat."

I do, but not before giving him a taunting grin.

He cups the back of my head and punches his hips. "Don't fucking move,' he growls.

I relax my jaw, and he fucks my throat, keeping me right where he wants me—nose to his pelvis. He moans, and I moan around him, my cock starting to rally once again from the desperate sounds he makes.

It's sloppy, his balls coated in cum and saliva when I massage them.

"Don't you dare fucking stop." His precum bursts along my taste buds. "That's it, baby boy. Fuck, *you take me so fucking well.*" The last part is a strained groan.

His fingers shake in my hair, he thrusts one last time, and his cock jerks, filling my mouth with cum. I swallow and suck him lazily until he yanks me away, gasping for breath.

"Come here." He draws me to him and devours my lips, his heart pounding with mine. After a few minutes of kissing and cuddling, he stands from the bed, his long, glistening cock hanging between his colossal thighs. "You better not be too tired for the game tonight."

I collapse onto my back, gloriously spent. I haven't bothered to check the time, but the muted gray light filtering through the sheer curtains suggests it's early. That, or there's another snowstorm. We don't, or *I* don't, have to be anywhere until noon. He'll leave much sooner.

My lips and jaw are sore, and my erection thickens at the sight of him. I flash him a smug smile. Now that I've let myself truly *see* him, I'm obsessed with every inch. "What will you give me if I win tonight, Coach?"

He narrows his eyes, peering down at me with annoyance and a hint of intimidation. He may appear threatening, but I don't miss how his gaze trails down my body to my hard cock. "What do you want?"

"I want your teeth marks as a tattoo."

Chapter 14
Reece

Aurora sleeps beside me, nestled close. I don't dare move, afraid to wake her, but sleep evades me. I'm used to getting up early, and as the sun's rays sneak into the bedroom, I get restless.

My shoulder and arm are also killing me, but I didn't bring any pain meds. I'm sick of being sluggish and irritable, and I can't tell if it's the pain or the pills.

A gentle nudge or kick to my side brings me a smile; then, my heart sinks, and the smile fades into a grimace. It's not the pregnancy or the baby. It's that it's not mine, and it feels like intruding on another man's territory to experience it, to enjoy it.

Strange, since I'm fond of caring for her, but unlike Ethan, I don't relish the taboo aspect of this situation. And I'm not Jax. I'm not entangled with both Aurora and Ethan, obsessed with anything related to them.

I'm deeply in love with Aurora—a love I'll never share with anyone else—yet I can't shake this uncomfortable feeling, this yearning for more. Sometimes, I still feel like I'm leading a double life.

I rake my fingers through my hair. It's not Aurora, it's not the polyamorous relationship—I don't need her all to myself—but maybe purpose and security I'm lacking. I'm not used to being idle, not used to…freedom.

She and Jax are soulmates, bonded for eternity or some shit, and she's having a baby with Ethan, who also loves Jax. The three of them are solid. She wanted something exclusively hers, and she has that with me, but what do I want? What's my place in this family? Where do I fit in this foursome?

This is why I stay focused; If not, my mind is chaos. But Jesus, I could use a fucking break.

I shift, and Aurora groans, reaching for me.

"Sleep. It's early." I kiss her forehead. "I'll get you breakfast."

"French toast and strawberries," she mumbles without opening her eyes.

"We'll see. You need protein. You eat too much sugar."

She makes a grumpy, pouty noise and falls back asleep. I go to the bathroom, shower quickly, get dressed, and find my phone on the counter. Wrestling with my clothes and the sling is agony, and once again, I regret not packing pain meds, but I'll manage.

I hadn't planned on sleeping here, but releasing her from my arms felt impossible, and we were undisturbed. The isolation was heavenly after the pandemonium of recent weeks.

When I arrived yesterday, I thanked my team then kicked them out. I saw them enough during my hospital stay. My commander hasn't mentioned me returning to the field, and I'm not pushing it. The case is in the investigative stages, and my recovery has been harder than I expected.

Plus, Jax and Ethan are traveling. My place is at home.

My place.

Being at home, protecting Aurora and this family, strengthens my sense of purpose, brings me peace. I'll forever be her bodyguard, and I'm okay with that. I am.

I enter the kitchen to blissful silence. The solitude is serene. I've never appreciated this house more.

The last time I saw Charlie, he grabbed a pizza box and headed toward my room. I'm assuming he hung around playing video games or went to the pool house. He stays close—another thing I need to figure out.

I doubt my partner will be on twin duty much longer. There's no way HSI will prosecute Desi and Dante. They were defending the house—my home—with weapons belonging to Charlie and me, issued by Homeland Security. A defense lawyer would eat that up, and neither of us would testify against them.

While coffee is brewing, I text Ethan. I'm surprised he hasn't checked in already.

> You got a moment to talk?

ETHAN

> Is this about you sleeping in my bed last night?

Startled and using only one hand, I fumble with the phone, dropping it on the counter.

Ethan is possessive of Aurora and Jackson, as in, they're his, and you're not allowed to hurt them or keep them. If I'm treating Aurora right and not stealing her, he's not bothered by me being with her.

Jax, on the other hand, watches our every move.

> It's your wife's bed also, and we agreed there'd be no cameras in the bedrooms, stalker.

Jessica Lyn

The coffeemaker beeps, and I pour myself a cup while I wait for his response.

JACKSON
Believe me, I don't care to see your ass. Wash my sheets. 🙄

Did you just put us in a group chat?

JACKSON
You slept in our bed, dude. I think that qualifies for a group chat. In fact, I'm naming it "Men Who Have Slept in My Bed."

Please don't. Where's your boyfriend?

JACKSON
In the shower. Where's my wife?

Asleep. She must not be used to a man who lasts longer than ten minutes.

JACKSON
Did you crack a joke? Holy shit. 😳 And I can't believe you'd say that about Coach.

I ignore his antics—it's clear we're getting nowhere—but he texts me moments later.

JACKSON
Fine, Viking. What's the problem?

I'd like to discuss my position here.

JACKSON
Okay... Is this blackmail? Are you suing me? If so, go after Kyle's homeowner's insurance. Or workers' comp? Is that a real thing? Technically, you were on the job.

> I'm not suing you, dumbass. Ethan offered me a position as security. I want to stay here with Aurora while you're away, or travel with you. I want an established place here.

JACKSON

> I'm confused. I thought you were already working as security. I built you an apartment. I'm expanding the pool house for your partner. You took a bullet for me... What am I missing?

> I have to pay you. Makes sense. How much?

He types far faster than me, especially since I only have one usable thumb.

> It's not about money. I have an income.

JACKSON

> You want to sleep in my bed. Gotcha. I'm not attracted to you in that way, but I'll consider it.

> I have no interest whatsoever in sleeping with you. Have Ethan text me.

JACKSON

> For a second there, I thought your sense of humor had improved. I'm kidding. That'd be awkward as fuck. Whatever you need. I planned to ask Charlie, but it's up to you, as head of security and all.

> You can be the funny one. I'll be the good-looking one.

JACKSON

> Two jokes? Damn, that must have been some good sex. Or was it head? I'm getting hard just thinking about it.

Jessica Lyn

> Fuck off. I hate you. What about the twins? Where will they stay?

JACKSON

> The pool house is currently only a studio, and they all managed just fine last night, so...

Jesus, I don't want to know.

Chapter 15
Reece

My partner shuffles into the kitchen in yesterday's rumpled clothes, hair a mess, eyes heavy-lidded, head down. He smothers a yawn with his fist and pours a cup of coffee.

From the breakfast table, I clear my throat. "They, ah, don't have a coffeemaker over there?"

He takes a massive gulp of caffeine before collapsing into the seat opposite me. "Didn't want to wake them." Eyelids nothing but slits, his body slumped, he sips his coffee.

A wide grin spreads across my face. "I've never seen you do the walk of shame. Did they get you drunk and kidnap you?"

"No alcohol. Not a walk of shame. We were up late playing video games."

"Oh…okay." I bite my lips and nod, feigning contemplation. "So, was one of the characters a vampire? And did he climb out of the TV and *maul* your neck?"

His eyes widen, and his hand flies to his throat in a clumsy attempt to cover the bites and hickeys left behind.

"Shit! I have a meeting with Bennett this morning." He drops his hand and stretches his neck. "Is it bad?"

"It's…a threat. Luckily, it's December, and you can wear a turtleneck or something."

Leaning in, he hammers his fists on the table, his face flushed. "I don't own a turtleneck. Do you own a turtleneck? No one owns a turtleneck. They went out of style with low-rise jeans. Fuckity-fuck-fucking shit on a waffle. How will I explain this to Bennett? I'm a horrible liar. I'm getting hives just thinking about it."

A chuckle rises in my throat, but I hold it in. "I think you have bigger problems than hickeys and love bites. I wouldn't mess with those two psychos, but hey," I relax into the seat, "at least you'll always be protected…and thoroughly fucked by the looks of it."

His face reddens further. "It was only one night," he mumbles into his mug.

One night, my ass. "You might wanna tell that to whichever twin—or both—marked you, claiming their territory."

He tries to hide a smile behind his coffee cup. "He was just being passionate."

I bark out a laugh, delighted my partner is finally finding his own happiness. "Yeah, passionately possessive. I'm not sure if you've noticed, but it runs in the family. No one gets out of here sane."

"You're here. It's *your* family."

"Exactly. Have you seen how jealous Aurora is? I'm stuck. She'd hunt me down."

He shakes his head and rolls his eyes. "Says the guy who assaulted a team of nurses after being shot to reach her."

My insides stir with agitation, a lingering effect from the fragmented visions. I vaguely remember being gripped with panic, believing she and our family were in danger, a mix of reality, dreams, and trauma.

It happens in a flash. My mind plays tricks on me, blending past and present events, skimming through memories as if they were pictures in a flip book. A sharp, phantom pain slices through my thigh where I was shot, point-blank, in another life, and my thoughts threaten to turn dark.

My mood plummets. Guilt strikes me, a tug of war between Aurora and my career. Can I truly step away from the intensity, the adrenaline, the reward of taking down bad guys? A part of me recoils at the thought.

Another thought stands out, though, greater than the guilt of not saving lives: I wish I were here when they broke in. "I should've been here—with her." I failed, and failure is deadly.

Fingers snap repeatedly in my face, the sound jolting me back to existence. "I was here. I'm not going anywhere."

I release a heavy breath. The tension in my chest and shoulders ease. Resolve spreads through me. I *need* to step away. I need peace. "I'm not returning—after medical leave. I'm not taking another case."

He forces a tight, awkward smile, the corners of his mouth twitching. "I figured as much. It was difficult to accept at first, but I understand."

My heart hurts. We've been together since Charlie was eighteen and thrown into a life he wasn't prepared for—*no one is prepared for a life of violence and death*. We've only been separated briefly while transitioning to the agency.

"Jax asked if you'd stay on as security. Said he'd expand the pool house for you."

He stares blankly, and then his gaze shifts to the patio, to the pool house, to the twins. "What about them?"

"I'm sure they'll return to New York soon. There's nothing here for them."

He winces, and I feel like an ass. "I mean—you know what I mean," I backtrack. "My brain is a mess lately."

His Adam's apple bobs, and he hangs his head. "Yeah. No, you're right."

I mentally punch myself for my poor choice of words. "Don't do that. You're worth it. Whatever you choose—whatever they choose—we'll work it out."

He doesn't seem convinced. "Yeah, okay." He rises and brings his mug to the sink. "I'm taking off. I need to shower and figure out…" He gestures to the warning sign marking his skin.

"Hey," I jut my chin, "wear a quarter-zip or a hoodie and get your ass back here after. That's an order. We have plans to make."

His face brightens before he stands at attention and salutes. "Aye, aye, Captain."

He's a damn good guy. Desi and Dante better not fuck this up.

It's not fifteen minutes before a set of pissed off and shirtless twins storm into the house.

"Where's Lucas?" Dante demands, as curt as ever.

I tilt my head. "Charlie?" I know very well who he means. I know my partner's full name.

"Stop calling him that." He balls his fists. "He shouldn't constantly be reminded of what he's been through. Maybe that's why he hasn't moved on. Maybe you don't *want* him to move on."

Today is not my fucking day. "Okay, Dr. Phil. Calm down."

Desi extends his hands in front of him, palms out. "Did he leave?"

Stalling, I take a generous sip of lukewarm coffee. "What about it?"

Dante's dark, bloodthirsty eyes stare me down. "Where'd he go?"

"Meeting someone." I give a half-assed shrug, feigning

nonchalance for the hell of it—and maybe because Dante's comment stirred up more guilt and agitation. "Might be gone for a few days. I'm sure you'll be in New York before he gets back."

Desi rakes his fingers through his hair. "No, we won't."

"Why not? They released Charlie—I'm sorry, *Lucas*—from monitoring you. You're free to go wherever you please." They haven't released Lucas yet, but I'm certain that's what his meeting is about.

They exchange a look, a silent plea in Desi's eyes.

"We're waiting on Ethan. We'll discuss it with him," Dante reassures him. "Let's get our stuff from the condo."

They turn to leave and just to be an ass, I call out, "Jax wants to know if you three need a bigger place or a bigger bed."

Chapter 16
Ethan

I'm with the entire team, so why is my phone blowing up? I glance across the private room of the hotel restaurant. Jax is staring down at his screen, snickering. Hoping it's Aurora texting us both, I raise my phone discreetly, never knowing what I'll find.

What I'm not expecting is a group chat between me, Reece, and Jax named Triple Power Play. Only Jackson would mess with my phone, change his name, and make a hockey joke about having two extra men.

> **REECE**
> No need to expand the pool house, only the bed.

> **BABY BOY**
> Are they fucking? Seriously?

Jax always jumps straight to fucking. In his eyes, everybody is fucking.

> **REECE**
> Yes, and the twins are obsessed. Be prepared.

Okay, maybe everybody *is* fucking.

> **BABY BOY**
> That's awesome! 😊 Your partner gonna stick around?
>
> **REECE**
> I'll let you know soon. He's at a meeting with Bennett.

Holy shit, Jax and Reece are getting along, talking civilly. When did that start?

> **BABY BOY**
> When do we leave for your sister's wedding?
>
> **REECE**
> Tuesday. You don't have to come.
>
> **BABY BOY**
> And miss spending Christmas with my other boyfriend's family? Never.

Three dots pop up and disappear. I stare at Jax until his head lifts and our eyes connect. I arch a brow, and he gives me that shit-eating grin.

My phone buzzes in my hand, a message from him outside the group chat.

> **BABY BOY**
> Don't give me that death glare unless you plan on doing something about it.

I type, "He's your boyfriend now too?" then delete it. Am *I* his boyfriend? He jokes about it, but do secrets really need labels? We're together as a unit, including Reece. But...I don't want him with Reece—not that Reece is interested in him. I don't want Jax with anyone other than Aurora...who I share with Reece.

What does that say about me? About Jax and me?

My phone vibrates in my hand, and my mental crisis is averted.

REECE

I know you're only fucking with me, but you can't say that shit around my parents. Not at my sister's wedding.

Jax and I exchange a glance. Reece doesn't talk much. We know little about his past, except that he grew up in the South, played football, and joined the military at eighteen or nineteen. When Reece was in surgery, Charlie called his family. We weren't present for the conversation, and they never visited. A week ago, after I mentioned planning a Christmas babymoon, Reece brought up his sister's wedding. We were reluctantly invited, for Aurora's sake.

BABY BOY

Are you trying to tell me they're homophobic?

REECE

My parents are, but my sister isn't, and I refuse to ruin her day.

BABY BOY

Dude, I'm bringing my boyfriend.

Despite this conversation—and our unconventional relationship—warmth blossoms in my chest, and I bite my lip to suppress my ridiculous smile. I guess that answers my question.

REECE

Again, you don't have to come. I'm not causing drama at my sister's wedding.

> **BABY BOY**
> Drama? You're bringing Aurora. My wife. How will you explain that? How will you explain she's pregnant, and not by you?

So much for them getting along.

> This is supposed to be a babymoon, remember? We'll attend the wedding, be polite, do whatever we have to do, then vacation somewhere together.

Reece is slow to respond, and while Jax waits, his knee bounces, his lips pressed in a tight line. He has no patience, no tolerance for indecision or disloyalty.

> **BABY BOY**
> I don't want Aurora going to the wedding if she'll only be hurt and disappointed.

> She'll be okay.

Reece will figure this out before we arrive, and if not, the first tear in Aurora's eye will bring his world to a halt—guaranteed. He won't allow anyone to upset her.

> **REECE**
> No one has to attend. I'll take my partner. If you'd like, you can still meet my sisters.

> **BABY BOY**
> Charlie? Who spent the night with two men?

> **REECE**
> His real name is Lucas and he understands my family.

BABY BOY

> Your family? You keep saying that word, but you can't even be yourself around them.

>> Bickering is getting us nowhere. Let's discuss this at home and come up with a game plan. We can pretend for a night.

Reece is trying, but Jax only has two options: in or out.

He throws his phone down, catching Grant's attention. Huddled close, they whisper, and that prickly sensation returns with a vengeance. It's a tremor beneath my skin, a tightness in my chest, a knot in my stomach.

Jax refuses to hide his true self. He'll play it safe around the team, fearing I'll be fired, but not elsewhere, certainly not with people who dare call themselves family.

Strangely, I feel his frustration. I, too, want to show my love whenever and wherever the fuck I want, without judgment or consequence.

The crowd is a dull roar, the arena packed full—a sea of faces behind the glass, all buzzing with excitement. The music pounds, a visceral thrum vibrating in the air, and adrenaline pumps through my veins.

It's surreal to be coaching after what we've been through. Puts things in perspective, you know? Winning matters, but it's not the be-all, end-all. Losing won't kill me. I'll hate it, but I won't be obsessively replaying the game in my head. I'll be thinking about home…and Jax.

Since lunch, he hasn't spoken to me. He's been off somewhere with Grant, and my mind has been plagued with my incessant need to fix things.

Jessica Lyn

Maybe sex with my captain wasn't the greatest idea, but fuck, I'm not stopping now.

A pang of guilt hits me. Jax is giving more than I'm reciprocating, and he's constantly forced to silence himself when all he wants is to shout his happiness to the world. He has every reason to be frustrated.

Still, Reece's family is his problem, not ours. I'm unsure what Jax expects.

"Do you golf?"

I blink a few times, coming back to reality. "What?"

"Do you golf?" my equipment manager, Blayne, asks again, a bundle of hockey sticks piled in his arms.

"No. I injured my neck." It's an excuse. I could golf if I wanted, but it's not worth the risk. It's boring and a poor use of my limited time.

"That's too bad. I find it relaxing." He stacks the extra sticks in a row behind the bench. "You need something to help you relax, Coach."

What makes him think I'm tense? Is it the tapping fingers or the hard gaze?

I'm staring at my relief—and my headache—six-three, two hundred pounds, the body of a god, and a smile straight from the Devil. He's warming up on the ice without a helmet, chewing on his mouthguard like bubble gum, and making me twitchy. Jackson's piss-poor mood and agitation are palpable.

"Maybe you need a girlfriend," Blayne suggests, his voice filled with humor.

I scoff. "I have one, thanks." And a boyfriend—both of them brats.

"You do?" He glances over his shoulder. "Does she come to the games?"

"Yup." She's just not here because she's taking care of her *other* boyfriend.

"What's she look like? Have I met her?"

"You know Aurora Embers, the model?"

He turns to face me with lowered brows. "O'Reilly's wife?"

"Yeah," I say with a curt nod and a smirk. "Her."

Mouth open and a deep scowl etched onto his features, he studies my expression, searching for any sign I'm teasing him.

He must live under a rock. Certainly, everyone has seen me with Aurora or at least heard a rumor. Our house was broken into. Both Jax and I took time off. Someone must've connected the dots.

My mood shifts to amusement at his utter confusion. "What? You don't think I can pull a twenty-two-year-old supermodel?"

His eyes widen. "What? No," he stammers. "I didn't think you'd *want* to."

A chuckle escapes me. "See? Now you know why I'm stressed."

Warmups end, and the game begins. Jax plays aggressively; he's temperamental, drawn into every fight and spending too much time in the penalty box, leaving us down a player. At the end of the second quarter, the score is tied.

"We should be winning." My gaze sweeps across the slumped figures, the silence in the locker room heavy and suffocating. The only sound is the rhythmic *thump-thump-thump* of my pulse in my ears. "What's the problem?"

Fucking Jackson. That's the problem.

Heads hung, nobody dares say a word. This, right here, is why having a close relationship with my captain was a horrible idea. No one wants to speak up.

I guess I'll have to be the asshole.

"O'Reilly, how many power-play goals do they have? How many did they score while you were sitting on your ass in the penalty box?"

Jessica Lyn

He doesn't respond, and players shift uncomfortably.

"Check your fucking emotions at the door."

His jaw clenches, the muscle furrowing, the only indication he hears me.

"They're drawing us into penalties," I tell the team, "and it's working. Play smart. Rest, refuel, let's go."

The game goes into overtime, then a shootout. I'm tempted to bench Jax and not let him take a shot on goal, but that'd punish the entire team.

He scores, as well as Grant and the rookie, a last-minute decision that thankfully paid off, and we win by one, thanks to Kill's ability to read the play.

With a fifteen-hour flight ahead, we leave straight from the arena for the airport, bound for Toronto. Jax and I don't talk—he doesn't even glance in my direction. My stomach churns. Apparently, he's pissed at me. For what, I have no clue, but it's driving me crazy, my thoughts ping-ponging off one another.

On the private plane, he sits with Grant as usual. It gets late, players and staff fall asleep, and I wonder if he's sleeping on Grant's shoulder. *He's not. He's probably not even sleeping.*

Are they touching? Is he attracted to his best friend physically, even though he dislikes his playboy behavior? *No, Jax doesn't work that way.* But Grant has changed. Does that change how Jax feels? *He'd never touch anyone else; it's unfathomable.*

This is ridiculous. Someone put me out of my misery.

Chapter 17
Jackson

Lights off, it's somber and quiet on the private jet. Only the gentle hum of the engines and the occasional rustle of clothing interrupt the peace.

Travel-induced sleep becomes routine as a hockey player, but I rarely doze on the plane, and currently, insomnia torments me. I'm restless, and I know someone else who's awake—I can sense his rising panic.

Headphones over his ears, eyes half-shut, Grant stretches his neck, peering out over the cabin, then angles himself toward the aisle and gestures with his head. We're the ultimate wingman team.

I drop into the seat beside Ethan. "Did you save this seat for me?" I whisper.

It's an overnight flight, and he's still in his suit, for fuck's sake. He should be in a hoodie and a pair of sweats, letting me slip my hand down his pants.

He recovers from his surprise quickly and gives me that perma-scowl. "No. No one ever sits next to me."

The corner of my lip quirks. "Because you snore?"

Despite his grouchiness and pinched brow, a flicker of

amusement glints in those stormy eyes. "I do not. It's because I'm the coach and I need my space."

I relax into the leather. "For that enormous brain of yours? I could hear you thinking all the way over there. What are you panicking about now?"

He glances behind me. "You shouldn't be sitting with me."

"Please." I wave off his paranoia. "We've sat next to each other and argued since the day you started coaching. No one cares."

He shakes his head. "We did not argue."

"You're right. It was thinly veiled flirting, but nobody knows any different with the way you *ride my ass* in the locker room." I allow my voice to rise, just a tad.

His eyes widen in warning. "Shut your fucking mouth," he grits through clenched teeth.

I bet his ears are burning.

A reckless thrill pulses through me. I live to break him, break that rigid façade.

The urge to kiss him and feel that tightly coiled control snap is *everything*. I crave his raw power in the same way I crave the pain and violence of the game.

His intense gaze becomes a challenge. "Don't, you little shit. I can hear your thoughts."

"Can you?" I bite my lip and envision him blowing his load down my throat—head thrown back, mouth open, neck strained, veins popping, his fingers gripping my hair, that rumbling moan... So fucking delicious.

His Adam's apple bobs and his chest heaves.

He attempts to dismiss me by turning toward the window. "Return to your seat, O'Reilly."

Following his lead, I stare into the aisleway. "No thanks. I'm good." Then, I get one of my brilliant ideas. "Unless you *want* me to go play with Grant."

I'm reminded of all those times he taunted me with Aurora. Now, I get to taunt *him*—with *me*.

He whips his head around, his eyes dark. "You wouldn't. Don't forget you're married."

He's right—I wouldn't. Plus, Grant is obsessed with Sloane. Still…

I shrug, feigning indifference. "I doubt she'll mind. She lets me play with you."

His nostrils flare. "Try it and see what happens. Don't fuck with me, Jax. I've had enough of your shitty attitude today."

The sweet taste of revenge turns bitter, and my mood sours. I lean in until I feel the heat radiating from his body, smell the sandalwood and amber shampoo I bought him. "Why not? I'm only yours until it makes you uncomfortable, so what does it matter?"

Let him try to hide us. He thought Aurora provoked him? She has limits; I don't. I can handle his brutality, and I'll do whatever it takes to drive him over the edge. Maybe I'm being petty, but I gave him secrecy around the team. Any more than that is hurtful. He wants me to *be polite* and *pretend* just to appease a bunch of homophobic assholes? Fuck that.

Ethan's hand shoots out, fisting my throat. His fingertips dig into my jaw and neck with bruising strength and pull me closer. We're chest to chest, his voice a growl in my ear. "If you've got a problem, use your fucking words, brat."

"Nah. I'd much rather piss you off."

"You itching for a fight, baby boy? Is that it? You're mine whether I tell anyone or not." He pushes me away with a final, hard squeeze. "Make no mistake."

Our eyes lock in a furious glare, neither one of us backing down.

He cocks his head. "Were you injured today on the ice?"

Confused, I curl my lip. "No. Why?"

He sinks into the leather seat and removes his phone from his pocket, dismissing me—again. "Means I don't have to take it easy on you once we get to the hotel room," his tone deepens, "and I correct that *fucking* attitude of yours."

"You're a dick," I mutter.

"And you're a pain in my ass."

It's been a while since I riled Ethan up—*really* riled him up—and after fifteen minutes, I regret it.

He must've forgotten how long this flight is. Even irate, there's no way he'll stay mad about that Grant comment for ten hours.

I definitely won't last.

Unsettled and thirsting for him, I lay my hand on his thigh. Just that slight touch sends a jolt of electricity through me. I want him so fucking bad—and therein lies the problem. Anything less than everything might as well be nothing.

Except that's not true. I'm waging a war with myself. I'll take whatever he gives—but I won't be sated until I've crawled under his skin. I'm obsessed.

His muscles tense beneath my palm, and, preoccupied with his phone, he throws me off him. This repeats until, curious, I rest my head on his shoulder and peek at his screen. He's texting Rocco, but before I can read the messages, he slips the phone into his suit pocket.

"Jax," he growls in warning. "Why are you being clingy?"

"I want you." I switch tactics to flirting rather than provoking his jealousy and possessiveness. "It's a new day. I need my Ethan fix."

"You're a head trip. I'm working." His words are clipped and callous. "We agreed to keep this between us. You *promised* you were okay with it."

Rejected—again.

Numbness washes over me, and a defensive wall snaps into place. "Whatever." I sit up and stare into the dim cabin.

I'd return to my seat, but I'm positive Grant has taken over the entire row by now. "You should've traded me."

He scoffs. "Are you *trying* to infuriate me? Since you clearly need my attention and won't stop until you get it, why don't you explain why you're so pissy?"

"This." I gesture sharply between us. "*This* is why. One minute, you want me, the next, I'm nothing." My body vibrates with pent-up aggression; my eyes burn with tears of frustration. "Maybe I wouldn't have to infuriate you if you gave a shit."

His harsh gaze softens, and he seizes my wrists, his tight grip oddly comforting. "You're shaking—take a breath." Only after I comply does he continue. "That's not true, and you know it. Stop listening to your toxic thoughts—they're lying to you. Tell me what I did wrong. What did you expect me to do about Reece?"

It comes spilling out, all my insecurities and vulnerabilities whispered in the dark. "Defend us. Tell him we're together. You haven't once said it. I respect your need for secrecy around the team, but is this it? Fuck buddies while traveling, nothing more?"

He glances away, bites his lip, and hesitates before replying. "Does this have anything to do with me not…reciprocating?"

It takes me a beat to understand. Then it hits me, and my face twists. "No. I'm a giver. You're a pillow princess. I don't mind."

"What?" His brows knit tightly together, and his lip curls. "I am not."

"Ahhh…" I tilt my head and eye him pointedly. "You are, but you're a giver in other ways. I'm good with it."

He releases my wrists and strokes his trimmed beard. He relaxes into the seat, the two of us facing each other. "But I'm not…giving in other ways. That's what you're telling me. You don't feel secure. You're hurt and lashing out, pushing me to fill the void." He doesn't ask. He states what I struggle to identify inside my own head. "I didn't tell Reece because he knew I loved you before I admitted it to myself. He'd tell me my love for you blinded me to the way you treated Aurora."

I roll my eyes. "And yet, you always keep the peace for him. You two have *meetings* to discuss issues while I get throat grabs and threats."

A wicked grin lights up his face. "Would you rather we had meetings, baby? You were itching for a fight a minute ago." Leaning closer, he lowers his tone. "I bet if we were alone, I'd have that anger and shitty attitude fixed real fucking quick—with my fist wrapped around your throat and my cock stuffed in your mouth, a few threats for good measure."

My gaze drops to my thickening erection.

"Exactly." His grin widens and crinkles his eyes. "Reece and I don't have that dynamic."

"Thank fuck." I'd become totally unhinged, worse than I already am. I can't even imagine.

He grazes his thumb over my cheekbone. "Reece is responsible for himself, his family—*Aurora,* and their relationship. I keep the peace for our girl." He weaves his fingers through my hair and cups the back of my head. "*You* are my responsibility, not Reece."

His mouth meets mine in a slow, languid kiss, forbidden and intoxicating.

"I want you," I whisper against his lips. "I have the urge to burn down anything that keeps you from me."

He stifles a chuckle, and his warm breath caresses my skin. "I see you've amped up the crazy."

"Crazy in love with you."

He releases a heavy sigh and presses his forehead to mine.

"Give me until the end of the season. I'll figure it out. Do you want to go elsewhere, skip the wedding?"

"No. I'll go...and fuck you in their house."

"Shut up," he hisses. "You will not be fucking me."

"Okay, fine. You fuck me, but we're fucking."

"No, we are not." He retreats, ending the debate. "We'll go to the wedding, help Reece through it, and then fly to New York for Christmas. You can love me all you want there."

"You promise?"

"I promise." With one last kiss, he reclines his seat and shuts his eyes. "Set up the loft. Rocco says it's mostly complete. Surprise Aurora. Fill the entire place with gifts. We have an amazing life and a baby on the way—focus on that."

Why does he always end up being right? I mirror his posture, rest my head on his shoulder, and interlace our fingers. Just for a few minutes, I tell myself. "Does this mean you're not punishing me when we get to the hotel room?"

"Oh no, baby boy. I'm still punishing you. Get some rest."

Chapter 18
Reece

Could I possibly pick a fight with anyone else today?

I stare across the kitchen and sunroom—which currently lacks any sun, thanks to the thick plastic covering the accordion doors—and contemplate my texts with Jax.

For five seconds, we got along, not just tolerated each other. I haven't spent quality time with my parents, a term I use loosely, in nearly a decade. Do I want to jeopardize my future family for a family that's dead to me? Other than my sisters?

Still, my sister, Sadie, deserves a perfect wedding. Any woman does.

"Were the twins here?" If there's anyone who can pull me out of this sullen mood, it's Aurora in candy cane flannel pajamas and her hair in a messy bun. "I thought I heard their voices."

"Yeah." I stand to intercept her before she reaches the coffeemaker. "You're going to have some stories for Gram."

She encircles my waist and narrows her sleepy eyes. "Are you blocking my once-daily dose of caffeine?"

I cup her nape and drop a kiss on her lips. "No, I'm

blocking your sugar rush. Can I make you tea with honey instead?"

"Ugh," she groans dramatically, a playful lilt in her tone. "Fine. I'll have the cinnamon, but only because I know you'll worry about me."

Her choice doesn't surprise me. The cinnamon tea has the most caffeine, though far less than coffee and without all that fake, sugary creamer.

While I prepare the kettle on the gas stove, she perches on a stool at the island.

"What were you saying about the twins?" She yawns.

Facing her, I rest my forearm on the granite surface. "They're infatuated with Charlie—*both* of them."

She sucks in a soft gasp, and her eyes widen. "For real? I thought Desi might be, with how he teases him, but Dante too?"

I'm not into chitchat, but I love the way her face lights up when she's enthusiastic about something, so I keep it going. "Yep. Charlie—well, his real name is Lucas—did the walk of shame this morning. Came in here with *hickeys*," I raise my brows and pause for dramatic effect, "all over his neck."

"Oh my God!" she gasps, covering her mouth with her hand. "This is so awesome, and I love the name Lucas. Did they all come over together?"

"No. Lucas snuck out to meet Bennett. The twins were here in a panic, demanding to know his whereabouts. I'm guessing possessiveness runs in the family."

The whistle of the kettle drowns out her laughter, and a lull comes over us as I prepare her tea.

I set the mug in front of her, cautious not to spill it. My muscles are sore, and my balance is off from using only one arm.

"Thank you," she singsongs with a happy little wiggle.

"We have to get groceries. There's not much to eat unless you want leftover pizza."

She scrunches her nose, shakes her head, and takes a careful sip. "I'll order food. How about a movie marathon? You need to rest."

"I ain't gonna lie. The peace and quiet here is nice. I've missed this place."

"We're boring, aren't we?" A tender smile curves her lips. "Like an old married couple. Gossiping, drinking tea and coffee."

"I've had enough action to last a lifetime. I don't mind."

"Jax and Ethan will be traveling the world, and you and I'll be on the couch, binging true crime docs with Gram."

She lets out an infectious laugh, and I can't help but join in.

"I'd have it no other way, angel. I love our life." Decision made, I draw a deep, steadying breath. "Your husband is not happy about the wedding."

She furrows her brows and sets down her mug. "Why?"

"He's worried you'll be hurt when I don't claim you as mine." I reach up to twirl my earring, only to find, with a familiar pang of regret, that it's gone. "If I do, my father will either kick us out or spend the day preaching how I'm living a life of sin, along with Ethan and Jax. We both know that'll set him off, and I'm not ruining my sister's wedding."

"Oh." Her head bows, and that single sound speaks volumes.

I hate it. I hate her disappointment, especially in me. "*But my sister, Sadie, is ecstatic to meet you, although she doesn't believe we're dating or whatever.*"

Large, golden-brown eyes, hesitant and questioning, peer up at me. "Why not?"

I scoff at her utter lack of self-awareness. "Because you're *you*—a *Sports Illustrated* model—and I'm their chunky jock brother."

"You are not chunky!" she insists, but her voice is laced with a chuckle.

"I was. Wait until you see the pictures. I'm sure they'll show you."

She hops off the stool, stumbling and nearly giving me a heart attack. Pregnancy hasn't helped her clumsiness.

Arm outstretched, I round the island. "Where are you going? Jesus, you make me nervous."

She scans my outfit. "Is that all you have to wear?"

I look down at my T-shirt and athletic shorts. "Yeah… I need to wash some clothes. Why?"

"That'll do. We'll go out to the beach." She dismisses me with a wave of her hand. "We're doing a photoshoot for your sisters."

"What? No, that's not needed." I am not photogenic. I do not fake a smile well.

Ignoring me, she turns toward the bedroom, presumably to change. "Grab your baseball cap. I like it."

I stand there, dumbfounded. What the fuck just happened? What about my parents and the wedding? "Aurora!" I chase after her.

"Was it a hoop or a diamond?" she calls over her shoulder.

"What?"

"In your ear, Viking. Is the hole still there?"

"What?" I repeat. I swear, I'm more intelligent than this. "Yes, it's still pierced. Why?"

Undeterred, she rifles through drawers in her mammoth closet. "I have a lot of jewelry given to me that I never wear or only wore once for a photo." She hands me a stack of small boxes. "Here you go. Diamonds."

I thrust them at her and shake my head. "No. I'm not taking these."

"Pick one. You don't have to keep them—unless you want to." Stepping back, she unbuttons her top, effectively silencing my argument. "Put it in for today, and we'll take a bunch of couples photos for your sisters." Then, a thought hits her, and she gasps. "We can FaceTime them!"

"Aurora, no. What about the wedding? We were having a conversation."

"I don't care about pretending—I get you every other day of the year—but did you ask your sister what *she* wanted?"

My mind goes blank when Aurora's shirt falls to the floor, then her shorts. "No, and I'd rather not discuss my family while you're naked."

"Okay then. It's settled."

"You had one here." She traces a tiny scar below my bottom lip, her finger cold on my heated skin.

We sit facing each other in the sand, the roar of the ocean in the background, her legs over mine, my hand resting on her hip. We took the obligatory picturesque beach selfies. I tried to hide my face by kissing her neck or shoulder, but I'm sure out of the hundreds she snapped, there are bound to be a few she deems worthy to send to my sisters.

I suck my lip into my mouth, pinching it between my teeth, a habit born from years of chewing on the missing ring, and nod.

"And here." She points to a barely visible scar above my brow, the site of another former piercing. "Do you want them back?"

I'm wearing the sizable square diamond earring she insisted on—her favorite one. It has a tint of blue; she says it matches my eyes. Just thinking about it drives me to touch it.

"Yes and no. I miss them, but if they're there, I'll play with them."

"What's wrong with that?" She gives me that flirtatious smile that gets her whatever she wants. "I wanna play with them." She wraps her arms around my neck and bites my bottom lip, tugging slightly to emphasize her point.

"You can play with any of them any time you want." My words come out raspy, my mouth chasing hers. Now that we've consummated our relationship, my body is revved up and fiending for her.

"You're secretly rebellious, aren't you?" she whispers between kisses.

I cup her ass with one hand and lift her higher on my lap. "Maybe that's why I like you. You're naughty."

She encircles her legs around my waist, and my cock stirs, but just as our tongues intertwine, we're interrupted by an exaggerated throat clearing.

I raise my head to find the twins staring down at us, the picture of gloom in all black, a stark contrast to the sparkling ocean and bright sunshine. Do they not own any clothes other than mafia garb? What am I thinking—*I* don't own anything other than tactical gear, save for workout clothes, which is all I've been wearing.

"Get a room, will ya?" Dante gripes, lip curled. "Groceries are here." He's typically the aloof twin, but today, he's unusually grumpy. Lucas must not be home yet.

I rise to my feet, help Aurora, and brush the sand off my shorts. "Don't act so disgusted. Didn't you both sleep with the same person last night? Together?"

Desi turns to his brother, his eyes wide. "The robot speaks," he whisper-yells with feigned astonishment.

Dante arches a brow. "What did you do to him, Aurora?"

"Recharge his batteries? Unplug him and plug him back in?" Desi grins.

She gathers her towel and phone, shaking her head at his never-ending jokes. "You're as bad as Jax."

I lace our fingers and lead the way through the sand dunes and along the path to the backyard.

"I miss the crazy fucker—wait! I know! You short-circuited his motherboard."

Desi laughs at his own stupid joke while Dante grumbles about refusing to wear shorts in December.

We go around to the side of the house since the back doors are boarded up—a simple fix if I had two working arms. By the time we enter the kitchen, Aurora is lagging and breathless.

"Sit down," I tell her. "We'll put away the groceries."

She doesn't rest, nor does she change out of her bikini. She unpacks and organizes our food orders by household, her cute baby bump and popped-out belly button on full display. It's utterly domestic. Some might find it boring, but I find it blissful. What's not to love about Aurora walking around half-naked and pregnant?

I can't wait until it's mine.

The thought takes me by surprise, although it shouldn't. The more I consider it, the more I accept our relationship, the more my chest swells with what can only be love and fulfillment.

I swear, I don't have a pregnancy kink. Maybe a slight hero complex, but I've only felt this way, only want this, with her.

And boy, wouldn't that piss Jax off if she ended up pregnant by me?

Shit, Aurora is right—I *am* rebellious.

Now that I'm no longer living in survival mode or following orders, I'm discovering a lot about myself. She once asked me where I wanted to go on a date, what my hobbies were, and I honestly didn't know how to answer. I've had no time or freedom for leisure activities. That's something we'll have to explore together.

On her toes, she reaches into a bag and pulls out a five-pound sack of dark-roast coffee beans, breathing in its rich aroma with a satisfying sigh.

"Give that to me!" I seize it from her one-handed, aggravating the dull pain in my shoulder in the process.

Only to have Desi snatch it away. "That's ours."

I chuckle. "Oh, right. Can't have your boyfriend going without coffee. He might escape."

Dante tucks a paper grocery bag under his arm, packed full of chips and sweets. "Speaking of which, where's your partner? For real? No bullshit."

"Have you tried—I don't know—texting him?" I ask, heavy with sarcasm.

"Yep." Desi bites off a piece of oatmeal cookie. "Only a dozen times."

"I'm sure he'll be here soon." I shrug, the movement causing sharp pain to shoot down my spine, and I wince. "Or maybe he doesn't want to see you."

Aurora tosses me a glare. "That's what you get for being mean." She grabs a bag, circles the island, and snags my T-shirt. "Let's go. You're going to bed."

I take the bag from her and peek inside to find fancy water, fruit, cheese, and prosciutto. Looks like we're having a picnic in bed. "Only if you're coming with me."

Chapter 19
Ethan

We enter the hotel room in Toronto, and my traitorous cock immediately perks up. I clench my jaw. *Haven't you done enough?*

I'm supposed to be punishing Jax, but I can't recall precisely what for. My gaze shifts to the man in question. He's already gazing at me with a smug smirk. Oh yeah, that's right—he was being manipulative, taunting me with his best friend.

I scoff and turn away, placing my luggage on the bed farthest from the door.

He follows and sets his bag beside mine. He toes off his sneakers, drapes his jacket over the back of a chair, and removes his shirt.

Trying to stay strong—because all I want is to cuddle the little shit, who's now shirtless, displaying my marks—I toss his duffel onto the other bed. "You're sleeping over there."

I decided making him choke on my cock wasn't a punishment, not to Jax, so I'm going in a different direction.

"Seriously?" He throws his hands in the air. "I might as well leave. Sleeping separately from me and denying me your affection is not a punishment; it's abuse, legit emotional abuse."

A threat *and* an accusation all rolled into one; he knows how to hit me, and I lose my temper. "Who told you that? Google? Certainly not a psychiatrist."

He stares pointedly until guilt flushes my face, forcing me to glance away. *Me and my fucking mouth.*

Awkward silence fills the room. I unzip my baggage and begin unpacking as he does the same.

I hang my suit then stop. You know what? No, I'm not in the wrong here. "It's funny how you keep track of everyone else's abuse but your own."

About to pull off his sweatpants, fingers on the waistband, he hesitates. "What the fuck does that mean?"

"Your level of possessiveness—*if I can't have you, no one else can*—is astonishing. You're willing to jeopardize my entire career, all I have, because you're not getting enough attention."

"All you have?" Brows raised, he presses his lips together and slowly nods. "Wow, Coach. Did you take a giant leap back in time?"

"That's not what I meant." I drop my bags on the floor, desperate to get into bed, and loosen my tie. "I meant besides us—you and Aurora."

Honestly, it was a slip of the tongue. I'm struggling, grabbing at anything to keep from falling to my knees for Jackson O'Reilly, the captain of my team. It sounds silly, even shallow, but that's exactly who he is—to everyone else. I'm his coach, he's my player, and no matter how much I try to fight it, he affects me wholly. Tonight's clusterfuck of a game proved that, along with his inability to keep his hands to himself.

He retrieves his shirt from the floor and yanks it over his head. "I'll get my own room or crash with someone. I'll keep my distance. That way, your reputation as a hard-ass straight guy remains intact."

"I am straight." There I go again. The words fly out of my mouth, a knee-jerk reaction, and I'm not even sure they're true.

"Hilarious," he deadpans. "Did you forget I sucked your cock? And you liked it?"

"That's *you*." I jut my chin. "You're the only man I'm attracted to." I pause then correct myself. "You're the only man I've *ever* been attracted to."

"Good to know you're at least attracted to me."

He reaches for his jacket, and, being a mature adult, I snatch it and chuck it between the bed and the wall.

"Like fuck you're staying elsewhere."

If he goes for the door, I may tackle him. I've lost all control.

He cocks his head. "See? You're as possessive as I am. The difference is I want you." His Adam's apple bobs. "I don't care who knows or sees. I'm *begging* for you. Not just your attention, *you*. Why is that hard for you to understand?"

How is he so open with his emotions and desires? He pours his heart out easily.

"Maybe because it's never happened before…" I shrug, palms up. "You. Aurora. Any of this."

"Because you never let it." He rakes his fingers through his hair and tugs at the strands. "If you don't want me destroying your career, then tell me what the fuck I'm supposed to do with this?" He slaps his chest. "This constant ache?" He takes a step back and gestures towards the door. "You want me to leave or stay? I'm done playing games—it's only fucking with my head."

If he leaves, his panic will only escalate. I know because mine will too. We won't sleep; we'll either seek each other out or do something reckless.

Tears well in his eyes. I snag his shirt and draw him into my arms.

"Stay. I'll fix it." Heat spreads through my veins and ignites every nerve ending, my body intensely focused on each point of contact. "Give me this season. It'll be worth it, I promise."

He doesn't answer, and the *ache*, as he put it, deepens.

I tangle my fingers in his hair and lean in to kiss him. He turns his head.

I grip his jaw and force his face to mine. "Kiss me, Jax. Feel how much I want you."

He remains tense, his gaze averted. Now I'm the one being punished. My pulse quickens, a frantic drum against my ribs that echoes the rapid beat of his own heart.

I sink my teeth into his bottom lip, biting down until his hips shift and he groans.

Jax doesn't do anything half-assed. It's all or nothing, in or out. He loves with his entire being and seeks the same in return.

It's not enough to hear that I love him—he needs to feel it in his bones, wear it on his skin. He wants to replace the pain of longing and loneliness with the pain of my love and lust.

I can do that, but first, I need to be sure of one thing. "I'd never hurt you—not purposefully. You know that, right? If you want me to stop, I will. Always."

He sucks his swollen lip into his mouth, his pupils dilated, and nods. "I know."

"Take your shirt off and hold your wrists out," I demand.

He complies, and I yank my belt free from my pants.

Using the buckle as the center, I swiftly fashion a double figure-eight then slip the leather over his hands to bind his wrists. When he shows no signs of revulsion, I jerk the loose end taut and rethread it through the clasp.

"Holy shit." He tests the restraints. "What are you going to do?" His voice holds no fear, only a curious edge.

This is the punishment he'd craved, the one he anticipated. I shouldn't have second-guessed myself.

I shove him in the chest, and he falls onto the mattress, landing flat on his back.

"Make sure you remember who you belong to." I kick off my shoes and unbutton my shirt. "Keep your hands above your head." I shut off the lights and strip to my boxers. "If you don't, I won't let you come, and you *will* sleep in that bed alone."

***

Jackson

The curtains are drawn tight, the room pitch-black. Ethan rummages through his bag, and my heart rate spikes, adrenaline shooting through my veins.

"Um…if you're searching for lube—" I stop mid-sentence at a sound I've known for over a decade, a sound that inhabits my dreams: the tearing of hockey tape.

"If you run your mouth, I'm taping it shut."

Keep my hands above my head, don't touch him, and don't talk. Got it. "I get to be the pillow princess tonight?"

He covers my smile with stick tape. "I swear, you're a brat just so I'll punish you."

Damn, he's catching on.

I was pissed earlier when he tried to force me to sleep alone. My emotions are a mess. The worst thing he can do is ice me out, because I will destroy everything. The idea of being without him triggers that furious scream inside me, the ticking time bomb.

Being away from Aurora doesn't help. Ethan's right—the

craziness has escalated. The darkness lurks just under the surface of my skin, waiting to be unleashed. Only his rough touch pacifies it.

The mattress dips, and my mind quiets, acutely focused on what he might do next. He settles between my thighs, his fingers finding my waistband, and I raise my hips to help him remove my sweats and boxers.

His hard body comes over me, our legs entangled, his clothed erection pressed to mine. He grabs my chin, tilts my head, and kisses my throat. His beard rasps against my skin, and goosebumps erupt on my chest.

"Can I mark you here?"

That deep rumble goes straight to my heavy balls.

I nod, lost to him. I'd let him do anything as long as he kept touching me.

His teeth sink into my neck, a searing brand. Endorphins flood my system, heightening my senses, and my hips flex, grinding against him.

"You like that, don't you? You like it when I claim you?" His body dips and applies more pressure to my aching cock, but it also makes it impossible to find friction.

It's maddening.

My reply is a throaty groan, thick with need.

Players will suspect something when I show up tomorrow with a bite mark—not that I give a fuck. I'll wear it proudly. Seems Ethan is okay with assumptions and rumors swirling around but draws the line at me clinging to him on the team jet when I'm insecure.

"I love you, Jax." His hot breath ghosts over my skin. "I think about you all day." His fingers thread through my hair. "I want you as badly as you want me." His mouth trails south, kissing, nipping. Then, his fist tightens in my hair, and his sweet pillow talk turns harsh. "You're. Mine." Each word is punctuated with a sharper bite. "Don't forget it."

The praise-pleasure-pain is a balm to my black soul.

Since I didn't win last night and caused him trouble, he probably won't allow the collarbone tattoo—but I'm absolutely getting it after the next game.

Lazily, he moves down my body, coming to rest between my legs.

He palms my shaft, and the air catches in my lungs. Wetness runs down my length, and I realize he's spitting on my dick. *Fuck yes.*

I'll die if he sucks my cock. Okay, maybe not *die*, but I'll definitely shatter the world record for the fastest orgasm. I can't imagine anything better than blowing my load down Coach's throat. Just the thought has me leaking precum all over his fingers.

He strokes me from base to tip, his grip firm and rough. His thumb circles my slit and swirls precum over the crown. "You want my mouth, beautiful boy?"

His touch…his words… I respond with a whimper.

Soft, pillowy lips engulf the head of my cock, and my hips jerk.

Holy fuck. This is real. I'm getting a blow job from Ethan.

He gently applies suction and curls his tongue around the ridge. I let out a stifled moan and fight to stay still, desperate to plunge farther.

Sucking cock is self-explanatory, and he quickly finds his rhythm, taking me deeper with each pull. It's fucking incredible, and I tilt my head back and shut my eyes. I'm so close…

Then, the suction disappears, and my eyes pop open.

No!

"You wanna come for me, baby boy?" He strokes me hard and fast while massaging my tight balls then stops.

Jesus, I might die after all—death from edging.

My angry dick throbs. I grip the bottom of the wooden headboard to stop myself from grabbing his thick hair and forcing him to end my suffering. The leather belt digs into my wrists from the effort of holding back.

Hard-fast-stop. "You gonna be good? Like you promised?" *Hard-fast-stop.*

I clench my thighs to prevent from releasing in his hand.

Here's the punishment I crave—the one where he edges me senseless and we both get what we want. I can pretend to be friends during the day if he wrecks me every night—but only with the team. Everywhere else is fair game.

I babble incoherent words behind the tape: *Yes. I'll be good. Please let me come.*

"You taunt me with Grant again, and I'll make you beg for it with my cock shoved down your throat. Understood?"

That sounds fan-fucking-tastic, but okay. I whine and rock my hips in reply.

His lips return, his fist working my shaft in tandem with his mouth. It's rough and sloppy, and I swear, his goal is to suck the cum right out of me.

I shatter in seconds, spiraling into oblivion. I shoot rope after rope of cum onto his tongue, the back of his throat. It doesn't stop.

My muscles jerk, and I'm so strung out, I'm incapable of speech. My brain is utterly blank. I'm dazed, lightheaded, breathless. My entire body tingles, each nerve ending vibrating, and a low hum resonates in my ears.

The hockey tape rips free, and I come back to planet Earth, realizing he's hovering over me. He grasps my jaw, squeezes my cheeks, and my lips open automatically. He leans down and spits into my mouth—*spits my own cum* into my mouth, mixed with his saliva.

One more way of him marking me, owning me, and my spent cock twitches back to life.

He brings his hand to my throat. "Swallow."

I obey, my Adam's apple grazing his palm.

"Good boy," he praises, dark and satisfied.

The high of the orgasm begins to fade, and I'm ready for another—an Ethan high. I need him.

"You want more?"

I nod, my eyes meeting his, unsure if I'm allowed—or able—to speak. *I want you.*

"You're insatiable." His thumb traces my bottom lip. "Can I fuck this pretty mouth?"

He's becoming less inhibited with his dirty talk, and for once, that word doesn't cause my stomach to roil, doesn't provoke the violent rage in my chest. He's rewiring my brain, linking words and actions to pleasure and love that were once associated with pain and fear.

I part my lips.

Chapter 20
Aurora

I read late into the night, a steamy vampire romance that leaves me aching. I message Jax a few times, but he doesn't reply. Given the time difference, he's probably asleep, and I don't dare text Ethan for the same reason.

After we ate, Reece settled into the pillows and passed out. I must have exhausted him. He woke briefly to check his phone, get a drink, and use the bathroom before drifting off again. The blackout curtains obscure the time of day, but he obviously needs the rest.

My eyelids grow heavy until they eventually fall shut. I toss and turn. Hot all over, I strip off Reece's T-shirt I put on before bed.

A muscled body presses to mine, an arm coming around my abdomen. "What's the matter, angel? Can't sleep?" His deep voice is deliciously husky and sexy as hell.

"No." My ass has a mind of its own, seeking his erection and grinding into him.

"You need me?" He nips my neck. "Are you sore?"

I shake my head. I am, but it's not terrible.

"Come up here and ride me then."

He rolls onto his back and kicks off his boxers. I waste no time straddling his hips, fisting his shaft, and positioning myself over him.

His arm encircles my waist. "Nope. Keep going." He guides me forward.

My hands land on his chest to steady myself. "What?"

"Bring that pussy up here."

My heart races, and I lock up. "Um…I'm pregnant."

"I'm well aware." He chuckles.

"I'll make a mess." My resistance is feeble.

"Please do. I love it." He scooches down and directs me onto his face. "Hold the headboard."

My legs tense, and I lean forward clumsily, grabbing the wood for balance. "I doubt I can come—"

His tongue slides through my slit, and my words cut off. Two fingers enter me from behind, and my hips rock.

"Lower, baby."

His breath is hot against my core. How much lower do I need to go?

I inch my knees wider, and insecurity creeps in. I'm not light, and I'm practically sitting on him, smothering him. That can't be enjoyable.

His palm pushes down on the small of my back, encouraging me to drop even farther. "Come on, princess. Ride my face."

Thick fingers move in and out of me, pleasure taking hold, and my nervous thoughts fade away. He circles my clit with his tongue, and my body assumes control, writhing and chasing my climax. I hear how wet I am but can't muster a bit of embarrassment, not when he feels so freaking good.

He doubles down, nibbling and sucking. I dig my fingernails into the wood, tip my head back on a sharp moan, and come on his face, just as he wanted.

I'm still dazed from the orgasm when he lifts me and sets

me beside him. His fingers collar my nape and press my chest to the mattress, my ass in the air. Keeping me in place, he spreads my legs wider with his knees.

"Your arm. You should lie down."

He notches at my entrance and thrusts deep, silencing my protests.

I suck in a gasp. He's massive in this position, and that bottom piercing? The ring above his balls? It's teasing my sensitive clit with each flex of his hips.

A searing wave of jealousy consumes me. I twist in his grasp and attempt to free myself. "There's no way you got those for yourself."

He seizes my wrists with one hand, binds them above my head, then delivers a sharp smack to my ass with the other. "You wanna fight about it, Tinker Bell, or would you like me to keep fucking you?" He withdraws to the tip then enters me slowly, allowing his five piercings to glide over my G-spot, one after the other.

"Oh, fuck." My legs twitch, and I clench around him, the sensation mind-blowing, especially after just coming.

Another stinging slap, and I nearly come.

"What do you say, princess?" He slams into me with a powerful thrust, smooth and firm, always maintaining complete control. "Do you want me to stop?"

The haze of lust overrides my jealousy. I've been dickmatized. "Keep fucking me," I whimper.

His strokes slow, each deliberate, leaving me suspended, teetering on the edge.

"I've already told you." His palm smacks my ass once more. "You're the only serious relationship I've had. You're the only one."

Heat spreads like wildfire across my skin and my nipples tighten. "You're gonna make me come."

"You want it soft while I tell you how much I love you?"

His teeth graze my earlobe. "Or you want it hard and I'll show you?"

I meet his thrusts. "Hard. I wanna feel you tomorrow."

"That's my girl." He shifts his hips and quickens the pace, hitting my G-spot harder, fucking me deeper. One hand pins my wrists over my head and the other clasps my nape, giving me the restraint I crave while his body drives me into the mattress.

I come with blinding intensity, crying out and pulsing around his cock.

My gushing orgasm triggers his, and he follows me over the edge with a growled, "Mmm, fuck," his forehead dropping to my temple.

He stays buried inside me and collapses next to me. He tucks me into his chest, his heart thundering against my back, and that's how we drift off, sleeping soundly until someone beats at the door.

Chapter 21
Lucas

A low groan drags me from the darkness, agony the first sensation I comprehend. My face is throbbing, and my throat is raw.

My head is tipped back, resting on a solid wall, my legs stretched out in front of me, my shoes missing. Dried blood crusts my chin, itching and cracking as I roll my tender lips.

Black spots dance in my peripheral vision, and I struggle to remain awake. I attempt to lean forward, and intense pain shoots down my spine.

My memories resurface, bringing with them panic-inducing fear. I twist and wrench my wrists against the binds behind my back until my arms shake and my shoulders scream in protest. Blood drips from my fingers, and I blink in and out of consciousness.

I wake, cursing myself. I'm an idiot, an absolute fucking idiot. I was in a rush, distracted by thoughts of getting railed by two men, and ended up instead stuffed in a trunk.

Maybe Jackson was right; I'm nothing more than a police academy dropout.

He doesn't think that. He wouldn't have offered you a job working security if he did.

I squeeze my eyes shut, fighting the headache, and my mind drifts. I never went to a police academy, but I bet they teach their officers how to avoid being kidnapped in an alleyway during broad daylight.

Crap, I parked illegally behind Ethan's apartment building. Jackson's Land Rover must've been impounded or stolen by now. That tank disguised as an SUV probably cost a couple hundred thousand, if not half a million. Few civilians own military-grade protection vehicles. I wonder whether Jax or Kyle purchased it. Did the perps who jumped me track the GPS? Can Jax?

Not important at the moment. You're delirious. How about you focus on staying alive?

What do I know? I'm caged in some sort of cellar. A musty smell clings to the back of my parched throat. Dim light creeps through a discolored, cracked window set high in a cinderblock wall. A train rumbles approximately every half-hour, the clickety-clack of the wheels echoing in the bitter silence.

I'm underground near the LA Metro.

Everything after I stepped out of the car is a blur. Ambushed from behind, I landed face-first on the concrete, smashing my forehead. Dazed, I flipped over and kicked out, connecting with an attacker's nose. Another assailant retaliated with a boot to my cheek and temple. Despite the brutal pounding in my skull and my eyes watering, I kept fighting until a final blow to the head knocked me out.

I got complacent in my cushy new life and let my guard down, leaving my weapons and gear behind. It was careless and reckless.

You should've let Dante kill every intruder. Dead men can't talk. You wouldn't be in this situation.

This has to be related to the case. Why else would I be kept alive in a decrepit basement besides ransom?

They may seek to trade me for Jax or Aurora, a pointless endeavor, or they may demand the freedom of their imprisoned colleagues—also unlikely, given the excessive red tape and bureaucracy involved.

Hopefully, this isn't revenge, and I'm not about to be used and sold off for sex. I'm in a cell similar to the picture Hugo sent to Jackson.

Either way, I'm fucked.

The thought sends a fresh wave of panic splintering through my chest, and my fingers tremble. I suck in a breath, my nostrils filling with dank, moldy air, and tug my hands with all my strength.

It's no use. The unforgiving plastic of the zip tie bites into my skin, sending sharp, searing pain through the cuts from my last escape attempts. The restraints were fastened too tightly. There's no give, and rubbing them on the concrete will only further damage my raw wrists.

Exhausted once more, I hang my head. At least I was smart enough to throw my dog tags on before I left Santa Monica. Reece will find me. When I don't come home, he'll know what to do.

Chapter 22
Reece

Dante slams his fist on the granite countertop. "What's the plan? It's been an entire fucking day!"

Aurora places three water bottles in the center of the kitchen island, twisting one open and setting it in front of me. "Should I call Ethan?"

Her words shake, and I flash the furious Italian a sharp glare.

I intertwine our fingers in an attempt to comfort her. "No, they'll only freak out. It won't do any good."

She squeezes my hand and smiles gently before turning away.

I shift my attention back to the map on my laptop. Lucas' dog tags pinpoint him inside an abandoned building in Skid Row, an area plagued by homelessness and drug use. The problem is, we don't know *where* in the building he is.

If my partner were here and we were rescuing someone else, he'd be hacking into the security feed, but I doubt this place even has cameras.

Unless it's not what we think. Unless this seemingly worthless structure is a front... Holy fuck, that'd be perfect for a criminal. A drug and human trafficking hub right in the heart of the city's most vulnerable. Kyle and his crew were seriously perverse.

"We need eyes inside the building," I tell the twins. "Are you still in contact with a hacker?"

Desi glances up from his screen. "Text me the address." He's been the opposite of his seething brother—deathly calm.

A moment later, Aurora returns with a cheese-and-fruit platter; it's likely to be ignored, but she has to stay busy. "Do you have Jackson's old phone?"

"Yes, why?" My tone comes off clipped, and I mentally kick myself.

It's not her fault my partner went missing while we were asleep, or playing on the beach, or screwing around. It's not her fault I'm injured at the absolute worst time. She's trying to help, doing her best to care for us.

"The Land Rover has an app with 360 surveillance and GPS." She shrugs. "It may show something."

"Good thinking, angel. You wanna get it for me? It's in the safe in the security room."

"We're wasting time," Dante grumbles once she's out of earshot.

"We can't go in there blind. He's avoiding contact for a reason. There's a hidden alert button in one of the links on his chain." I lift my dog tags from my chest to show him. I don't mention that it's designed to prevent accidental activation, requiring it to be pressed and held for five seconds. More worry will only fuel his rage. "Communication could be risky. There might be others around, too many for us to eliminate."

He connects the dots, however. "Or he could be injured… or *dead*."

Desi's head jerks up, eyes feral. "Don't say that, Tay."

Dante clasps his brother's nape, much like Ethan does to

Aurora and Jax. "Sorry, Des. I'm frustrated. We should have done something by now."

"This isn't New York," I remind him.

"It sure as fuck isn't." He draws a calming breath, his nostrils flaring. "None of this shit would happen in New York—*none*." He emphasizes his words with a wave of his hands. "That building would've been raided, and anyone who touched what was ours would be rotting in a morgue by now."

"You're the one who didn't want to call this in," I point out. "A raid is still possible."

"You call this in, it's out of our control, more time is wasted, and it becomes a hostage situation."

"This *is* a hostage situation. He's not missing by accident." Hurried footsteps clatter down the hallway, and I lower my tone. "But I'm with you. We gather intel then move in under the cover of darkness."

"Here you go!" She hands me the phone. "I've added the Wi-Fi. It's updating."

"Thank you. Could you do me an enormous favor?" I swap phones with her. "Call my sister. Tell her there's been a work emergency. She'll understand you can't say more. Let her know our attendance to the wedding is iffy. Ask if she needs anything. I'm sure she'd love to hear from you after receiving all those pictures."

Seeing right through my bullshit, Aurora cocks her head and narrows her eyes. "You don't want me here."

I press my lips together and nod. "I'd rather you weren't, but you get to FaceTime my family."

She stares me down before she relents. "Fine. I'll let the men talk. What's the passcode?"

"Same as your husband's."

Her face brightens, but it doesn't last long. "Te amo," she says with all her heart, her golden eyes burning into mine before she reluctantly leaves.

I offer the phone to the twins. "Do either of you know how to use this?"

Dante takes over, his fingers tapping until a video pops up on the screen. The dashcam footage shows Lucas emerging from the car, the bright sunlight glinting off the doorframe. Then, with a sickeningly swift motion, he crumples, disappearing from view.

Two uniformed figures appear, their movements harsh. Blood roars in my ears, the air evacuates my lungs, and my stomach clenches. Time stands still, each second dragging on as the fragmented video continues and Lucas never gets to his feet. It's not a good sign.

"Is there another angle?" I ask, monotone, my heartbeat pounding in my throat.

The view switches to the rear of the vehicle; my body goes numb and my mind races, preparing for what's next. I'm powerless, seeing my best friend's motionless form being laid in a trunk, his lolling head covered with a black bag.

"Motherfucker!" With a swipe of his hand, Dante sends the cheese platter flying, the ceramic shattering against the hardwood.

I don't flinch, don't so much as blink. My brain locks into crisis mode, separating emotion from reality. I'm laser-focused, calm, rational, but that doesn't mean I won't kill someone for this.

Everything's prepared. Thanks to a hacker, we know Lucas was dragged down to the basement, which has no cameras.

There appear to be only four men—two right inside the

back door and two in a surveillance room on the second level. The bottom floor is unknown.

We've studied the building's layout and are familiar with the optimal routes of entry and exit. Guns are loaded, tactical gear and medical supplies checked and rechecked.

Only one problem. "Who's staying? This might be another setup."

"You." Dante cinches the bulletproof vest tighter. "You're injured and can't shoot."

I scoff. "I can handle a gun with either hand, and Lucas needs me. I'm a medic."

He turns to his brother. "Des—"

"Nope." Desi shoves a government-issued Glock, which I hadn't returned yet, into his vest holster. "No way am I staying."

Dante mirrors his twin and secures his own weapon. "You're not going without me."

I toss them each a silencer. If I don't resign, I'm sure to be fired after tonight. "I'll call Ethan. He'll have an idea, or Jax may know someone who's not on the team."

"No," Aurora interrupts, coming into my bedroom. "Drop me off at Jax's penthouse. It's the safest place." She stops before me and, without me asking, helps me out of my sling with trembling fingers and into my own vest. "Promise me you'll be careful. Call for backup if needed. Once you're in, you're in; there's nothing Bennett can do about it but save your asses."

Chapter 23
Lucas

Commotion overhead rouses me. I crack open my stinging eyes, confused. Not a sliver of light penetrates the blackness. The night has turned cold, and my aching muscles tremble uncontrollably.

The noise upstairs abruptly ends, and an oppressive silence weighs upon me once more, heavy with despair. How long have I been here?

"You want to kiss me, Lucas?" Dante's smoky tone, a phantom memory, his black eyes taunting my broken dreams.

I want to kiss him again and again.

"Fuck, you're beautiful." Desi, softer and lighter than his twin, gazes at me like I've always wanted, like I *am* wanted.

I wish I had never gotten out of their bed. I was removed from the case anyway. What was the point?

Maybe minutes later, I'm startled awake by the thud of footsteps on the stairs, a hollow sound that reverberates above me. The cadence suggests more than one person, and an icy dread clutches my chest, my heart slamming against my ribs.

Despite the terror, my mind remains murky, time distorted. I await the next brutal interrogation, the next nightmare, but nothing comes.

I swear I hear something or someone moving around me, but my brain plays tricks on me. No energy, no struggle left, I fade out.

My body jostles, and my head swims, falling forward onto a soft, warm surface. A familiar scent envelops me, replacing the musty odor that clings to my nostrils, and a fragile whimper claws its way out of my raw throat.

"I got you, piccino." That deep, velvet tone haunts my dreams again. *"You're okay."*

"Dante, I need your knife." Why is Reece in my dream?

"Careful. They're embedded."

"Motherfucker, I hope we find one to torture. I'm slicing their wrists and letting 'em bleed out while I stomp their fucking face in."

"Save some for me, brother."

Relief washes over me. Nothing can harm me now, not with these three here, and I finally surrender to oblivion.

Searing, bone-deep pain has me bolting upright. Or at least I try to. A sharp spasm in my spine freezes me mid-motion, stealing the air from my lungs.

Reality crashes in. I'm caged in a basement, beaten unconscious by cruel, disgusting men, and hands are upon me. I tense, my breath coming in rapid puffs, and blink against the sudden light to clear my spotty vision.

Obsidian eyes stare back at me. "You're safe." Desi kneels between my legs, cups my nape, and gently guides me to rest on his chest, my head on his shoulder. "Hold still, baby. Reece is working on your wrists."

The binds release and my arms go slack, falling limp at my sides, and a weak groan pushes past my lips. Blood flows to places previously numb, and more pain follows. The world spins, a dizzying blur, and I shut my eyes to stop from throwing up.

Desi ghosts his knuckles over my swollen, throbbing cheek. "How many did this?"

I swallow hard to wet my dry, scratchy throat. "Four," I rasp, barely audible.

"We only found three. No one is down here. Dante is keeping watch," he explains.

"They say anything?" Reece unslings his bag from his uninjured shoulder and lets it fall to the floor beside me. "I need to clean and bandage your wrists first. They're bleeding."

I give a slight nod and mumble, "Wanted to know what O'Reilly turned over. Told them I was removed from the case."

If I'd given them what they'd demanded, I'd have been useless, killed.

With practiced skill, Reece swiftly retrieves and prepares the medical supplies. "That true?"

"Yeah." I've witnessed him work countless times as a medic, and the sight brings tears to my eyes. "Thank you," I whisper, my throat thick with emotion. "You didn't have to. You're injured."

"What kind of partner would I be if I left you here? Huh?" He rips open a package of gauze with his teeth. "Fuck, I'm sorry we weren't here sooner. I've called for backup; they're on the way, but you know how they are."

They'll need to clear the area before EMS can safely enter. Otherwise, these three will have to carry me out, which might be risky if someone is waiting upstairs to ambush us.

He flushes my open wounds with sterile solution and wraps them while Des talks me through it.

"Now that you're free…what are your plans for Christmas? Are you going to New York with the rest of the gang? If not, you should. You could meet our parents." He places a tender kiss on my forehead despite the likely blood and grime. "Or we could meet yours. That's fine too. We'll split our time."

For the love of caffeine, no. "Can we just lie in your bed?"

"He doesn't like people," Reece tells him. "He has a severe concussion. His breathing is shallow. He's lost some blood. He needs to be in a hospital." He takes my hand, rests it on his thigh, and cleans my skin, the biting smell of alcohol reaching my nose. "Slight prick." He inserts the IV needle, secures it, and clips the bag to the shoulder of his vest.

The cool liquid floods my veins, and I shiver. Desi wraps his arms about me tighter, his heart beating a steady rhythm in my ear, and my eyes grow heavy, exhaustion threatening to drag me under.

Reece resumes his assessment. His hand skims down my spine, across my back and ribs, where I baulk. "Might be broken," he mumbles. His fingers brush lightly through my hair, searching for injuries, but come to a stop when the stairs creak.

Chapter 24
Dante

I drop the piece of shit onto the filthy cement of the makeshift jail cell. The dumbfuck is not deadweight, but damn, he could lose a few pounds, preferably in blood and flesh.

His head hits the floor with a sickening crack—well, not sickening to me; I enjoy it—and the air whooshes from his lungs.

I press my boot to his windpipe just in case the asshole gets any ideas. "That one of them?"

The man my brother adores, the one I've become addicted to overnight, gives a sharp nod then averts his gaze.

People joked I got the brains and Des got the charm. It bothered him far more than it did me, because I don't care and he's not stupid.

One thing holds true, however: he has all the emotions, the humanity, and I have none. "Live or die?"

Lucas' answer is no surprise. "Live." But he shocks the hell out of me when he continues, "I want you to send a message to the rest of them." His bloodshot eyes, surrounded by deep red and purple bruising, connect with mine. "Let them know what happens when they mess with us."

Us. Welcome to the dark side, my addiction. The Rossi side. There's no going back now. You don't rehabilitate from murder and torture. It becomes you or it breaks you, and we won't allow Lucas to break.

My twin kisses his temple. "You got it, baby." Then, he glances up at me. "Make sure they know who it's from."

Des holds Lucas while Reece staunches the flow of blood from an open wound on Lucas' scalp. Reece mutters something about being surrounded by psychos but otherwise doesn't intervene. The way he violently responded to Aurora's voice while fighting to come out of anesthesia leads me to believe the same darkness flows through his veins.

He also didn't flinch when I shot someone in the forehead upstairs. Instead, he lifted his gun and shot the next dickwad square between the eyes. He's competitive.

I don't consider myself a psycho. I'm not dysfunctional. Jax tends to lose his tether to reality at times. Me? I know precisely what I'm doing, and I don't give a fuck. I'm not saying I'm a vigilante, but the world could use fewer predators. I have zero remorse. Maybe I'm a sociopath.

The wheezing prick whose throat is under my boot doesn't have much consciousness left, and I need him to escape.

When he stepped out of the stairwell, I snuck up behind him and tore through his shoulder with a serrated knife—my favorite weapon. He went straight to his knees and dropped his gun.

Typically, I'd say jumping someone from behind or stabbing someone in the back was cowardly, but they showed Lucas no mercy, and I have none for them. I stomped on the fucker's face and ribs until the damage exceeded what was done to our boy. Fair is fair.

Apparently, Lucas doesn't care for loud noises, particularly grown-ass men shrieking. He covered his ears and tucked into Desi's chest. I shut the bastard up quickly with an uppercut to the jaw, but he's bound to wake and scream like a banshee when I slice through his skin.

"You got zip ties, Viking?" I plan to let this dickhead loose on Skid Row for his friends to find. All he needs is a working set of legs.

Reece uses his free hand to search through his bag. "Hurry. He can die in the alleyway for all I give a fuck, but not here. Not with your monogram on his skin." He passes the plastic restraints.

His arm shakes, and I know he's hurting, but he doesn't complain.

Ain't no way this rapist piece of shit is ratting on us, not after kidnapping and assaulting a federal agent. He's lucky I'm letting him live with only a few scars, broken bones, and a horror story.

I crouch and make quick work of binding the douche canoe's wrists. He attempts to kick me, and I punch him in the nuts.

"Keep your feet to yourself. Didn't your mama teach you anything?"

He balls up into a fetal position, gasping for breath, his wrists tied tightly behind his back. It's his own fucking fault for being stupid, a predator, and for touching what's mine, but I digress.

I grip my blade in one hand and the idiot's hair in the other. "Tell me your favorite song, Lucas."

Des wears that unwavering grin, as constant as death and the sunrise. "Oh, I love this game. We used to play this as kids."

"My favorite song?" Lucas' voice cracks, and he whisper-sings the lyrics, *"Don't stop be-lieving..."*

"Journey?" Des asks, taken aback. "No shit."

"We listened to a lot of classic rock." Reece tosses medical supplies into his backpack and adds, "We only have a few minutes before backup arrives."

I position the tip of my knife at the motherfucker's cheekbone. "Brother, kick us off."

"Just a small town boy..." he begins, the lyrics altered. *"Livin' in a lonely world..."*

The ballsack howls and struggles beneath me as I carve into his worthless flesh. He arches his neck in agony, and I snag the corner of his lip.

"You ruined my masterpiece, cuntmuffin." I place a knee on his forehead to keep him still while I finish the jagged letter 'D'. "Now, I have to start over."

I bet Jackson would love this. I glance at my brother and, sure enough, he has his phone out, filming. I'm no psychiatrist, but revenge and violence can be quite therapeutic—and Jax is going to need it if these sick fucks sent him any taunting pictures of this jail cell.

"Just two city boys," Des sings louder.

I join in, confident of the next part. *"Born and raised in Staten Island!"*

Reece scoffs but slides in on the coming lyric, and the four of us drown out the pussy's whining.

Facial injuries are so messy, and blood drips from his nose and chin onto the nasty floor. I'm certain there's sufficient body fluids and evidence in this basement to keep crime scene investigators busy for years.

I yank the little bitch's hair, flipping his head to the other side as we drag out that high note. *"Searchin' in the night!"*

After I finish the 'R' and hastily cut 'Rapist' into his chest, I assist him up the stairs. He stumbles on the steps and collapses face-first, unable to extend his hands to catch himself.

Jesus, I need a cigarette.

"Seriously? You're the worst criminal." I pick him up by his belt and add a wedgie to his humiliation. "Get the fuck out of here before I change my mind and dismember you." I boot him in the ass. "Don't forget to tell all your fucked-up friends it was Dante Rossi who got you looking pretty."

Chapter 25
Ethan

I pull into the underground parking garage, find an open space, and kill the engine. Silence falls heavy between us, and we both stare out the windshield. I'd hoped never to see this hospital again.

In the passenger seat, Jackson's knee bounces. He's been a wreck since we learned Charlie—or Lucas, as we're told he prefers—was kidnapped, rescued, and admitted to the same unit Reece was only a few weeks ago.

My body sinks into the soft leather, utterly spent. I'm drained, but even in my exhaustion, I know Jax feels a hundred times worse.

He hasn't slept. He has been a zombie, focused on getting home and avoiding the media. How they associated Hugo and Kyle—and Jax by extension—to the latest raid on Skid Row is anyone's guess.

I place my hand on his thigh. "This isn't your fault. You know that, right?"

"Of course it's my fault." He swallows hard, his throat clicking, and hangs his head. "None of this would've happened—to any of you—if it wasn't for me."

"Look at me." I cradle his face and lift his haunted gaze to meet mine. "We *choose* to be with you, every day. I'd choose you in every lifetime, a thousand times over, no matter what." His eyes shimmer, and I press my forehead to his. "I love you. Your fight is my fight, baby boy, and we'll get through this."

Christmas in New York can't arrive fast enough.

We exit the elevator to the ICU. Agents and officers, men and women in various uniforms, flank the corridor. Their hushed conversations come to a standstill, and I feel the scorching heat of their stares on us—or rather, on Jax.

I straighten my posture and lace our fingers together. Let them have something new to gossip about.

The double doors at the end of the hall open, and the clickety-clack of fast-approaching heels captures everyone's attention.

Bennett sweeps her narrowed gaze over every officer. "Don't you all have somewhere to be?" she snaps, and the crowd swiftly scatters. "Come on, boys. We have work to do."

Jax and I trade glances then hustle through the doors. They slam shut with an echoing thud, followed by an eerie silence, broken only by the rhythmic *beep-beep-beep* of a monitor—a chilling soundtrack to the oppressive doom. Did I mention I hate this place?

She stops in front of a set of glass doors, the curtains drawn. "I asked Reece what you'd need," she tells Jax. "He said Aurora and space. Your girl is inside, but unfortunately, I can't give you space. This is the biggest raid yet. We've been searching for the cells."

The cells.

Aurora called me after our game, worried Jax would review the security footage and realize she wasn't home. Her voice shook as she tried to explain why she was at Jackson's penthouse. I was on the road, and the boisterous team made it hard to hear, but I gathered two key facts: Lucas was missing, and she was alone. Naturally, Jax picked up on my distress.

It was the longest seven-hour flight of my life, with sporadic text messaging. We were helpless, learning something new each hour. Lucas was in the ICU. Reece was admitted for observation and wound care. The twins were uninjured but refused to leave. Bennett escorted Aurora to the hospital herself.

It was utter chaos.

Everybody assumed Jax had received taunting pictures of Lucas in the cell being tortured. He hadn't—thank fuck—but I find it hard to believe this was only a ploy to force information from Reece's partner. These assholes attacked while we were out of town and drew everyone else away from Aurora. That can't be a coincidence.

She was smart enough to set aside her discomfort and stay at the penthouse. In the past, she may have called Emily for help. The thought turns my stomach. I don't trust the bitch not to be involved.

Aurora could've been in a cell next to Lucas. Again, we got damn lucky.

Jackson's fingers twitch. "I knew nothing about them. Memories from my childhood are spotty," he repeats the exact words he practiced with Rocco, which are not a lie.

I squeeze his hand and clear my throat. "Our lawyer is on the way from New York. You can question Jax with him. For now, could we see our family please?"

Bennett nods, and I creep the door open, quietly entering the dimly lit room. The twins flank the bed, Reece and Aurora cuddled on the couch.

She gasps softly, "Jax!" and jumps up, rushing into his arms after quickly kissing my cheek.

My gaze lands on Lucas' battered face. He's asleep, curled

on his side, blankets tucked under his chin. He's about Jackson's age but looks so young.

A chill runs down my spine, and my stomach clenches. My teeth rattle. What if it were Jax they'd taken and beaten? What if it were him lying in a hospital bed with a severe concussion, collapsed lung, and broken ribs? Or Aurora?

Most likely, if they were snatched, I'd never see them again. They'd never make it to the hospital. Jax would be killed, and Aurora would disappear.

I'd commit murder, and the words burst from my lips. "You kill them all?"

Dante glances behind me to ensure our privacy. "Yes, sir. Except one, but he's as good as dead."

I clasp Reece's uninjured shoulder. "You let one live?"

"To send a message," Dante continues. "It was Lucas' request."

At the sound of his name, his eyes flutter open and widen. "Holy shit," he rasps, his voice raw. "I didn't know everyone was here." He pushes himself up in bed with a wince, his arms trembling.

Jax lingers near the door. "Rest. Don't get up." He's terrible at comforting others, even worse than I am. He rarely touches people, except for me, Aurora, or sometimes Grant, but he's also perceptive and understands better than anyone that Lucas might want space right now. "Is there anything you need? Anything I can get you?"

Desi lifts a plastic pitcher with a straw from the bedside table and encourages Lucas to drink. "Get us to New York? My mom's a nurse; he can recover there."

"He's under observation and on oxygen." Reece sucks in a deep breath, his eyelids drooping with exhaustion. "He needs to remain in the hospital."

"You're one to talk," Lucas croaks. "Did they release you? Or did you sign yourself out against medical advice?"

"I'm still in the hospital, aren't I?" Reece raises his brows, presses his lips together, and collapses against the couch cushion. "I'll leave when you do, and you'll stay with me."

"He doesn't need you," Dante interjects, his dark eyes narrowed.

"He has us," Desi adds. "We'll take care of him."

Oh boy. I exchange a glance with Jax and Aurora, who now sit beside Reece, Aurora on Jax's lap, his hand on her belly. We have some important decisions to make, none of which I'm ready to discuss tonight.

"One day at a time. When the doctors release you," I tell Lucas, "we'll get you to New York if that's what you want. Same with you guys." I nod to the twins.

Desi stands and perches on the side of the bed, motioning for me to take his chair. He smiles down at Lucas and brushes his hair from his forehead. "Spend Christmas in New York with us—no people, just us."

Lucas returns the smile and whispers, "Okay."

Dante watches their every move. It's obvious the three are close, and I wouldn't expect the twins to allow Reece to care for their boyfriend.

A line has been drawn. Reece may have always cared for his partner, and perhaps he's feeling guilty, but he'll have to let him go. The twins are ready to return home—with Lucas—and I don't blame them.

We're all going to do what's necessary to protect those we love.

An hour later, Rocco arrives, and Bennett accompanies him into the room. With him is another man I vaguely recognize.

He doesn't look like Rocco or Shorty. He's taller and more muscular, with a full head of wavy, salt-and-pepper hair. The twins stand when he enters, and, despite the age difference, the resemblance is uncanny. He has to be their father.

After hugging them, he shakes my hand. "Wow, you've gotten bigger. You remember me?"

I furrow my brows and nod. "Yeah, vaguely."

"Dimitri. You stayed with me when you were about…"

"Five," I answer and swallow hard. "You called me little prince."

It's one of my earliest memories, etched in my brain. My mother had overdosed. I thought she was dead.

In footed pajamas and bawling my eyes out, I ran across the street to the only place I knew: the diner. I still remember the scrape of the rough, cold concrete under the thin plastic material covering my feet.

I was terrified and crying so hard, I couldn't talk. Shorty scooped me up, rushed me to his office, and sent someone to the apartment.

An ambulance took her away, and he brought me to Dimitri's. I stayed with him, his wife, and their baby for many nights.

When my mother eventually came for me, they argued. She threatened to call the police. She hated them.

They had spoiled me with new clothes and gifts, but after we left, she got rid of them all. She most likely sold everything for drug money. It wasn't long before she was using again.

I could've grown up with the twins. That's wild to think about.

Chapter 26
Jackson

Seated on the windowsill, Bennett tries to sneak in another question. "When did you first learn your father was holding women hostage?" If she's aiming for nonchalant, friendly conversation, she's failing miserably.

My impulse is to yell. *"I didn't know! I was a fucking child! It wasn't only women he was holding hostage, you fucking idiot."*

But we're at the hospital, in front of everyone, and I suppress the anger and embarrassment. Ethan predicted this. He was smart enough to call Rocco. I was focused more on my fear and guilt.

I peer over at Dimitri, who's also a lawyer, of the criminal type, and he gives a curt nod.

Her wording is open to interpretation, and I state my answer as advised. "I had no knowledge of the house on Skid Row. I listed all the properties I was aware of."

My body won't stop trembling. Forget having nightmares —I'm *living* a nightmare.

That's a stretch, I tell myself. Shit could be worse. *I could've been locked in a cell. I could've been tortured.*

But fuck, I'd rather it be me. I'd rather fight these fuckers than see any of our family hurt. I'd rather *die*.

I can't look at Lucas without wanting to end it all. If it wasn't for the woman on my lap and the man next to me, I'd do it. I'd end all this pain.

Aurora holds my hand against her stomach, reminding me of what I have to live for, but it also reminds me of what I need to protect, what I risk losing. There's no longer a possibility of her being hurt or worse; it's inevitable if we stay in LA.

Reece is injured, and she's pregnant, for fuck's sake. I should've listened to Ethan. She needs to go to New York, but I can't function without her.

My eyes find his. I blink away the tears and swallow the tight lump in my throat. I open my mouth, but before I can say anything, he leans in and cups the back of my head.

"I know, baby. I got it," he whispers, his warm breath tickling my neck. "I'll make sure everyone is taken care of. You focus on this interrogation, that's all." His lips brush my temple as he pulls away.

"According to this text from Hugo…" Bennett holds up her phone and reads aloud. "He wrote, 'I miss you, but your pretty girl will do. I'm saving the spot just for her,' and it's accompanied by a picture of a cell in the basement of the Skid Row property."

Aurora gasps and turns to look at me. I glare at Reece on the other side of her and clench my jaw so hard, the muscle spasms.

His face twists with remorse. "Sorry. In order to get a unit to follow Ethan and Aurora home and extra security at the hotel, I had to provide evidence."

Despite my fury, Bennett continues, "To me, that sounds as if you've been in that cell." She enunciates each word as if she's cross-examining me on the witness stand.

My body lights on fire then goes ice cold. *I want to die. I want to die. I want to die. I want to die. I want to die.* The intrusive thought repeats, though in this moment, I doubt it's intrusive.

The flashback hits violently. I'm rocking back and forth, my arms wrapped around my knees, repeating those exact words in my mind.

I stare down at my bright-white sneakers, a stark contrast to the damp, nasty floor I'm huddled on. They're scuffed, and when I try to wipe them clean, my smaller fingers smear blood and dirt across the canvas. It's impossible to get them clean, and I stare at those shoes for days.

Ethan clasps the back of my neck. "We're done," he growls, low and harsh. "You can bring him in if you need to question him. Don't contact us otherwise."

His thumb caresses my skin, and reality returns in waves. My heavy breaths whoosh in my ears, though I can't fill my lungs. My heart slams against my rib cage. I'm shivering, and Aurora is no longer on my lap. She sits with the Viking but holds my hand.

I lean forward and glance down at my boots. Brown, oiled and waxed, broken-in leather. Unnecessary relief washes over me—or maybe it's relief for twelve-year-old me who never wore white sneakers again, but the numbness remains.

Lucas clears his throat and breaks the silence. "You won't beat these sick bastards following the rules," he says to Bennett. "They're playing outside the law while you're restricting our abilities. I could've researched them a long time ago. Based on what I found, we would've known who to concentrate on. Instead, you had me focused on those in this room who've hurt no one. Then, you take me off the case for inappropriate behavior." He gestures to his best friend. "Reece isn't returning. He has a family to protect because you can't. If we want to put an end to these predators, we need to work together, not alienate our only source of information. What the fuck is wrong with you?"

Desi chuckles, and Dante glowers at Bennett, daring her to respond unkindly.

She cocks her head and raises her brows. "I'll let that last comment slide. You're asking me to allow you to hack into the LAPD and all its employees. Do you know what will happen in court if that information comes to light?"

"I'm not asking for your permission. I no longer work for you. I'm giving you the opportunity to have that knowledge and use it wisely."

"If not," Dante continues, "these assholes won't make it to court. They'll be dead."

The late-night air on the balcony is chilly, and goosebumps prickle along my arms. I grab a blanket from the back of a chair and wrap it around my shoulders. Aurora must have been using it; I can't imagine why else it'd be out here.

More guilt churns in my stomach. She hates this place—too many terrible memories. I've done everything I could to prevent her from having to return, yet here we are, at my downtown penthouse. It's safest and closest to the hospital, and she swears she's not bothered, but still…it only adds to my misery.

I find the farthest lounger from the door, away from the panoramic windows, and stare out at the never-ending lights. Everyone is inside, including Rocco and Dimitri, and I need a breather. This is the first I've been alone since this nightmare began.

For a moment, I allow myself to envision climbing the

glass barrier and taking a skydive. The free fall into oblivion is not as appealing as it used to be, but only because it'd kill Aurora too. And maybe Ethan.

The solitude doesn't last long, maybe five minutes, before I sense him approaching.

He swings his leg over the chair, sits behind me, and draws me into his chest. "Reece is keeping Aurora busy, and the other two are unpacking."

I make a sound of acknowledgment, my throat too constricted to speak.

His touch dispels the numbness, my emotions rise to the surface, and I pull out of his embrace to stop from shattering.

"Turn around," he demands.

I know he won't let it slide, and I shift to face him, my head hung, my eyes downcast. I can't meet his gaze. If I do, I'll break.

He raises my chin. "Look at me."

A part of me wants to defy him, to argue. Maybe he'll punish me, force me. I crave the fight, the physical pain, but I lack the energy and glance up.

"How bad is it? Don't lie. You promised to tell me."

My lips tremble. "I want to die."

A tear escapes, and he wipes it away. "You can't die. I can't live without you. *Aurora* can't live without you."

He wraps himself around me and lifts me onto his lap as if I'm not six-three and two-hundred pounds. He relaxes into the pillows, widening his knees, and tucks my face into his throat.

This would be sexy as fuck if I wasn't battling depression —that bitch.

"You need to let go, Jax." He runs his fingers up my neck and into my hair. "You don't have to be strong for me. Fall apart. I got you."

I've always had to be strong. For my mother, for my

father, for the media, for Aurora...but for Ethan, I don't have to pretend. He accepts me for who I am, and my walls crumble. I collapse into him, and my body racks with sobs.

I let it all out—the guilt, the shame, the torment...

He clutches me to him, his pulse pounding against mine. "You're breaking my heart, baby boy. Hold on a little longer for me. I promise I'll give you the life you deserve. I'll never leave your side. You'll wake each morning with your head on my chest, your arm around me. You want a yacht? Fuck it. Get a yacht. Buy a jet for all I care. We'll explore the world if that's your dream. And I'll be with you every step of the way, fighting your demons, until you're sick of me."

With each word, my tears and hopelessness subside. "I'll never be sick of you."

He kisses my temple and plays with my hair. "I love you. I love your scent. You smell like the beach and goddamn sunshine. I love how you taste. I love your snarky attitude. I love how you feel in my arms, as if you've always belonged there. You can't leave me, Jax." His tone turns rough, his touch desperate. "I wouldn't survive. Do you need to see someone?"

"No," I choke. "The last thing I need is to be locked away from you and Aurora. I won't harm myself."

"Will you tell me if it becomes too much? Anytime? Anywhere?"

I swallow hard. "Yes."

"Do we need to pinky promise?"

I stifle a weak, breathy chuckle. "No."

"You wanna talk about it? Reece said you have flashbacks—and before you get mad, he has them too, from the military. He's worried about you and pissed at Bennett for the way she handled that...fucking interrogation."

"Nope." I shake my head. "I don't wanna talk about it."

He releases a heavy sigh. "Okay. Just know I'm always

here. I'll never think differently of you. Is there anything you need?"

"I kind of like being on your lap."

He barks out a laugh, deep and throaty. "You wanna sit on my lap and listen to how I met Dimitri?"

"Yes. Of course."

He drapes the blanket over me and recalls the first time he remembers his mother overdosing, how he screamed for her to wake up, how he ran to the diner and stayed with the twins' father. "They gave me dinner and a bath every night. We went to the park and out for ice cream. I had new clothes and coloring books and shit I never had. That's when I realized my life wasn't normal. Kids aren't left alone. They don't go without food."

Again and again, he somehow eases my anguish, this time by giving me his to focus on instead of my own. "Fuck, I'm sorry. I'm sorry, I'm the same as your mother—an addict."

"You're not. I recognized it the first night we met. Even tipsy, you were full of emotion, full of fight. You wanted Aurora back. It was obvious you loved her. My mom had nothing left. Whatever love she had was locked away with my father."

Silence falls between us, but it's not awkward or uncomfortable. I meant it when I said I liked being on his lap. Honestly, I'm quite fond of it.

I slip my hand under his shirt and draw circles on his heated skin. "They kept me in that cell for days with no food or water." I start to tremble and stop. That was the least of it, and I can't go on.

"I'm sorry, baby. I'd kill every motherfucker who touched you if I could. The twins took care of the assholes who hurt Lucas—Des has a video for you when you're ready." Ethan rests his forehead on mine and kisses my lips. "Lucas will be okay. We're *all* going to be okay. I'll make sure of it."

Chapter 27
Ethan

Jax flops between Aurora and me. "Can we go back to how you love my taste?"

"Shut up," I say through gritted teeth and clasp my hand over his mouth. "Or you're sleeping on the couch."

His smile grows beneath my palm, and I release him. The four of us are crammed into one bed tonight—both guest rooms are taken. We're exhausted, but that doesn't stop Jax from running his trap.

"I'll sleep on the couch," Reece repeats for the tenth time from the opposite side.

"You will not," Aurora chastises. "You're injured, and your shoulders won't fit comfortably on the sectional. I'll go."

"No," we all reply in unison, appalled. As if we'd ever let her sleep on the couch.

There's a beat of silence before Jackson starts in again. "This is awkward as fuck. I miss my wife, and we can't do anything because the Viking is a prude."

Reece scoffs as if we're clueless, and now I'm curious.

Jax as well. He's too perceptive not to be. For that reason, I know what he's going to ask next.

"Did you two fu—"

I clamp my hand over his mouth again and draw him close until his back is pressed to my chest. "Leave them alone and go to sleep."

"God give me strength," Reece mumbles while Aurora huffs a frustrated breath.

Jax drives his ass into my groin, and my cock takes notice.

I grab his hip. "Stop it," I growl then bite his ear in retaliation. I'm actually getting fucking hard. Why is my dick such a troublemaker? I've never been attracted to any guy until Jackson. Despite what he argues, I doubt I'm even attracted to men, only *him*. "Don't be a brat, or *I'll* sleep on the couch."

He shakes his head emphatically, and I uncover his mouth. I slip my hand under his shirt and caress his skin to distract him—and because I'm utterly obsessed with touching him.

Bedding rustles, and Aurora turns on her side to face us, giving Jax the attention he's crying out for.

"I missed you too," she whispers, although nothing is a secret in this king-sized bed, which feels more like a twin right now. "Reece is uncomfortable because he took a bullet for you. Don't be rude."

"I missed you more." Jax kisses her and lowers his tone. "I'm teasing. Feel free to prove me wrong at any time."

Humor and sex: Jackson's healthy ways of coping, neither of which Reece shares with us. I bet Jax had fantasies of a threesome dancing in his head before this shitstorm hit. I admit, with our new dynamic, I imagined the same.

"He was unbearable without you," I add to break the tension. "An absolute terror. You need to get better, Reece, because I can't handle him alone."

"He's a liar. He *handled* me just fine." He grinds his firm ass against my erection.

Aurora brushes his hair from his forehead, weaving her

fingers through the top. "Will you sleep in with me tomorrow?"

She knows just how to persuade him to catch up on sleep. Plus, they need time together. I can only calm Jackson to a certain level; he needs her. This reminds me—I need time with her too. She can't stay in LA, and then there's my relationship with Jax. We have a lot to discuss.

"We have company, babe," he says apologetically.

"Right." She releases a heavy sigh. "Sorry. It's been a long few days."

"It's been a long few *weeks* for her," Reece chimes in. "She's been taking care of everyone and *needs* to rest."

I clear my throat. "We have the next week off, and the twins are heading home. I'll make sure she rests. I planned to get up with Rocco and Dimitri. You guys can sleep in."

"And I'm up with the sun." Reece yawns. "I'll start coffee and order food."

I wake and sneak out from under the covers. A beam of sunlight peeks into the room, softly illuminating the bed. Reece is already up, his side of the bed empty. I stare down at the other two. They're tangled together like something out of a movie—sickeningly in love.

When I found out Aurora was pregnant, I believed they were meant to be. I couldn't bring myself to come between them. I looked at them and thought they were perfect. And they are, except now I gaze at them and think, *they're perfectly mine.*

In no way am I threatened or jealous. I see them, and love swells in my chest. My heart beats just for them.

Chapter 28
Reece

The bedroom door closes softly, and Ethan pads down the hall. I know it's him by his long, assured stride.

He enters the kitchen, and on his way to the coffeemaker, his gaze lands on the blanket and pillow on the couch. "Was it that bad?" He smirks and pours himself a cup.

"Not terrible." Seated at the breakfast table, I sip my coffee and skim through my phone. "I'm a light sleeper. I'm usually up all night."

The dark calls to me, and I wake often. There's something about solitude in the dead of the night. I can't explain it, but time moves more slowly. It's tranquil, meditating.

He takes a seat across from me, blowing the steam from his mug. "That'll be convenient when the baby comes."

I wince, a knee-jerk response to the thought of caring for what's his. I don't know how they share everything, and I don't know why it bothers me.

Not only that, but the last time I was around a baby—my nephew when he was a year old—his cries evoked an agitation that made me want to put my fist through a wall.

Ethan quickly corrects himself. "While we're away...or we

could hire a nanny." His cheeks flush. "I didn't mean it was your responsibility. Sorry."

He's talking as if I belong, as if I'm one of them. Isn't that what I'd hoped for?

"No, it's fine. She won't want a nanny."

He makes a sound of agreement. "How would you like to do this? I know your dynamic differs from ours, and you want to work security." He swallows a hefty dose of caffeine and gets straight to the point. "I need her to live in New York. She can't stay here."

Of course, I'll go with her, but... "Permanently?"

He shrugs, but his gaze gravitates to the ceiling. He's worried about the cameras and Jax's reaction.

"What about her doctor? Her grandmother? The baby?"

"We'll figure it out. Obviously, I'll need your help." He shoves his fingers through his unruly hair. "If she stays, it's only a matter of time before it's her they come after—again. The twins won't allow Lucas to return, I guarantee it, and I'd much prefer she were with my family and safe."

I doubt Jackson will finish his contract in LA while Aurora lives in New York, even if he is in love with Ethan. He'll either quit or have an absolute meltdown.

"I'll go anywhere with her, but she's six months pregnant. She and the baby need stability. She's going to be worried sick again."

"She has you; you're her stability as well."

Panic sets in. I almost lost my partner. I'm struggling to care for myself right now. I don't know if I can care for her *and* a baby.

"Once you're healed," he continues, "she can travel with us, and we'll stay in New York when we're not playing. I'll talk to her, ensure she has everything she needs. Just help me get through this season. It's what's best for her."

"I don't disagree, but she'll have doctor's appointments.

She'll want a nursery." I gesture with my hand. "You're missing out. *She's* missing out."

He narrows his eyes. "What is she missing out on? There are three of us, and she can pick whatever nursery she wishes. I'll pack up and ship this one if that's what she wants. I'm trying to keep her safe."

Frustrated, I shake my head, a dull ache forming at the base of my skull. "She's missing *you*—the father of her child."

His scowl deepens, a puzzled expression on his face. "I'm not leaving forever."

I grip the edge of the table, and sharp pain shoots through my neck, adding to my annoyance. I need to go back to bed. Aurora was right—I shouldn't have slept on the couch. "The baby isn't mine! It's not the same."

He raises a challenging brow. "You can't love and care for someone who's not yours?" He holds my gaze, knowing he got me there. "It's not Jackson's either, but he's over the moon with excitement."

"That's because it belongs to you."

"Nope. His life changed the moment he discovered she was pregnant. He didn't know I was the father."

"He wants a baby."

"And you don't?" His voice rises. "Probably something you should've thought about before you fell in love with Aurora."

The bedroom door creaks, and Jackson's hurried pace echoes down the hall. He hustles into the kitchen wearing only black boxer briefs, his hair sticking up in places, marks and bruises on his skin, exhaustion darkening his eyes.

"What the fuck could you possibly be arguing about at six in the morning?" he whisper-yells. "Rocco and Big D must be jet-lagged if they're sleeping through this."

I stand. "Nothing. Never mind." I wave him off and go to

the coffeemaker for another cup. "I'm just agitated. Shit hasn't been easy lately."

"No, it's not nothing," Ethan hisses. "If you don't want a baby, it's a huge fucking deal."

Jax glances between us. "What? Like any babies? Or your own?"

I set my mug on the counter and pinch the bridge of my nose. "That's not what I meant." I drop my arm to my side and spell it out for them. "All I'm saying is, Aurora needs quality time with the baby's father. I'm not a substitute. It's yours. *You* should be going to appointments, feeling the baby kick, putting together the nursery—shit like that. I can't do it! Look at me!"

Fuck, I'm injured. I'm tired. *I failed my partner.* Who's next?

They stare at each other, having some wordless conversation.

Ethan slumps in his chair. "Thank you...for telling me how you feel. I'm not asking you to assume my responsibilities. I didn't know you drew a line between Aurora and the baby. *We'll* set up the nursery." He gestures to the three of us. "This isn't all on you. Does it make you uncomfortable to take her to appointments if needed? Or to care for my child?"

I clear my tight throat. "Not necessarily, but it doesn't feel right either."

Jax leans against the wall, arms crossed. "You have this picture-perfect, conventional idea of what having this baby should look like when we're anything but. In a *perfect* world, it'd be mine. *I'd* be there for every milestone. But that's not how it went." He places a hand on his chest. "I relapsed—a few times—and got punished with you two." He gestures to the man beside him. "He used a decrepit wallet condom on his oversized dick to screw an escort in the back of a limo while still married."

Ethan smacks Jackson's ass cheek in retaliation and snarls, "Shut up."

Jax motions to me. "You fell for Aurora, who was already pregnant—by said oversized dick—who you were pretending to protect, who wasn't yours, who you watched with two other men." He cocks his head and scoffs. "And *now* you're uncomfortable? Be for real."

Well, when he puts it that way…it does sound ridiculous. Maybe I'm still holding on to some of my parents' conservative views. Maybe I need to let that shit go. Maybe I'm shaken over the shitty month we've had. "I'm not uncomfortable. I feel like I'm trespassing, encroaching on another man's territory."

"Yes, because you've *never* done that before," he mocks, sarcasm dripping from every word.

I skewer him with a glare. "You were broken up, remember?"

His nostrils flare. "She never broke up with me!"

"Let's not take a trip down memory lane," Ethan cuts in. "Let's figure this out. Reece," his eyes lock with mine, "you won't be injured forever. Shit won't be this rough. Lucas wasn't your fault. You rescued him and you kept Aurora safe. I appreciate you. We're all in this together. Tell me what you need, and I'll make it happen."

Unable to speak, I swallow the lump in my throat and nod.

"Why don't we drop the whole 'whose kid is whose' thing?" Jax suggests. "You wouldn't want us to treat your kid any differently. I'm uncertain I want a biological child, and it would suck if we couldn't share." His voice strains with emotion, and his eyes glisten. He's moody—all over the place—and he's only been in LA a handful of hours. I'm not much better.

A frown contorts Ethan's face, etching deep lines into his forehead. "Why?"

Jax taps his temple and gives a half-assed shrug. "Not sure I should pass along this DNA."

Ethan pulls Jax between his legs until he's partly on his lap and wrapped in his arms. "It's not all DNA. Our life won't be like yours or mine. It may not be perfect, but it'll be pretty damn good. You're okay, I promise."

I return to my seat at the breakfast table. "I agree—with both sentiments. Our kids will have a much better life, and we shouldn't focus on whose baby it is." A crazy thought hits me, and I can't suppress my smile. "After this one, we won't know who it belongs to anyhow."

Jackson's gaze snaps to mine. "Is that a challenge? Are we playing Russian roulette, Viking?"

"I'm just saying." I full-on grin. "There's no guarantee who the father will be."

Chapter 29
Aurora

The mattress dips and I crack my eyelids to see Jax sneaking into bed. He cuddles close, and my gaze catches on a bite mark on his collarbone.

"Holy shit." I push him onto his back and straddle his waist. In the dim light, I ghost my finger over the angry red indentations, only inches above my name.

Eyes downcast, he caresses my baby bump. "Does it bother you?"

"You and Ethan? Why would it? Unless these aren't his bite marks," I joke to lighten the mood.

I've seen them touching, and I know they love each other. I'm nothing but grateful for Ethan and their relationship. Without it, Jax might've spiraled out of control by now.

He scoffs. "These came after I baited him with Grant. If they belonged to anyone else, he'd have killed me."

I bend down, ass in the air to accommodate my growing belly, and kiss his bare chest. "You don't need to hide anything from me." I trail kisses down his stomach. "Ethan loves you in a way I can't, and it only makes us stronger, more complete."

"I fucking love you, you know that?" He gathers my hair into a fisted ponytail. "I missed you like crazy."

I trace the defined lines of his abdomen with my tongue, loving how his muscles tense beneath my touch.

"How much did you miss me?" I work the waistband of his boxers down.

"Enough to drive Ethan mad." He lifts his ass to help me free his erection. "He practically tied me down and punished me for being so obnoxious."

"Sounds kinky." I wrap my lips around the head of his cock and cup his balls, massaging them gently.

His breath hitches and his hips buck. "Fuck, baby."

Gazing up at him, I circle the sensitive underside with the tip of my tongue.

His eyes darken. "Aurora..." His grip on my hair tightens. "Get up here and ride me."

The slight sting on my scalp shoots straight to my clit, and I moan around his length. Still, I ignore his demands and take him deeper until he hits the back of my throat.

I establish a rhythm, bobbing my head while stroking his shaft. The salty taste of his precum bursts along my tongue.

"Baby, please." He yanks my ponytail upward. "I need to be inside you. I need to feel you."

I release him and climb up his glorious physique. I remove my shirt, and his hands immediately go to my tits, his thumbs brushing over my hardened nipples. With my palms on his thighs for leverage, I slide my wet slit along his cock.

"You're so fucking beautiful." His gaze roams hungrily over my body, and then he gasps. "Your belly button!"

I glance down and smile. "Yeah, it popped out."

He twists his torso and reaches for his phone on the nightstand, forgetting all about getting inside me.

"What are you doing?" I ask, my annoyance barely contained.

"Sending a picture to Ethan," he says as if it's obvious.

Throbbing and needy, I grind against him. "Jax..." I whine. "Where is he?" I wouldn't mind fucking them both—or all of them? Too bad that's not happening anytime soon.

He returns the phone. "Probably in the living room doing mafia shit." Hands on my ass, he guides me over his length. "Now, fuck me."

I sink down onto him, and an embarrassingly lusty moan escapes me.

"Fuck," he hisses through gritted teeth. "I missed this."

I pause when he's fully seated and squeeze around him. "So deep," I whimper.

His jaw clenches, and his breathing turns ragged. "Move, baby. Give me that tight pussy." His phone vibrates on the nightstand, but he ignores it.

I lift until only his tip remains inside me, then slowly descend, and roll my hips.

Another buzz from his phone—I bet I know who it is.

I reach over and snatch it. A glance at the screen confirms my suspicion—Ethan.

COACH

Thanks, asshole. I'm not alone.

Wait for me.

I angle the camera above us to capture my swollen breasts and Jackson's defined abs, careful to keep his cock buried inside me. I snap the photo and send it with a simple message:

Hurry.

Jax takes the phone and tosses it aside. "You're killing me. It's been weeks since I came in this pussy. I'm dying."

His hands clutch my hips, and he drives up into me. The pregnancy has made me more sensitive, and each stroke sends ecstasy rippling through my core.

I lean forward, bracing on his chest, and match his rhythm. He hits the perfect spot, and I bite my lip to stop from crying out.

The bedroom door opens, and we both freeze.

Ethan kicks the door shut behind him and strips off his shirt. "Don't stop on my account."

Wondering about our guests, I glance anxiously toward the living room.

"Don't worry. They're headed to the hospital." He sheds the rest of his clothes, palms his hard cock, and slips in close to Jackson.

"Reece?" I ask.

"Going to see Lucas."

Jax hits me with a powerful thrust. "You don't need Reece."

Ethan grabs Jackson by the chin and grits, "Stop being a brat," then plants a firm kiss on his lips.

"Wow," I breathe.

I haven't seen them kiss yet, and it's so effortless, so natural, it's as if it has always been this way. It's beautiful, and, yeah, it's hot, but overall, it's *right*.

Ethan's hesitant gaze meets mine, his cheeks flushed. "Sorry. I meant to talk to you before now."

"No need. I'm not upset at all—about anything. I love that you two love each other. I saw you touching in the shower. I thought it was hot." I grin and writhe my hips. "Please proceed."

He turns to Jax and cups the back of his head. They kiss

open-mouthed and full of tongue. Jackson groans and drives into me.

I meet his slow, deep thrusts, wetter than ever, the sight of them igniting a fire in my core. I've never seen anything more erotic than them losing themselves to their desires.

Jax breaks the kiss, his eyes gleaming with lust when he meets my gaze. "Damn, you're soaked."

My response is a whimper and a roll of my hips.

"Our dirty girl. Made just for us." Ethan fists his cock, stroking with an unhurried pace. "I wanna watch you two finish. Then, I wanna fuck her while she's full of your cum."

"Jesus." Jax pounds into me harder. "You really have a thing for my cum, don't you?"

He fucks me with a punishing rhythm while our boyfriend whispers naughty words in his ear and I dig my nails into his pecs.

"Fill her cunt for me, baby boy." Ethan grazes his lips along Jax's jawline. "I want her dripping with your cum while I fuck her."

Jackson's head arches back into the pillow. "Bastard," he grunts. Urgency overtakes him, and his pace becomes raw and wild.

A flash of heat spreads across my skin, and my nipples harden. "I'm close." My eyes flicker from one beautiful man to the other—Jax's features contorted in pleasure and Ethan's lazy strokes. "Don't stop."

"Come on Jackson's cock, baby girl." Ethan reaches between Jax and me and teases my clit. "Get that tight pussy nice and wet for me."

His filthy words send a tremor through my thighs, and ecstasy explodes in my core.

I bite my bottom lip, but it's no use. I can't hold back. I climax hard, pulsing around Jax and crying out.

He finishes with me, his chest heaving, his moans swallowed by Ethan's kiss.

My legs still trembling, I slip off Jackson, ready to straddle Ethan—but before I can, Jax leans over and engulfs the head of Ethan's cock.

Holy fuck. Despite coming mere seconds ago, the sight of Jackson's lips stretched around Ethan has me aching again. "I wanna join."

With a wicked glint in his eyes, Jax scooches over, making room for me beside him.

Together, we work Ethan's thick length; I glide my tongue along the shaft while Jackson teases the ridge.

"Goddamn." Ethan threads his fingers through our hair. "Look at you two, my perfect, cock-hungry brats."

I trace a prominent vein from base to tip as Jax moves lower. Our tongues meet at the underside, sliding together. Ethan's dick jerks, and Jax's lips curl into a devilish smile.

"Christ," Ethan hisses through clenched teeth. "So fucking good. Keep that up, and I won't last long."

We suck the head of his cock in tandem, mouths pressed to each side, our tongues intertwining. It's honestly similar to kissing, but with our boyfriend's dick in between.

I cup his heavy balls, and they tense in my palm. I trace patterns with my tongue along his shaft, and Jax sucks the tip into his mouth.

Ethan's breathing grows ragged. "That's it." He fists my hair and pulls me off him. "Come here."

Jax releases him with one last hollow of his cheeks, and I crawl up Ethan's body.

He slides his fingers through my slit, gathering the evidence of my release mixed with Jackson's cum. "Such a beautiful mess you are. You like sucking my cock with Jax?"

I position myself over him and grind my needy clit along his length. "Yes."

Jackson flops onto the bed beside Ethan, sweat-soaked hair plastered to his forehead, and palms his erection. "And... yup, I'm hard again."

"Fuck her with me.' Intense gray eyes meet mine. "You want us both, baby girl? Can you take it?"

I imagine the stretch, the fullness of having both of them inside me at once, and rock my hips. "Please."

Chapter 30
Ethan

Why was I *ever* resistant to this full-on threesome? The way they sucked my cock together, their eager tongues around my shaft, their greedy mouths and moans…

"Fuck, I want you." Hands on Aurora's hips, I position her over me before I turn to Jax. "You have lube?"

"Hell yeah." He lunges for the nightstand and yanks the top drawer open.

She lowers onto my cock with a whimper that shoots straight through me. So fucking wet and full of his cum. The combination is obscene and filthy, and I throb inside her.

"That's my girl." I thrust upward, and her full breasts bounce. "Lean forward, baby. Get comfortable."

She braces her palms on my chest. Jackson kneels behind her, slicking his fingers and then stroking his cock. He drops the bottle to the sheets and reaches down. Her body tenses, and her inner walls clamp around me.

A soft touch grazes my sac, and my dick jolts. Devilish green eyes lock with mine, his lips curling into that crooked grin I can't resist. He cups and rolls my balls, and I clench my jaw.

"Jax..." I warn, barely hanging on.

Aurora moans, her pussy fluttering and hips rocking. Jackson never stops working my balls as he preps her, occasionally sliding up to trace where she and I are joined before returning to torment me.

"For fuck's sake." My voice is thick with lust, my body aching for release. "You two are going to make me come before we even get started."

"Please, Jax," Aurora begs. "I'm ready. I want you both."

He removes his hand from my balls, giving me a momentary reprieve. I tighten my hold on her hips and still her movements. He gets into position behind her, clasps her shoulders, and eases forward with excruciating slowness.

The pressure of his cock through the thin barrier separating us increases, and I grit my teeth to stop from rutting into Aurora and coming.

Her mouth falls open, her breath hitching. "Oh God," she whimpers. "So full."

Shockwaves of ecstasy race through my veins, tingling my fingertips. No matter how many times we've fucked, it's always mind-blowing. Aurora's wet heat gripping me while Jackson's hard length slides along mine doubles the friction, the sensation, the pleasure. The three of us coming together as one is unlike anything I've ever felt—sexual or otherwise.

"Fuck, I love this," Jax groans, his hips flush with her ass. "So fucking good."

We remain still, giving her time to adjust. He cups her breasts, pinches her nipples, and kisses her neck while I circle her clit.

Her face is a portrait of desire—eyes glazed, bottom lip caught between her teeth. "Move. Please." She writhes her hips.

We establish a rhythm—I thrust up and he pulls back. He pushes in and I withdraw.

"Such a good girl." Her seductive moans and the drag of his cock along mine have my balls hugging my shaft already, no thanks to them edging me. "Taking both our cocks so fucking well."

Our bodies reach a fever pitch, racing toward release—then the door opens, and Reece slips into the dim room.

Jesus, fuck, will I ever get to come?

My rhythm falters. Jax freezes. Aurora gasps, her walls clenching around us. Reece comes to a standstill, mouth agape, eyes wide with shock. What did he think we were doing in here? And why hasn't he left yet?

His expression flickers from surprise to confusion to something darker. His brows furrow, and he stares, his hungry gaze drinking in the sight of Aurora naked between us.

Jackson recovers first, his cock buried deep and throbbing with mine. "Jesus, it's not like you haven't seen us together before. Pull up a chair, man," he barks, but there's no bite behind it.

"What's up?" I manage to shake off the awkwardness, my voice strained from the effort of holding still.

Not moving from the doorway, Reece clears his throat. "The ICU is crawling with LAPD."

"That's it?" Jax flexes his hips. "Shit, Viking. This meeting could've been an email."

I ignore his snark. "My uncles?" My tone is harsher than intended, my restraint collapsing by the second.

Reece shifts his weight and avoids direct eye contact. "Dropped 'em off and came here just in case. They're worried about the twins."

"Fuck," I curse. Looks like we're cutting this fuckfest short.

"In or out, Viking?" Jackson rolls his hips again. "We need about two minutes."

Aurora whimpers. I shoot Jax a glare, and he gives me that shit-eating grin.

Reece's gaze snaps to our girl, the conflict in his stare undeniable, his jaw clenched so tight, the muscle bulges.

His Adam's apple bobs. His hand goes to the doorknob but hovers.

"Fuck it." He throws his arms in the air, steps farther into the room, and stalks to the leather armchair tucked in the corner.

Jackson grabs the lube from the bed and tosses it to him.

He catches it and grumbles, "I hate you."

A smug smirk on his face, Jax reclaims Aurora's shoulders, pulls back, and thrusts with renewed purpose.

Reece drops into the seat, his eyes never leaving our girl.

She glances between him and me, her cheeks flushed, breathy moans escaping with each snap of Jackson's hips.

The bottle cap clicks, she grows wetter, and her cunt squeezes around my cock. We pound into her from both sides, and her nails dig into my chest.

"You like that?" I drive into her and circle her clit. "Like him watching while we fuck you?"

She gives a gentle nod, her attention on whatever he's doing.

I spank her ass and command, "Use your words."

"Y-yes, Sir."

***

Reece

What the fuck am I doing? I should've walked out, but the sight of her—damn.

Aurora, sandwiched between them, her pregnant belly

and full breasts on display while she takes both their cocks... It's the most erotic, frustrating thing I've ever seen.

I stroke my erection, matching their rhythm. Her eyes meet mine before her gaze drops to my fist gripping my shaft. Her lips part, and her moans grow louder. Her tits bounce with each thrust, and I work my hand faster.

There's something wrong with me, something fucked up about jerking off while watching the woman of my dreams get railed by two other men. But the way she's looking at me, pleading with me to unravel... My cock pulses in my palm.

"You gonna come for us?" Ethan's deep voice fills the room. "Show Reece how much of a good girl you are."

By *good*, he means submissive, willing to surrender to our desires.

"Yes," she answers him, but her words are aimed at me. "I'm so close."

The slick sounds of their bodies moving together, their masculine grunts clashing with her feminine whimpers—it's a sensory overload in the best possible way.

I pump my length harder, twisting my wrist at the crown. Barbells along the underside graze my rough palm, and pressure builds in my balls, drawing them up against my shaft.

Jackson wraps his fingers around her throat and slams into her ass with a low growl. Her lips form a perfect O, and she cries out, her entire body quaking.

The sight of her orgasm pushes me over the edge, and my breath shudders. My head tips back, thick ropes of cum shoot from my cock, and my vision blurs. I hiss through clenched teeth, my hips bucking, my dick jerking violently with each pulse.

Chapter 31
Jackson

So I only had to talk about babies to get Reece to come around? *His* babies? We might actually have something in common, the same kink—a breeding kink? I can work with that.

While I may not love Reece the way I do Ethan, I want our family to be harmonious. I want him to be happy here.

I place kisses along the curve of Aurora's neck, my body still flying high in post-climactic bliss. "Babe, you'll never believe what Reece said."

She arches her back, hooks an arm behind her head, and threads her fingers through my hair. With her tits on full display, she glances at the Viking. "Hm?"

His gaze traces over her, lingering on her breasts and belly. There it is—that longing look.

When Aurora was pregnant and alone, I bet his hero complex was at its peak. Now that we're all in the picture, he seems to struggle. Maybe he needs the fantasy of having her—or at least a piece of her—all to himself. He had no problem sleeping in my bed while I was away, and he changed his tune earlier when I mentioned his kid.

"Don't start," Ethan grumbles, but his eyes gleam with amusement. He loves me and my ridiculousness.

I cup Aurora's breasts, leaving Reece with no choice but to watch me. "He said after this baby, we won't know who the father is, since we're all fucking." I bite her earlobe. "He's challenging me, racing to get you pregnant first." My taunting gaze meets his, a smirk playing on my lips.

His eyes narrow, but he doesn't deny my words. He moves to pull up his boxers, but not before I catch a reflection of light glinting off his dick—*several reflections*.

I can't help myself. I glance down, and—holy shit. He's pierced.

My smirk falters.

A smug grin transforms his face from annoyed to cunning, and he winks—fucking *winks*.

Of course his cock is pierced. Karma is a cruel bitch.

Aurora drops beside Ethan, releasing me from her warmth. I collapse onto him, drawing the sheet over us and letting my arms flop.

The air whooshes from his lungs. "What the hell is your problem?" he grunts.

I suck in a breath and exhale forcefully. "The Viking's dick is pierced. I can't unsee it. I may never get hard again."

Behind me, Reece snorts. "Somehow, I highly doubt that."

Aurora shakes her head. "Jackson…" she chides, but it's written all over her face—pure carnal satisfaction.

My stomach twinges. He fucked her with his pierced Viking cock, and she loved it.

I take back everything I said about us living harmoniously. I hope those piercings become infected and he ends up impotent.

Okay, maybe not. I'm being dramatic.

A little erectile dysfunction wouldn't hurt though.

Ethan fists my hair. "Why are you checking out his dick?"

"You can't miss it!" Partly feigned sobs rack my body. "Is he bigger than Coach?" I whisper-yell at Aurora.

Ethan whips his head in her direction, and we both stare, waiting for a response.

She clamps her mouth shut, and the silence stretches on. "What?" she snaps, raising her brows. "I'm not answering."

My lips twist into a disgruntled frown. "Seriously? We're supposed to be best friends. I tell you everything about Ethan."

She rolls her eyes. "I know everything about Ethan. Besides, you have that Captain Hook curve that hits all the right spots. You've got nothing to be jealous of."

Male pride swells in my chest, and I can't help but smile.

Still... "That doesn't answer my question." I widen my eyes and gasp. "So it must be true."

"Shut up," she grits through her teeth and slaps my bicep. "It's not true. They're...' she lowers her tone, "different. Now, be good. There'll be no more freaky-foursome sex if you can't control yourself." She tilts her head and cocks a brow, as if to say, *'You want that, don't you? You want to watch everyone fuck?"*

Yes. Yes, I do. I might get another erection after all.

Plus, there are cameras in this room, which Reece is aware of. I can analyze everything later.

My smile stretches into a salacious grin. She gets me. "I'll be good."

She clears her throat. "Unless it's twins," she says for all to hear. "Ethan has twins in his family."

"Jesus," he curses. "I'll wear a condom. I was only kidding about having twins."

He claims that, but he also likes the idea of her being pregnant with his baby.

I lift my head, cross my arms over his chest, and rest my

chin on them. "I think a bunch of little Ethans would be absolutely adorable."

His face flushes. "Fuck no. One is enough." He pushes me off him softly, since Aurora is beside us. "You're sweaty. Go shower. I need to call Rocco."

"You'd be sweaty too if you weren't the pillow princess."

He grabs me by the throat and brings me in for a rough kiss. "I'm going to fuck you into next week if you don't shut your mouth."

"Stop talking dirty to me." Damn, I love instigating him.

Reece stands, goes to the other side of the bed, and extends his hand to our girl. "And you need to use the bathroom. Come on. I'll start you a bath."

Ethan leans against the door frame, his phone pressed to his lips, head bowed.

Sitting on the bed, Aurora on the floor in front of me, I take the rubber band from my mouth and tie off her braid. "What's the verdict?"

He spent an hour on the balcony talking to Rocco and Big D. The rest of us have showered and changed into whatever clothes we have.

"The Skid Row building caught fire. They've taken off for New York."

Our eyes meet briefly before Reece asks, "Lucas?"

The Viking has been reclining in that leather chair, pretending to be distracted by his phone while sneaking peeks at Aurora and me. Maybe he wants to learn to braid, or maybe he doesn't know what to do with himself.

Ethan blows out a breath. "With them. Rocco says not to

worry; the doctor and Bennett approved a transfer to New York, and they're taking a med-flight."

Jaw clenched and nostrils flaring, Reece returns to his phone—no doubt trying to contact his partner. He's quite stubborn. Loyal to a fault, and I swear, he holds a grudge for life. The twins will be next on his shit list. Finally, someone other than me.

I gently loosen Aurora's braid to create a relaxed style. "What's the plan?" I ask Ethan.

"We need to head out as soon as possible. I'd rather not be trapped at the airport." He holds my gaze.

He's worried about the LAPD grilling us or possibly detaining me. I'm surprised they haven't already—unless they're watching the penthouse and know we've been here the entire night.

Or they're waiting to ambush us.

He rakes his fingers through his messy hair. "Can you arrange a flight?"

"Where to?" I turn to the Viking. "We going to your sister's? Flying into Charleston?"

"Yeah," he replies, focused on his screen. "We'll leave for New York right after the wedding."

The wedding is the day after tomorrow.

"You have your ID, birth certificate, and passport?" I ask Aurora.

Clutching my knees for balance, she gradually rises from the floor. "Yes, but I don't have a dress or makeup or anything. The only clothes I fit into are leggings, loose sweaters, and your hoodies."

"We can get whatever you need." Ethan cuffs the back of my neck with icy fingers. "Secure a private jet, please." He's anxious.

I remove my phone from my pocket. "I got you. It won't take me long." A few clicks—that's all.

Reece grabs his backpack from the closet, drops it in front of the bed, and takes a seat beside me. "Angel, can you get this off me?" He gestures to his shoulder.

"I like this brace much more than the sling." She comes between his legs and guides a strap over his head. "Are you gearing up?"

His new bionic-looking brace attaches at multiple points along his arm, with metal, hard plastic, and an adjustable hinge at the elbow. He's finally accepting that this injury will take time and effort to heal.

"Yeah, just in case I need to appear official."

While Ethan and I watch, completely amazed, she pulls his bag toward her, takes out his bulletproof vest, and helps him into it. "Your badge?"

He nods, and she threads it through his belt while he attempts to buckle his vest.

"Here. Let me." I extend my hands, then, unsure what to do, I pause.

"Slide the four pieces together. It'll lock into place." He observes as I follow his direction. "We should get you one, actually. Have you ever shot a gun?"

"A few times in my backyard. Not something I'm interested in. Not something I want to worry about around Aurora and kids, you know?"

"Understood." He twists his torso so I can attach the other side. "Someone did try to shoot you though."

Ethan clears his throat. "We can talk about it later. That shit won't be necessary in the future."

No matter what he has planned—even if it's moving Aurora to New York, which will kill me—security will always be a factor. But I'm not the smartest choice for a gun. I have no training. I become paranoid and overwhelmed at times, and misusing or misplacing a deadly weapon is not something I ever wish to experience. I'll leave that level of responsibility and focus to Reece.

Our girl straightens, stretches her back, and hands him his dog tags. "You want me to get your boots?"

He slips the dog tags over his head and tucks them under his shirt. "Please. They're by the door."

While he holsters his firearm, she rushes out of the room, a soft smile on her face.

"She needs to rest," Ethan grumbles, his gaze following her. "Fuck, I can't wait for this to be over."

"She likes to help. It eases her anxiety." Reece rifles through his backpack. "I've got her passport and birth certificate. I'll grab her ID and prenatal vitamins. I've taken pictures of her..." He waves with a flick of his wrist toward the bathroom, "products. I'll see what my sisters can find."

My brows knit together. "Why do you have pictures of her stuff?"

He meets my scowl head-on. "For times like this, when we have to run. Don't you have a bug-out bag?"

"Yeah, it contains cash, keys, and cards, not her skincare routine."

He smirks. "I like to make sure she's well taken care of."

"Is that another joke? Holy shit. I'm proud of you. Keep it up, and I'll think you're flirting with me." I knock my shoulder into his.

Ethan scoffs, Reece's expression falls, and I burst out laughing. He's so serious. Has he *ever* been in a situation that wasn't fucking stressful, where he could joke and fool around? I'm almost afraid to meet his parents.

Chapter 32
Ethan

I'm about to throw up. I trust no one in this city. I don't know what I'll do if the LAPD tries to arrest Jackson or take him in. I'd never let it happen. I'd lose my mind—and my temper.

"Let's go over this." Reece tosses his backpack down in front of the entryway. "The only information they wanted from Lucas was what you told investigators," he says to Jax. "If the LAPD stops us, you're the one they'll be after."

"Yeah, no shit," Jackson quips and drops his own bag to the floor.

"I'll step in," Reece continues, "and claim jurisdiction." He turns to Aurora. "That's when I want you to call Bennett. Remain behind me until I have to intervene. Then, you go with Ethan. If you can't get in touch with Bennett, call Lucas."

Dimitri offered to stay in case Jax needed a lawyer, but I declined. He should be with his boys. The twins cause enough trouble.

"Got it." She nods. "Only one thing: I already texted Bennett. She'll meet us downstairs shortly." Becoming occupied with her phone, she asks Jax, "Are we taking an Uber or one of your cars?"

A scowl forms on my face. "Baby girl, what are you doing?"

We've come to an agreement with Reece's commander. Still, I'd rather Aurora wasn't involved.

"I'm ordering Bennett a coffee from the cart in the lobby. With this clusterfuck of a morning, she hasn't had a single cup." She peers up at Reece. "Do you know how she likes it?" Her lip twitches.

My little brat is up to something. She can't hide her emotions. It's one thing I love about her.

"Probably as black as her soul," he replies. "Why are you communicating with Bennett?"

She drops her phone into her purse. "Remember when she escorted me to the hospital?"

We all stare at her blankly.

"Well, she's newly married and having trouble with her wife, Kelsey. Bennett has been in LA, and things have been rocky between them." Aurora talks with her hands, a mischievous glint in her eyes. "She's miserable, just wants to end this case and see Kelsey, who lives in Arkansas. So, I found her on Facebook and..." She grimaces, bracing for our reaction. "Yesterday evening, I flew her wife in, *secretly*. I put her up in the Laguna Beach penthouse—"

"Babe!" Jax cuts her off, his brows nearly hitting his hairline. "No—"

"Quiet." She raises a hand. "It gets better." Her smile grows wicked. "You know the concierge, Sam, who adores me? I texted him and told him to make sure they get the royal treatment. Anything Kelsey wants, Kelsey gets. Couples' massages? Done. Spa visits? Done. Lobster and steak? Midnight strawberries and whipped cream? You got it. I paid him a bonus to ensure he was at their beck and call. Whatever you gave him in the past, I matched it."

She grins, proud of herself, and I bite my lip to stifle a chuckle.

Reece stares in shock while Jax drags his hands down his face.

"Aurora," he groans. "You can get into trouble for that. How did you pay for it?"

As if I'd ever let her get into trouble. She's cute when she's devious.

"With my grandma's credit card." She shrugs, palms up. "I was careful."

He tilts his head and narrows his eyes. "Your grandmother has a credit card with that kind of limit? Sam's bonus was not small."

Her sharp gaze meets mine. "*Someone* gave her a black card."

I'm pretty sure that card is listed under Rossi Investments. Rocco handles the nursing home's finances. I only approve or deny—and I would never deny Aurora's grandmother anything.

"And you two arranged this?" Jax asks, skeptical. "You and Gram?"

"I did. The in-suite couple's massage was her idea though."

"Babe!" he repeats, his tone higher-pitched. "You can't bribe a federal agent."

"We're friends," she dismisses him with a wave, "and this job is shitty. Besides, I'm not bribing her with the penthouse. I'm bribing her with your old iPhone."

He whips around to glare at Reece. "What?"

"Don't look at me. I'm confused as fuck right now."

"Please." She shakes her head. "It wasn't hard to figure out. Why would Reece have your phone and Lucas know about the videos? Why would you lock it in the safe in the security room?"

He throws his arms in the air. "Because it contains videos of you."

"Yup, and other people, and I'm turning it in. What's the worst that can happen? I have leaked sex tapes with my hot husband?"

"There are videos of *all* of us." He points to Reece. "The Viking's supervisor will see his *pierced* dick." He stresses the word 'pierced' as if it's a personal insult.

"Shocker—she already has," Aurora retorts with a tight smile. "After a night of dollar margaritas at the bowling alley." She singsongs the words, all sassy.

I can only gawk in disbelief. Dollar margaritas at the bowling alley? Reece bowling? I can't picture it.

Jax gasps and widens his eyes dramatically. "Holy hell, dude. You slept with Bennett? I did not see that coming. She's… Is she into Dominatrix shit?" He scrunches his nose and draws air through his clenched teeth. "Is that your thing?"

"What?" Reece recoils in horror, his mouth hanging open. "Fuck no."

"Fuck no to which part?" Aurora asks. "You being into Dominatrix, or…"

"Wait!" Jax throws his head back in laughter. "This is the best day of my life." He inhales sharply, trying to rein himself in. "You don't remember? Were you blackout drunk wearing bowling shoes?" He clutches his stomach and doubles over. "Please tell me you were wearing matching bowling shoes while you fucked."

Reece's face turns a deep shade of red. "Shut the fuck up before I toss your ass over the balcony." His hesitant gaze finds Aurora. "I did not sleep with Bennett…or anyone else I work with."

Aurora crosses her arms over her chest and cocks a brow. "Are you sure? You *were* drunk."

She's faking. If she actually thought he'd slept with a co-worker, she'd be pouting or shooting daggers at him. Instead, there's an amused gleam in her eyes. She's busting his balls—Jackson too.

Welcome to the family, Reece.

"Not that drunk. I remember going home."

"With someone?"

"No." His chest heaves. "Did Bennett say I did?"

Her lips curl into a naughty smirk. "She said she saw you taking a piss in the alleyway with your pants around your ankles—her exact words. She said your dick scarred her for life."

"Jesus Christ." He blows out a breath. "I'm going to spank your ass so fucking hard." He lunges for her. "Give me your phone. You're not allowed to talk to my co-workers anymore."

Jax and I exchange a sidelong glance. Piercings and spankings? Reece might be kinkier than we thought.

Aurora squeals and turns away. "You can have it after Bennett and I discuss where to take her wife shopping while she fucks over the patriarchy."

Chapter 33
Ethan

"How can you be friends with her?" Jax glowers at Aurora from his plush leather seat on the private jet. "She called you a doormat—*death's* doormat."

"I'm pretty sure that was aimed at me." Facing them, I stretch out my legs and get comfortable for the five-hour flight ahead. "Bennett was saying I'm death and Aurora is my doormat. She was pissed I wouldn't let Aurora out of my grip. She thinks I control you both...and maybe the Rossi family too."

Leaving the condo and boarding the plane was uneventful. Bennett and two other agents escorted us. I could tell Reece's commander was itching to get Aurora alone, which wasn't going to happen. Even when our girl turned over evidence, I kept her and Jax close, my hand clasping Aurora's nape the entire time.

Bennett glared at me as if I were the enemy. I don't blame her, nor do I care. I did end Jax's interrogation, and I am a *tad* controlling when it comes to what's mine—none of which is about to change.

Am I annoyed with Aurora for going behind my back and

setting up something with Bennett? A little. Am I surprised? No. She'll always protect Jackson. Will I allow her to continue working with Homeland Security? Absolutely not. I'm about to lock her in the loft in New York.

Our girl casts a glance at Reece, who's next to me, before turning to Jax. "I'm not her friend." She holds his heated stare. "But I'll play along if I have to. You think I don't know that vacant look? The one you had at the hospital?" Her voice breaks, and she swallows hard. "I haven't seen those lifeless eyes in a long time, and if I need to act ditzy and bubbly to keep Bennett focused on me and not you—fine. I've got a lot planned."

His gaze softens, but his jaw remains tight. "I don't want you involved in this. I never have."

"But I am." Imploring him to understand, she steeples her fingers at her chest. "From the moment we met, I've been a part of this, possibly even before then." She shrugs. "Who knows? Without you, I might have followed in Emily's footsteps."

He shakes his head and furrows his brow. "You wouldn't have. That's not you."

"It doesn't matter." She waves him off. "Think about it, Jax. Emily was associated with your father and Hugo. She dated one of your best friends, who she lost interest in once we moved in together. You knew nothing about her, but she knew everything about you. You hated her, but she still hung out with you and the guys after we broke up. Why? I thought she wanted to be a wealthy hockey wife. How stupid am I?"

"Aurora," I growl. "Watch your mouth."

Of course, she ignores me. "I was pretty fucking dense. Who was at the Laguna Beach penthouse the day before Kyle showed up?" she asks Jax. "How did he find out I was pregnant and staying with you? I didn't trust Emily enough to tell her about Ethan. Kyle found out about him by following me to New York, where Emily was supposed to be. She knew the address. Kyle assumed the baby was yours, which is what we let Emily believe. Throughout our entire relationship, your dad has always known what we were up to."

"And that's how Kyle discovered the loft, took pictures of us, and shared them with Hugo," Reece adds. "God-fucking-dammit, I hate her."

Jax drops his head into his hands and pulls at his hair.

My stomach plummets. "We're lucky Emily didn't harm Aurora or the baby to appease him."

Jackson snaps upright, his face pale and eyes wide. "Are we sure she didn't?" His breathing grows rapid and shallow. "Aurora was sick in New York, and we never figured out how Kyle drugged me."

Rage floods my veins, and my heartbeat pounds in my ears, drowning out Aurora's response. I turn to Reece for answers.

Thinking, he peers up and to the side. "I ordered all her food, made all her meals. She was only out of my sight once —at Emily's. Still, it's highly unlikely. I would've become suspicious if Aurora were suddenly sick."

Thank fuck he was there, takes his job seriously, and caters to her every whim.

It doesn't ease the fury in my chest though.

"I was throwing up from the beginning of my pregnancy." Her words shake, and her lip trembles. "The baby is fine—he has to be—and each ultrasound has been perfect."

Jax wraps her in his arms. "He's perfect, babe. I promise. I'm paranoid, that's all. I'm sorry."

He comforts her while I ponder homicide. What constitutes a murderable offense? Where do you draw the line? Assisting a predator in harming what's mine? Definitely crosses the line, right?

I flip my phone over in my hand and contemplate texting

Rocco or Dante. Maybe I'm not so different from my father after all. I just needed love to understand hate.

"Lucas will find her," Reece says quietly. "We should watch her anyhow."

"Thank you."

"Anything else?"

"No, Dimitri is getting me the name of the obstetrician his daughter uses. The loft is almost finished—furniture came last week. I'll let Aurora pick the nursery..." I inhale deeply then exhale slowly. I still have to tell her she's staying in New York. "And we'll get it put together before the baby is born."

Aurora lifts her head and wipes away her tears. "Well, I guess that ends my idea of personally connecting Bennett with Emily."

A collective "Absolutely fucking not" echoes in the plane's cabin.

My tone drops an octave. "We need to have a serious conversation, baby girl."

Those whiskey-brown eyes flash with defiance. "What's the point of having a conversation? You're sending me to New York no matter what."

"Your safety," I retort, not denying her accusation. "Bennett is a wild card we can't control, and Emily is a snake. As much as I'm trying to be patient and appreciate all you're doing, I'd rather you didn't."

Her eyes narrow, her hand cradling her swollen belly. "I'm not a child."

"No, you're not." I lean forward, elbows on my knees. "You're the mother of *my* child and the heart of this family. There's no *us* without you. Your safety is nonnegotiable. Befriending Bennett is one thing; making plans to meet up with Emily is completely different." I rub my tired eyes with the heels of my palms. "This isn't a game, Aurora.

These people have proven they'll do whatever it takes to harm us."

"You think I don't know that?" She cocks her head, her voice rising. "Again, I'm involved in this. They were after *me* too."

"That's precisely why you're going to New York," I cut in, my tone brooking no room for argument. "The loft is secure, and you'll have round-the-clock protection. The twins and Lucas plan to stay in the apartment below ours. *No one* will mess with our family in New York."

Her eyes, brimming with tears, hold mine, and the weight of her unspoken anguish crushes me—and pisses me the fuck off. She should be happy, dancing around the house, dressing up, buying tiny baby clothes, baking damn cupcakes if she wants…not holding back her emotions for our sake and making deals to protect us. Jesus, that's my fucking job.

Except I haven't been home, and Jackson is going through hell. Reece is injured, and then there's Lucas. She's carrying it all on her shoulders.

I undo my seat belt. "Come here."

She doesn't.

"Now," I rumble low.

She huffs, unbuckling with deliberate slowness, and Jax snickers. When she stands, I drag her onto my lap and wrap her in my arms.

She tries to maintain her stubborn stiffness, but after a moment, she softens and lays her head on my shoulder. "I'm getting too big to sit on your lap."

"Never." When she says nothing more, I continue, "I'm not trying to punish you by sending you to New York. I'm fucking terrified."

"Then you know how I feel."

"Won't being in New York be less stressful? You can set up your studio and start designing."

"For how long?" She sucks in a shuddering breath. "I hate being useless."

"You're growing our son. That's far from useless."

She shakes her head. "That's not what I mean."

"I understand what you mean. You wanna help. I get it." I press my lips to her forehead. "But if you're not happy and safe, everything we do is pointless. Our world crumbles."

Her fingers fidget with the hem of my shirt. "Don't say things like that. It makes it impossible to be irritated with you."

"Good." I caress her stomach, hoping to feel the baby move.

"I hate this," she sighs. "I hate being separated. I want *our* house. I want my grandma close by."

"I know." I twist her braid around my fist and try to find the words to soothe her.

There's nothing I can promise, nothing I can say with certainty. We will be separated—not always, but at times, when Jax and I travel—and I can't replicate the beach house.

Jackson clears his throat. "Properties are investments, babe. I can sell ours and design another. I don't mind. I actually enjoy it."

He's talking as if he realizes this isn't temporary, and I meet his gaze over Aurora's head. His eyes are shadowed with worry, his brows furrowed, but there's trust there too. Trust in me to figure this out.

The connection between us—between all of us—tightens something in my chest and fuels my need to protect this bond we've built.

"And Gram can come to New York," Reece offers. "We'll find her the best assisted-living facility, or I'll help with her. There's in-home care. We have plenty of options."

"Talk to Gram." I clasp Aurora's chin and raise her mouth to mine for a gentle kiss. "Let me know, and I'll arrange it—

although I'm not sure I can handle the trouble you two will get into."

"You'd do that for me? Move my grandmother all the way to New York?"

"I'd do anything for you."

"What about the baby? Doctor appointments. The delivery?"

"I've got it covered."

Her eyes narrow to slits. "You've been planning this."

"I spent a long time talking with Rocco and Dimitri."

Jax leans forward, his sandy-blond hair falling across his forehead. "We'll be in New York between games, even if it's just for a day. We'll make every appointment, without question. I'm not missing a single ultrasound."

She turns her head to peer at Reece. "You'll be with me?"

"Where you go, I go. Remember?" He tucks an unruly wave behind her ear. "But you better stop keeping shit from me. We don't lie to each other."

"We don't lie to each other?" Her brows raise. "You lied to me about your birthday."

"Fuck," he curses, his lip curled. "Did my sister tell you?"

"Sadie did, yes. You didn't think they were planning to celebrate your *thirtieth* birthday?"

He throws his head back into the headrest and groans, "This is a nightmare."

"Thirty?" Jackson smirks. "Damn. Now we know why you wear cargo pants, Grandpa."

"They're tactical pants," Reece shoots back. "And I'm pretty sure the cutoff age for skinny jeans is twenty. It's time to retire the nut-huggers."

Jax kicks his leg out. "These aren't skinny jeans! They're a normal fit."

The corner of Reece's mouth twitches. "Normal for middle schoolers."

I stifle a chuckle. "Speaking of your family, what are we doing? Are we pretending Jackson is with Aurora?"

"Oh." Our little devil scrunches her nose. "I kind of took care of that too."

Reece's expression falls. "What did you do?"

"I made a tiny…" She stretches out the word, pinching two fingers together. "…donation to their church to improve the daycare. I saw it on their website."

"They don't have a daycare, Aurora. They have an empty room."

"Well, they do now," she singsongs. "I told Sadie it was a surprise and not to tell you. So, surprise," she finishes with jazz hands.

"I left you alone for one fucking day—not even a full twenty-four hours—and you managed to bribe a federal agent *and* my parents?"

"I know, right? I got a lot done."

She grins brightly, once again proud of herself, and a snort escapes me.

"Aurora," Reece scolds.

"What?" she snaps playfully. "I used my own money, and, per Sadie, your mom is thrilled to furnish the daycare. She's also been showing off pictures of us and is *over the moon* about you coming home."

"You sent pictures to my mother."

"No, I sent pictures to your sister, which you approved of."

Jackson shakes his head. "I've never been happier not to have siblings."

Same.

She adjusts herself on my lap to face him. "Maryanne, Reece's mother, loves cooking and baking—that's your in." At his blank stare, she adds, "You can be charming when you want to be. I know you can. This is important."

I tug her braid. "What about me?"

"His dad is a pastor." She shrugs. "Probably not gonna have a lot in common."

Definitely not.

"Holy shit, dude." Jackson's brows shoot up. "Your dad is a pastor? That explains *everything*."

Chapter 34
Reece

Aurora pauses on the sidewalk, a few feet from Sadie's downtown Charleston rental, a frown creasing her brow. "All jokes aside, your sister is fantastic. I already love her. But if you're uncomfortable, we leave. No questions asked."

It's late Thursday, less than a week before Christmas. The air is crisp, the historical streets are decked out for the holidays, horse-drawn carriages clop along, and the pastel houses twinkle with lights. All this charm to appreciate, and she's staring at *me*, worried about *me*.

"I'm fine, princess. We're only seeing my sister tonight." I hoist my bag higher on my uninjured shoulder while Ethan and Jax grab theirs from the trunk of the Uber. "Being here with you makes this easier."

It's true, even though I thought it'd be the opposite. I feared my family would offend her, reject her and our relationship, and ruin my sister's wedding when I stormed out of here. I dreaded Aurora's reaction to my parents' conservative views, but she seems to have embraced them, at least for now.

Jessica Lyn

She hasn't met them yet. They haven't met her. My mom can be intrusive and loves to give backhanded compliments. My dad is judgmental and self-righteous, all in the name of his religion. I still may end up pissed off and storming out.

"I know how much Sadie's wedding means to you." Aurora's eyes search mine. "And she wants you to be here above all else."

Between my two sisters, I've always felt closest to Sadie. She's the youngest—nearly five years younger than me—so it's only natural I look after her.

Jax joins us, tilting his head back to admire the pink three-story townhouse with its ornate white trim and wrought-iron balconies. "I've never been to Charleston. It's beautiful. If anything, we'll have a fun babymoon." He shrugs.

Ethan steps up beside him. "No matter what, we leave here together. We have Christmas together. We go on with our life *together*."

I twist the diamond in my ear and release a heavy exhale. Never did I imagine these three with me—*supporting me*—during my first return home in years. "My parents will be at the rehearsal dinner tomorrow," I warn as I guide them toward Sadie's porch. "They'll have opinions about everything. Just ignore them."

The door swings open, and I hear my sister's shriek before seeing her.

Bright-eyed and beaming, she launches herself at Aurora, wrapping her arms around her neck. "You're here!"

"Oh." Aurora stumbles backward, cheeks flushed.

I steady her with a hand on her lower back. "Careful, Sades. If you hurt her, Ethan will never let her come again," I joke—partly.

"Sorry." She pulls away to examine Aurora's baby bump. "I'm so excited to meet you! My brother tells me absolutely nothing. I was shocked when you called. I still can't believe you're dating."

"It's fine." Aurora gives her a warm smile. "I'm glad to be here."

Sadie turns her attention to Ethan and Jackson. "And these must be your other...partners?" she asks me, not Aurora, a genuine question in her tone, her brows raised.

Is that what they're called? My first instinct is to reply, "Fuck no." But we're something more than friends, aren't we? Maybe?

"We're a family," Jax explains. "He's Aurora's *other* boyfriend. I'm her husband."

He says it with attitude, and she laughs.

"Don't listen to him." I shake my head but can't hide my grin. "Sadie, this is Jackson." I gesture to him. "And this is Ethan. They are..." I pause, looking at Ethan, who gives me a subtle nod. "They're partners."

My sister gently embraces me, careful not to touch my arm. "Well, any rare friends of my brother's are friends of mine." She glances up at me, her eyes glistening. "Harper is here with Danny, but y'all can have the upstairs guest suite."

I tighten an arm around her. "We can stay at a hotel if you'd like."

"Nonsense. I miss you, and you're in desperate need of a haircut."

My cheeks hurt from smiling. "You wanna give me one? I wanna get a tattoo."

Her fiancé is a renowned tattoo artist who has done a few of my pieces, and I have another planned.

"I guess I have to, don't I?" She slaps my bicep before breaking away and leading us into the foyer.

The interior is as charming as the exterior—exposed brick walls, plank hardwood floors, rustic wooden beams, well-loved furniture, and a Christmas tree glowing in front of the window.

Harper, my older sister, stands in the living room archway with my nephew on her hip. "Look who finally showed up," she says with a mix of teasing and scorn. "Your Uncle Reece."

Her demeanor is similar to my own, whereas Sadie is the bubbly one.

Danny, now four, peers at me with big, blue eyes—eyes that match mine and my sister's. He buries his face in her neck, suddenly shy, and my chest tightens. The last time I saw him, he was learning to walk.

"Hey, Harp." I step forward, unsure if I should hug her. She hasn't been my biggest fan, and she hasn't had an easy life as a military wife either.

She decides for me and pulls me into a one-armed embrace. "It's nice to see you smiling. I almost didn't recognize you." Her gaze shifts to Aurora. "And this must be the model I've heard so much about."

Her tone is neutral, but I don't miss the assessment in her eyes as she scans our girl from head to toe.

Determined to win over my family, Aurora smiles and extends her hand. "Aurora. It's lovely to meet you."

Harper moves Danny to her other hip and takes Aurora's hand. "It's nice to meet the woman who finally got my brother to come home." Her focus drifts to Aurora's stomach. "And with a baby on the way."

"Harper," I interject. "Enough."

Aurora laughs nervously. "It's complicated."

Harper's attention slides to Ethan and Jackson, who stand close behind Aurora. "And you two are…?"

"The complicated part." Ethan steps forward to shake her hand. "Ethan."

Jax follows with his usual smirk. "Jackson, the husband, the fun one, the good-looking one..."

"Obviously," Harper says dryly.

"Dad is going to have a fucking aneurysm," Harper mutters. "I hope you warned them. He still believes any day now, you'll have some epiphany, retire, and come home. Follow in his footsteps."

She sits on the rug in front of the Christmas tree, Danny between her legs while he colors on a sketch pad. As his assistant, holding the box of markers, I sit beside them.

Aurora rummages through Sadie's closet for a dress to wear to the wedding, Jax wanders around, examining the architecture, and Ethan reclines on the couch, working on his phone.

"That'll never happen. Why do you think I'm staying with Sadie?"

My parents' carefully constructed world of church potlucks and prayer circles doesn't include their only son being in a polyamorous relationship. It also didn't include Sadie attending college and marrying a tattoo artist. Harper was the only one who followed the traditional script, and she's not exactly happy.

"Is that why you're here?" I ask gently. "To avoid Mom and Dad?"

When we went upstairs to unload our bags, it was clear Harper and Danny were living in one of the bedrooms— boxes stacked in the corner, clothes draped over a chair, dinosaur toys scattered across the floor, a twin bed against the wall with a portable crib wedged between it and the dresser.

She avoids meeting my eyes. "It's only temporary. We needed somewhere to stay, and Sadie offered to watch Danny while I worked at her salon."

Upon hearing his name, my nephew lifts his picture for her to admire.

She brushes his pale blond hair back from his forehead and kisses his crown. "Good job, buddy."

I hand Danny a blue marker when he points to it. He's awfully quiet for a four-year-old. "You've been here a while, Harp. He's too big for that crib. You should've called me."

Her gaze snaps to mine. "And say what?" Her voice is sharp, bitterness lacing her tone. "Hey, brother who dropped off the face of the Earth, can you save me from my failed marriage?" She shakes her head. "You helped Sadie; she helped me. End of story."

Guilt hits me hard, twisting in my gut, and I force myself to breathe through it. I can't turn back time.

I *helped* Sadie by paying her college expenses—because my parents refused. They disapproved of her getting a business degree, or any degree at all. She earned the scholarships and worked her way to owning and managing a successful day spa. All I did was ensure she had food, books, and a roof over her head. Harper was already married.

"I'm sorry I wasn't there. I couldn't sit in church and listen to Dad talk about God's plan after Afghanistan, you know?" And I couldn't bear to let my sisters see me broken.

Her expression softens. "You had your own shit to deal with. I get it, and Dad has only gotten worse."

How much worse can he get? He's pretty much set in his ways.

"I'm here now." I bump my shoulder into hers. "Things have changed."

"I noticed." She gives me a sidelong glance. "What's up with that?"

"Exactly what it looks like. We're a family."

"The oddest family I've ever seen."

"It works." I run my hand through my overgrown hair. "I love her, Harp. I can't picture myself with anyone else."

She studies me for a long moment. "And the other two?"

"They're part of the package. It's new, but we all support each other."

"You're okay with that?" She arches a brow in disbelief. "Y'all sleep together? In the same bed?"

"Ah…" I waver, uncomfortable with the direction of this conversation. We *are* sharing a room with only one bed. "Not usually. I still don't sleep well, and the guys are away half the year."

"And you're with her?"

"Yes."

"Is the baby yours then?"

"No, and it doesn't matter," I reply with conviction, believing it myself. "Enough with the interrogation. Jesus, should I grill you about your husband? You're sounding like Mom."

Her eyes narrow to slits. "That's rude. Really fucking rude."

"Language," Sadie hisses, suddenly in front of us. "Don't start, you two. Tonight is drama-free. Tomorrow will be a shitshow." She claps her hands and beams at Aurora, who stands beside her with a wary expression. "We're going out—for a girls' night."

"What?" I ask, dumbfounded. Ain't no fucking way Aurora is going out for a girls' night. Not to be controlling, but it's not safe.

"We're going shopping. You too, Harp. Come on, you could use a break."

Harper scoffs. "Danny is heading to bed soon."

"We'll wait, and Reece can watch him." Sadie flashes a self-satisfied grin in my direction.

I push myself up from the floor. "Just the three of you?"

She nods. "Your girlfriend needs a dress and shoes. She's taller than I am."

"She's being nice. My belly is too big," Aurora adds, her hand on her swollen stomach.

"Not happening." Ethan sets his phone down, his stormy gaze fixed on our girl. "You're not going out alone."

Sadie's brows furrow. "But Macy's is only a few blocks away, and I know the formal staff personally."

"It's not up for discussion. One of us goes with you," he tells Aurora. "Take Jax; he enjoys shopping."

"What if I want you to come with me?" She crosses her arms over her chest, cocks her head, and purses her lips.

Jackson snorts from across the room. "Pick me up some sneakers so I can do some jogging. I forgot mine."

Ethan releases a heavy sigh, stands, and slides his phone into his pocket. "Fine. Let's go."

And that's how Jax and I end up alone with a toddler.

Chapter 35
Jackson

Danny refuses to stay in his crib. Every time Reece puts him back, he lets out an ear-piercing scream, and my insides crawl.

I cover my ears to block out the shrill noise. "Why won't he stay in bed? Why is he screaming?"

"Because he doesn't fit in this bed and he wants his mother."

Red-faced, his cheeks wet with tears, his leg stretched over the side of the portable crib, Danny peers up at Reece. "Mama," he cries.

My stomach churns with nausea, and my heart races. "You need to call her. She needs to come back."

Reece gives me a blank look as he lifts Danny with one arm and cradles him against his chest. "I'm not calling Harper." He bounces him gently. "Every kid misses their mother. He'll be fine."

The crying subsides into shuddering sobs of "Mama," and he reaches for the door. It's the saddest thing I've ever seen; my eyes actually water.

If our baby is like this, I'll never leave. I can't imagine

abandoning a screaming child, or abandoning a child period. Where is his father? I'd go crazy without my son.

I cast a doubtful glance between Reece and his mini-me dressed in dinosaur pajamas. "He doesn't seem fine. He seems traumatized."

"He's overtired," Reece snaps, his frustration palpable. "You wanna try?"

In response to his agitation, Danny wails and flops sideways. The Viking grimaces in pain and nearly loses his grip on him.

I lunge forward. "Give him to me before you drop him."

Big blue eyes stare at me suspiciously, but the boy doesn't fight when I take him from his uncle. The weight of him surprises me—solid and lanky yet so damn small. His tiny hands grab fistfuls of my shirt, and he continues to sob. I've never held a child that I remember, and the feeling is unfamiliar—strange, terrifying, but freaking incredible. I can't wait to have one of our own.

"Hey, buddy." I rub his back. "It's okay. Your mom will be home soon."

He hiccups and presses his face to my neck, his tears dampening my skin.

I pace the small bedroom, mimicking the way Reece bounced him. "So...you like dinosaurs, huh?" I spot a well-loved, fuzzy orange T-Rex in the crib and reach for it.

Reece sinks onto the edge of the bed and massages his injured shoulder. "You're a lot better at this."

I scoff at how disgruntled he sounds. "I'm not. He senses your agitation, that's all." I hand Danny the stuffed animal, and he snuggles it to him. "You don't like children, do you?"

"I do—well, I used to." He rakes his fingers through his hair and releases a heavy sigh. "I hate listening to them cry. Makes me wanna kill something."

I recall Lucas mentioning they worked in an orphanage

while deployed. Hearing other kids cry or seeing them hurt is a whole lot worse than hearing my own crying in my head, I suppose. "I understand. It'll get easier. He doesn't know us. Our baby will know you. He's learning our voices even now, and he'll recognize yours, the same as he does ours."

Seemingly impressed, he nods and presses his lips together. "You've thought about this."

Danny's weight grows heavier, and his breathing slows.

"Of course I have. Ethan and I will have to FaceTime while on the road, even when Eli's a baby, so he hears our voices often. Our kid is going to have four parents who adore him, not to mention Gram and the twins—your sisters," I add. "He'll never be alone or feel abandoned."

"You're not what I expected." He twirls the diamond in his ear. "I was certain you'd be a nightmare and guard this baby like a pit bull."

I sway side to side, rocking Danny. He clutches my shirt, and his soft hair tickles my chin.

"I mean, I might, but not with you." I stifle a yawn, exhausted from traveling and everything else. "I want our life to be peaceful. I don't want our kids going through the shit I went through." Parents arguing nonstop, tension in the home, walking on eggshells… That's not a family, at least not the one I dream of having.

Studying me, Reece tilts his head and narrows his eyes. "What did Ethan do to you? Did he finally snap and choke you out? First, you let me in your bedroom, and now, you're sharing your kid?"

I suppress my laughter, not wanting to wake the sleeping child in my arms. "I saw your dick. You brought me home to meet your family. We're basically dating—engaged."

He flips me off, but there's no heat behind it. "You're ridiculous. Don't fucking start."

I shake my head and dismiss the joke. "Should I lay him in his crib?"

"No. I bet he sleeps with Harper," Reece whispers, not saying her name too loud, and stands. "Let's sit with him downstairs until she gets home. She shouldn't be much longer."

Chapter 36
Aurora

Ethan's large hand slides over my swollen belly from behind. "Fuck, look at you."

His beard brushes my ear and sends shivers down my spine.

I catch his heated gaze in the dressing room mirror. "You're supposed to be getting the zipper, Blackwood."

Sadie wandered off to look for shoes, leaving me with several options to try on, while Harper never made it past the kids' area. It's just me and Ethan—and a handful of others in the upscale formal section.

He slips beneath the neckline and cups my breast. "I like it better down."

"Ethan…"

His thumb brushes over my hardened nipple, and my protest dies. Why is everything so sensitive, every touch heightened? Oh yeah, I'm pregnant.

"You have no idea what you do to me." He pinches my nipple then moves to seize my throat and jaw, tilting my head back to rest on his shoulder. "Wearing this dress," his teeth graze my neck, "carrying my son."

Jessica Lyn

Reece's sister insisted I try on this dress—a figure-hugging black gown—claiming it complemented my complexion perfectly. I'd only wear it to the rehearsal dinner, not the wedding. I'm not that bold.

Ethan guides my lips to his for a possessive kiss. I feel exactly what I do to him pressed to my back, hard and insistent. Heat pools between my legs, and I arch into him. His hand on my stomach drifts lower, bunching the fabric around my thighs.

"E—" My breath hitches when his fingers find my bare center.

"No panties?"

"They don't fit well." My ass is too big, along with my hips.

"My dirty girl, always ready for me." He traces my wet slit from entrance to clit and back, slow and deliberate. "How are you feeling?"

"You're not serious," I deadpan.

I know where this is headed. This is Ethan. He has a taste for the taboo, craves the forbidden.

"Deadly." Two thick fingers plunge into me. "The door is locked; no one can come in."

Hangers glide along a metal rack in a neighboring stall, and my pulse quickens. "There's someone beside us."

"And you're dripping for me." He captures my mouth again, swallowing my soft whimpers. "You want me to stop?" he mumbles between kisses. "Tell me to stop."

I can't. I don't want to. "No, Sir."

"That's my girl. Hands on the mirror."

Leaning forward, I place my palms on the glass and arch my back.

His fingers work deeper, curling to find that spot that weakens my knees. "Spread your legs for me."

I obey without hesitation, widening my stance as much as the tight dress allows.

A door shuts nearby and I bite my lip to stifle a moan. The danger of being caught, of someone hearing us, only intensifies my arousal.

"Fuck," he curses. "Try to be quiet. I need you."

He withdraws his fingers and frees his length before he lifts the back of my dress and fills me in one powerful thrust.

I gasp at the slight soreness from earlier, and my inner walls clench around him.

He hisses through his teeth, and his fingertips dig into my hips, threatening to leave marks. "Look at us." His stormy gaze meets mine in the mirror. "Watch what you do to me."

The sight is obscene—me in a silky black gown, at Ethan's mercy while he towers behind me, fully clothed in his faded jeans, brown dress boots, and a button-up rolled to his elbows, his jaw tight, eyes hooded with lust.

The submissive part of me, the part that lives to please him, loves being taken like this—claimed by him.

One hand comes to my throat. "You're mine." His pace increases. "Say it."

"I'm yours." My voice is breathless, barely audible.

"You gonna be a good girl for me?" He punctuates his words with a deep thrust. "Obey me?" Another slam of his hips drives him even deeper. "As you *promised*?"

Oh, no. This is more than him appreciating my pregnant belly in this dress. This is a punishment, a manipulation using his dick, and, dammit, it'll work.

In the mirror, his gaze locks with mine, dark and unwavering. "Answer me." His grip tightens on my throat—not enough to cut off air but enough to remind me who's in control.

"Yes," I exhale.

"Yes, what?"

His thrusts grow more forceful, and my legs shake.

"Yes, Sir."

"No more going behind my back. No more secrets." Each demand is emphasized with a sharp snap of his hips. "Understood?"

"I understand—oh God," I moan, unable to keep quiet.

"*I* protect you and this family." His hand slides to my belly, cradling our baby. "Not the other way around."

"Y-yes, Sir."

"You better not lie to me, Aurora." His fingers move to my clit and circle with skillful precision. "You won't ever leave the loft if you do."

His possessive words and rough rhythm... My fingers press into the glass as ecstasy crashes through me. My vision blurs at the edges, my body convulses, and his palm clamps over my mouth, muffling my scream.

"That's it, baby girl." His pace grows erratic. "Fucking perfect." His hips jerk, and he comes inside me with a rumbling groan.

We return home with half a dozen dresses, along with new bras and panties, to find the other two asleep on the couch, side by side, Jackson with Danny snuggled against his chest. Markers are everywhere, and both Jax and Reece have new, colorful tattoos. It's the sweetest thing I've ever seen.

Ethan slides his phone from his pocket and snaps a picture. "Fucking perfect," he repeats.

Chapter 37
Ethan

I wake with Jackson's arm around my neck, fingers in my hair, cheek pressed to my shoulder, leg between mine. So fucking clingy.

Dusky morning light filters through the blinds, and I lift my head to find Reece and Aurora in a similar position, both asleep. Danny must have worn him out last night; Reece is usually the first one up.

An interesting fact I learned about the former soldier—he'll only sleep closest to the door, even at his sister's house. That leaves me on the opposite side of the bed.

I turn and nuzzle Jax. He smells so fucking good, musky and enticing, and my semi-erect cock takes notice, thickening between us.

He wraps a leg over my waist and presses into me, his own arousal hard and ready. "Mmm," he groans, raspy with sleep.

I place kisses along his sharp jawline. "Morning, baby."

His lips curve into a lazy smile, and he grinds his erection against mine. "Missed me?"

"Always so smug." I brush my thumb across his bottom lip.

He catches it between his teeth then sucks it into his mouth, and my cock jerks. The brat has trained my dick to expect to come multiple times a day. How did this become my life?

"Keep that up, and I'll stuff your mouth with something else." I envision rolling on top of him, pinning his wrists above his head, and...I don't know. Whatever he'll let me do, I guess.

He releases my thumb, snakes his hand down between us, and palms my cock through my boxer briefs. "Promise?"

I devour him in a hungry kiss, sliding my hand under his shirt to trace the ridges and valleys of cut muscle. Our tongues intertwine, and he moans softly, rocking his hips.

I break the kiss to glance at Aurora and Reece, still dead to the world, and slip beneath the waistband of his boxers to fist his length. "Shower with me," I whisper.

"Fuck," he breathes. "I don't want the marker to wash off before we get tattoos."

Shit. I forgot about today's bachelor tattoo party while the girls are at the salon. Now I really need him, need the release. "I took pictures. Can't they use those?" Jesus, I sound whiny, desperate.

His breath hitches as I stroke him, my thumb gliding through his precum.

"Please," I beg, only for him.

Before he can respond, Reece's husky voice interrupts us. "Yes, please go into the bathroom. Anywhere but here."

The moment we're naked and the water is heated, I push Jax against the shower wall, capturing his mouth in a bruising kiss. His fingers grasp my waist, pulling me impossibly close. Our bodies align perfectly—hard cocks sliding against each other, creating friction with every movement.

I grip both our shafts in one hand, stroking us together. "This okay?" I bite the sensitive spot below his ear. *This* is still new to me. With Jax, I have no idea what I'm doing.

"Fuck yes." His head falls back, his wet hair darkened, water droplets clinging to his long lashes.

I quicken my pace, transfixed by his pleasure—those wicked green eyes half-lidded, those perfect lips parted. I'm tempted to get on my knees for him, just to witness him shatter, but again, I'm the rookie here.

Though he seemed to enjoy my mouth last time. A blow job is a blow job, right?

No, definitely not. He and Aurora have proven otherwise.

His hands move up my body, over my shoulders, and tangle in my hair. He thrusts into my fist and whimpers, actually whimpers, and I nearly lose it then and there.

My chest aches with something beyond lust at the sight of him coming undone for me. He's fucking mesmerizing—all sharp angles, six-pack abs flexing with each roll of his hips, water cascading down his defined muscles.

"Goddamnit, you're beautiful." I tighten my grip and rest my forehead on his. "Give it to me. Come for me, baby."

His eyes lock with mine, pupils blown wide. My free hand reaches around to grab his ass, fingertips dangerously close to places we haven't discussed, and that's all it takes.

His entire body tenses, his fist clutches my hair. "Ethan—fuck—" He comes with a cry gritted between his teeth and spurts hot cum all over my fingers and cock.

My name on his lips sends me careening over the edge. My balls draw up tight as my orgasm tears through me and steals my breath. I follow him with a guttural groan, my release joining his.

We stand there panting, our foreheads pressed together, the water streaming over our shoulders. Feelings and emotions hit me hard, and all I can think is...*fuck, I love him*. I *really* love him.

I want this every day. The more time I spend alone with him, the less I want to go back to coaching him, to pretending and hiding.

"We should stop," I blurt out for absolutely no reason. I know damn well I'm not stopping this. I'd let him ruin my life, happily.

He knows it, too. He gives me that cocky smirk I've grown to love. "Whatever you want, Coach."

I glide my hand up his stomach, rubbing our mixed release onto his skin, although it's only washing down the drain. "What if I wasn't your coach?" My heart pounds from more than blowing my load, and I hold my breath, waiting for his answer.

He stiffens. "Don't say that."

I pull back to meet his gaze. "I'm being serious, Jax. We can't—"

"I won't play for anyone else." He cuts me off, a stubborn glint in his eyes, the muscles in his jaw bunching.

I was going to save this for New York, but I'm having some sort of post-sex breakdown.

"You can and you will if you want to be together."

We can't hide this. It's impossible. And no matter how hard he tries to convince me otherwise, he can't control himself. Being together and on the same team affects his mental health and his performance on the ice.

His chest rises and falls rapidly as he straightens to his full height. "What are you talking about? You love coaching."

"I love you." Wholeheartedly. Unconditionally. He's broken me.

"Hockey is your life."

I shake my head. "Hockey isn't my life. You're my life. Aurora is my life. This family is my life."

"You could win the Stanley Cup." He places his hand over his heart. "I can give you that."

"I'd rather be yours." Emotion tightens my throat, and I force myself to swallow. "I'd rather be with Aurora. I'd rather be a father."

His eyes glisten, his brows furrowed. "You're serious?"

"Yes." My decision was made during the flight, but seeing Jax cuddling a toddler...that sealed it. I've lost my damn mind, but this is what I want. *Them.* The house, the kids. I want to hold my son proudly in the arena with Jax's hand in mine. Always.

"What happened?"

Despite his heartbreak, I can't help but chuckle. "You. *You* happened, baby boy. You and Aurora."

Chapter 38
Jackson

I want to rage. I want to cry. I *am* crying—a little. "Your pillow talk needs fucking work. Were you hoping to soften the blow with an orgasm?"

"No." He rinses the shampoo from his hair, his face tilted up into the spray. "I was going to wait until New York."

I'm pissed off, but my cock still tries to rally at the sight of soapy water sluicing off his bulging muscles.

Then, realization hits me, and panic splinters in my chest, my hard-on forgotten. "Oh my fucking God. Are you staying in New York too?"

"No—" He releases a heavy sigh. "I don't know."

"What the fuck, Ethan?" My voice rises, and I glare at him. Not even the snake between his legs could distract me at this point. "What the hell am I supposed to do? Go to LA while everyone lives on the other side of the fucking country?"

A blush creeps across his face. "Shh, quiet. I wouldn't do that to you."

I angrily wash my body, thinking of Ethan and Aurora and the entire family in New York while I'm traveling. Tears burn my eyes. "What *are* you doing?"

He moves aside to give me space to rinse. "I don't know yet. Take a breath."

"Take a breath?" I stare at him in disbelief. "You drop this bomb on me and tell me to take a breath? You planned this and didn't even talk to me."

He thrusts a hand toward me. "There is no talking to you about this."

"So, what? You tried fucking me into submission instead?"

"We're not fucking," he dares to say with a straight face.

I give him a blank expression. "You're joking, right? Is that your way of compartmentalizing? It's okay as long as we're not fucking?"

"You're ridiculous. Are you listening to anything I'm saying?"

About to explode, I step out of the shower, and Ethan follows, shutting off the water.

"Why?" I yank a towel from the rack and wrap it around my waist. "Why are you doing this? Is it because I had a shitty game?"

I snatch another towel and toss it at him. I refuse to be sidetracked by his bare skin glistening with water and all that damn chest hair.

Thank fuck—he covers his dick.

"Your shitty game is the least of my worries—although it had to do with *us*, remember? You wanted a commitment, something solid. I'm making that possible."

"By leaving me? Abandoning me in LA?"

"No..." He shakes his head. "You said you were okay with being traded if it meant you could have me."

I throw my arms in the air. "That was before. I would've said anything to be with you. Now, I don't want to be separated. I want this every day." I gesture between us.

"That's exactly what I'm trying to achieve."

He reaches for me, but I pull away. I'm too agitated and overwhelmed to be touched.

"How?" Before he can respond, I jump in. "Oh, I see." I laugh incredulously. It sounds broken and pathetic, my throat tight with emotion. "Quitting is your way of giving me a commitment without anyone knowing. You're hiding."

"Fuck you." He steps up to me, the vein in his neck pulsing, a deep scowl etched between his brows. "I'm sacrificing everything for you, for us to be a family. You're married. You already have a very public commitment. What do I matter?"

I lean in, our noses nearly touching. "We're not married—legally—we have a domestic partnership. Marrying her in New York would mean the baby was mine. He'd have *my* last name. I wasn't taking that from you. Neither was Aurora."

I storm out of the bathroom, leaving him standing there, staring after me.

The bedroom is empty, thankfully—Aurora and Reece must have gone downstairs. *Reece*. Damn him. He probably convinced Ethan to quit with his 'you're the father—it's your responsibility' speech.

Fuck him.

I pull on clothes with jerky movements, my mind racing. The fucking audacity. Ethan makes this life-altering decision, excluding me, and then casually mentions it after getting me off? The worst part is, I can't even argue. This is what good men do—they take care of their families.

He's such a good guy, it's sickening. How am I supposed to live without him? He's the reason I'm sober and functioning—he and Aurora.

My brain scrambles for a solution, a way to keep him from quitting. I come up with nothing.

Fuck it, I'll quit too. We'll quit together. If this is what he wants, then fuck hockey.

I'm dressed and heading out of the bedroom before Ethan

finishes in the bathroom. I'm so consumed with my thoughts, I almost trip over Danny, who's lying on the floor, peeking under the door.

I come to a halt, gripping the doorframe to stop from stepping on him. "What are you doing, little man?"

He leaps up and roars, hands out, fingers curled like claws.

Despite feeling hopeless and angry, I laugh. "Holy shi... znitzle, you scared me." I feign a gasp and clutch my proverbial pearls. Is shiznitzle a word? Wienerschnitzel? I have no idea, but it's better than the alternative.

He giggles, bounces on his toes, reaching for me, and I melt. He's so damn cute, with his big blue eyes and chubby cheeks.

I scoop him up. He's still in his pajamas, and I glance at his room. "Did you sneak out of your bed?"

He nods and smiles proudly. They need a gate to prevent him from tumbling down the stairs, but he'd probably climb that too.

Can four-year-olds go up and down the stairs without falling? I'll have to ask Reece.

"Is Harper—your mom sleeping?"

He nods again, pointing to my forearm, where he'd drawn me a stick figure T-Rex. It looked more like a vertical, misshapen dog, but nobody is judging here.

"Sorry, buddy. It washed off in the shower. But you can color me another one. How about that?"

He beams as I descend the stairs.

"Have you had breakfast?"

He shakes his head, his blond hair falling across his forehead.

"Well, let's make some. Do you like eggs? Pancakes? Waffles?"

"Pan-cakes," he says quietly.

It's the first full word I've heard him speak, other than Mama.

Aurora and Reece are sipping their coffees at the kitchen table when we enter.

"Morning." Aurora smiles. "Someone made a friend."

Danny points at Reece. "King."

The Viking *grins*. "Good job, buddy," he praises then asks me, "Harper sleeping? You want me to take him?"

Tiny arms tighten around my neck, nearly choking me. "No. Jax," he pronounces clearly.

Reece rolls his eyes, and I chuckle.

"Uncle Reece is scary, isn't he?" I gesture to my wife. "Can you say Aurora?" I articulate her name slowly.

Danny opens his mouth wide and unleashes a sound somewhere between a lion's roar and a war cry, sending us into fits of laughter. I guess Aurora equals roar. Close enough.

After raiding the pantry for ingredients to make pancakes, I have Danny perched on the island beside me, his legs swinging as I whisk eggs and add them to the dry mix.

"Milk?" He lifts the full measuring cup.

It sounds like 'miwk,' but I understand him perfectly.

"Yes, Chef," I reply with exaggerated seriousness, earning a giggle from both him and Aurora. "Go ahead, Chef."

He pours the liquid with surprising precision. Not a drop spills over the edge of the bowl—a stark improvement on our earlier egg-cracking fiasco that left me fishing out shell fragments and cleaning yolk from the floor.

Reece sips his coffee, his posture relaxed for once. "Harper might murder you for stealing him and allowing him to make a mess."

"He was outside our door. What was I supposed to do, leave him in the hallway? He could've fallen down the stairs. Besides, I'll clean the mess."

Reece shakes his head with amusement. "I'm having a hard time believing you didn't sneak in and take him."

Ethan breezes into the kitchen, wearing worn jeans and a light-gray Henley that matches his eyes, a manila envelope in hand. His hair is damp and extra wavy, his jaw tight with tension.

He takes a seat at the island across from me, his cologne filling my senses, and my stomach dips.

"What kind of pancakes do you want, little man?" I struggle to keep my voice light and unaffected.

"Chocwat!"

He grabs the package of semi-sweet morsels and, before I can stop him, dumps the bag into the batter. A good portion misses the bowl entirely and spills onto the counter. His small hands chase after the chocolate chips, stuffing handfuls into his mouth.

I chuckle and poke his belly. "Hey, save some for the pancakes."

He lets out a melodic laugh that warms my chest.

Ethan's gaze locks with mine, his eyes soft. "What conference has the fewest travel miles?"

I look away, unable to handle the emotion swimming in those stormy depths, and stir the chocolate-chip-laden batter with more force than necessary. "Eastern." It's common knowledge that the Eastern Conference travels much less.

I pour the first pancake onto the hot griddle, and Danny claps with excitement. "Now, we wait for bubbles," I tell him after I finish pouring the rest of the batter.

Ethan sets the envelope on the counter. "What teams specifically?"

My hand freezes, spatula in the air. "Both of the New York teams, New Jersey, and Pittsburgh." I eye the envelope with suspicion. "What is it?"

"An early Christmas gift."

"What kind of gift?" The words come out harsh, my mind racing. Is he going to one team and sending me to another? "If you're not coaching, I don't want it."

He leans in and raises a brow. "You're a stubborn little—"

Before Ethan finishes, Danny squeals. "Bubbles! Bubbles!"

"Let me take over." Reece appears at my side, nudges me out of the way, and steals the spatula. "I think I can manage pancakes."

I hesitate until his mini-me is slapping his arm and chanting, "King! Bubbles!"

Aurora slips between Ethan's legs, her back to his chest. "What's going on? What is it?"

His arms wrap around her, a hand splayed protectively over her belly. "Just open it, Jax."

I unfold the envelope and slide out a stack of documents. The top one bears the New York Stars letterhead.

The kitchen becomes too small, too hot. I glance from the papers to Ethan and back again. "How? Why do you have this?"

Players usually learn about a trade only after it's finalized and they're en route to their new team. Sometimes they find out on social media—not from their coach, over Christmas break, with no one else present. If it were a done deal, my agent would've called.

The corner of his lip twitches. "Read it."

The first few pages are a standard trade proposal. My heart skips a beat when I see my name and a decent offer. "You're trading me to New York?"

"*I'm* not trading you." The twitch stretches into a full-blown smirk.

Quickly, I scan the document, my thoughts a whirlwind of questions. Who will be my coach? I'm still holding out hope it's Ethan, although he made his decision clear.

There's no way he's just *staying home*. Ethan, a stay-at-home dad? Nope. He'd go crazy.

I flip to the signature page, and my breath catches in my lungs. His name is there: Ethan Blackwood, in fresh black ink.

But it's not as the coach, and it's not on the Huskies' side.

"You'd…" I stare at him, completely dumbfounded, "own me?"

Chapter 39
Ethan

"I'd own part of you," I correct. "Thirty-three percent of the Stars is mine. Rossi Investments owns the rest—privately." Turns out, I wasn't drafted to the team by accident. The Rossi family has held majority ownership in the organization for two generations. Now, we own it all.

"Same thing," Jackson mutters as he reads the documents. "You'll be the GM?"

"If you agree. If not, we rip up the contracts and forget about it." I shrug, feigning nonchalance despite the anxiety coursing through my veins. I won't be general manager without Jax. That requires staying in New York. The Rossi crew knew this, which is why Rocco showed up in LA with two offers in hand. "The transfer of ownership is almost finalized, though. I won't be your coach much longer."

Aurora peers up at me, brows pinched. "You're leaving the Huskies?"

I nod. "They'll be letting me go."

She glances between the two of us. "Why?"

It's Jax who answers. "Because he can't own one team and

coach for another. It's a conflict of interest. He'll have to choose, and he's choosing to be in New York."

"Not without you." I tighten my hold on Aurora while locking eyes with Jackson. "I'll divide my time if that's what you want."

"No. Please, Jax," our girl pleads, hands steepled at her mouth. "We could all be together."

He draws a deep breath, and the kitchen falls silent, save for the scrape of the spatula and Danny's lip-smacking.

"You're willing to give up coaching and work for your family?" Jackson's voice is quiet, controlled. "For me? For us?"

He was back in LA for only a few hours before he wanted to end his life. Lucas was jumped and locked in a cell, tortured. If it were Aurora or Jax in that hospital bed, I'd die—after I killed someone. *Many* someones. I won't risk them again, and I never want to feel as helpless as I did when Jackson was crying in my arms or when Aurora was under that desk.

"I'd do anything for the two of you—to ensure your safety, your happiness." I swallow the puck-sized lump in my throat. "I want to be there for it all—the pregnancy, the birth, watching you with *our* baby." I thrust a hand toward the man flipping pancakes and pretending not to listen, though I know he hears every word. "Reece can't live without his partner, and you know the twins won't let Lucas return to LA." I shoot for lighthearted and blink away the tears.

"What happens if I don't fit in with the team?" Jax clenches his jaw. He's going to give himself a headache if he doesn't stop. "What happens when they don't want me anymore?"

"I'll want you," I say without hesitation, because I know that's what he's asking. Will I be disappointed? Will I still want him? "Always."

He has the freedom to choose—whether it's playing for a different team, not playing, dabbling in real estate, or staying home and helping raise our children. He's not worried about his career or finances. He's worried about me. Us.

His expression hardens and his eyes narrow. It's not the reaction I was expecting, and my stomach churns.

"I'll do it under one condition." He crosses his arms over his chest. "I want more than Carmichael. That prick doesn't deserve to be paid higher than me."

My shoulders relax, and I let out a breathy laugh. "I'm working with a strict budget. We're trading two players for you."

"Who?"

"McArdie and Botterill."

He tilts his head, and his scowl deepens. "I'm worth at least three."

I jut my chin. "Prove it."

"Fine. Add Grant and Kill, and we have a deal."

"Don't push it," I warn, but my heart is soaring. This is happening. We're going to be together, safe, in New York. "Maybe next year."

Fuck, Reece is right. I'm a sucker for this kid.

"Now you're my boss *and* my boyfriend?" A slow, devilish smile creeps across Jackson's face. "Will you have an office?"

God help me and my office staff. "Soundproof, so I can choke you."

He lowers his tone. "Pretty sure being the owner and fucking a player is way worse than being the coach and doing the same."

I lean in and cock a brow. "Yeah? Who's gonna stop me?" Not like they can fire me.

He rounds the island and squeezes himself between my legs. Jax is on one thigh, Aurora on the other—except they're standing, or we'd break this stool.

His arm comes around my shoulders, and he gives me those puppy-dog eyes. "I'm sorry I was a dick to you."

"You didn't scream and destroy shit. I'm proud of you." I press my lips to his.

"Ew! Kissin'!" Danny shrieks from his perch on the counter. "Icky!"

Laughter ripples through the kitchen, and the knot in my stomach finally unravels. "Sign the contract, Jax." I sneak in another kiss. "Let's make this official."

"But New York is so cold." He pouts dramatically. "I'm a Cali boy. I'm not meant for freezing weather."

"A brat, that's what you are. I'll buy you a fucking jacket… and get a tattoo today." I grumble the last part and glare into his teasing green eyes. He's got me by the balls and he knows it.

"Reece James!" interrupts a sharp Southern voice.

Jax and I jolt apart, heads snapping to the doorway.

Harper stands with her hands on her hips, her hair in a messy bun. She marches to her son, who has chocolate smeared across his cheeks and covering his fingers and pajamas.

"I swear to God, if he crashes out today after being hyped up on all this sugar, you're dealing with him." She surveys the chocolate disaster and shakes her head. "And you're giving him a bath."

Reece points the spatula in our direction. "Don't blame me! This was Jackson."

"Traitor," Jax hisses. "You fed him. I would've done a much better job."

"I only have one arm!" Reece fires back.

"Ugh, here we go again," my *boyfriend* groans. "Always using your injury to get attention and sympathy. You were shot. We get it. Jesus."

Chapter 40
Reece

Never in my wildest dreams did I envision shooting the shit with an old Army buddy while getting tattoos with Jax and Ethan. Yet, here I am, laughing my ass off, mostly at Jackson.

He leans over the table, gawking at my freshly buzzed sides and the half-finished tattoo etched in my scalp. "Are you fucking serious?" He draws a deep inhale, readying for the tantrum he's about to throw. "You always have to show me up, don't you? First with your dazzling dick, and now you get Aurora's name tattooed across your head? What the actual fuck, Viking? You look like a walking billboard for fuckboys and bad decisions. Stand next to Ethan, and you'll be his goon. Fucking Christ," he curses, loud enough for the entire shop to hear. "Fine, I'm getting my tongue pierced. Compete with that."

The needle hits a sensitive spot, and a spike of adrenaline rushes through my veins. "I don't need my tongue pierced to have your wife gushing on my face, but go ahead, do it. Then I won't have to listen to you bitch and complain for at least a few days."

"You're not getting your tongue pierced," Ethan cuts in. His expression is contorted in horror—by the thought of a needle going through Jackson's tongue or the sight of the tattoo gun at my temple, I'm not sure. "It's against league rules."

Sadie's fiancé, Cal, a buddy of mine I asked to watch over her—another story for another day—chuckles as he works on my head. "You're all insane. I love it."

***

Ethan

I follow Kelly, Cal's apprentice, to a tiny room in the back of the shop, away from Jax's prying eyes and Reece's knowing smirk. The door clicks shut behind us, and suddenly, my legs are made of concrete. A wave of dread washes over me—not because I'm second-guessing the tattoo, but because I doubt I'll make it through this without passing out cold on the floor.

"Decided what you want?" She pulls on a fresh pair of gloves and snaps me out of my panic.

I clear my throat. "Yeah." I slip my phone from my pocket and show her a simple design I found on Pinterest—fucking Pinterest. Who have I become?

"Two black bands?" Kelly studies the image. "Classic. I like it. Ring finger?"

"Yup." I swallow hard, my heart palpitating. I'm bound to go into cardiac arrest one of these days.

"Have a seat." She nods toward the leather chair, similar to those in a dentist's office, which does nothing to help my fear.

I ease into the chair, rigid as a board, and place my left hand on the armrest.

Kelly preps her station, setting out small bottles of ink and assembling her torture device. "First tattoo?"

"That obvious?"

She grins. "Your white-knuckle death grip and pale face give you away." She cleans my trembling finger with alcohol. "Try to relax. Don't forget to breathe."

Easier said than done. I stare at the ceiling tiles and focus on why I'm doing this—for Jax, for Aurora, for our family, a permanent commitment no one can question.

"You sure you want this?" Kelly asks, tattoo gun in hand. "Once it's on…"

"I'm sure." I've never been more certain of anything. Besides, it's just two black bands around my finger. How painful can it be?

Reece has Aurora's name on his head, for fuck's sake. Jax has intricate wings across his shoulder blades. I got this.

The gun buzzes, and I count the ceiling tiles.

One. Two. Three. Four. Fi—*fuck*!

***

Jackson

I glance over at Reece, who's admiring his new ink—Aurora's name written in script from his temple to the base of his skull. Such a suck-up.

Next is my turn. Ethan has been gone nearly twenty minutes, and I'm getting antsy.

"What's taking him so long?" I ask no one in particular. "It can't be that complicated."

"Maybe he chickened out," Reece answers with a shit-eating grin. "Maybe he decided you're not worth it."

"Fuck you," I retort, but it lacks any anger. My mind is too preoccupied with Ethan and what he might be getting.

Something hidden, I bet. Something safe. "What if he fainted?"

"They'll finish the tattoo while he's asleep," Cal jokes as he takes a seat at my station. "Got a picture?"

"Many." I grab my phone and flip through photos. "This, on my collarbone."

"That's sick." He takes the phone and zooms in. "I'll need to send myself a few of these pics. That okay?"

"Yeah, but make sure it's *this* one." I point to the bite mark I've been obsessing over since the day Ethan and I first kissed.

Reece snorts. "It's his teeth, Romeo. They haven't changed in thirty years."

"The placement is slightly different, fuckface," I shout back before removing my shirt. "Has he always been a dickhead?" I ask his soon-to-be brother-in-law.

Cal chuckles while preparing the transfer paper. "Since day one. We were deployed together. He was the most serious motherfucker I'd ever met—stoic, by the book. He didn't talk unless it was to correct someone or give orders, but you'd want him by your side. Nobody was better."

"Yeah, no shit," I agree. The Viking might be an asshole—sometimes—but he did take a bullet for me. "You just can't trust him with your girlfriend," I tease to lighten the mood.

"I can hear you." Reece adjusts the ice pack on his scalp. "Pay no attention to a thing he says, Cal. They were separated."

I grind my molars. "I'm going to separate your teeth from your gums if you don't stop repeating that."

Cal bursts into laughter. "You two are a riot." He positions the transfer sheet on my collarbone and presses firmly. "I can't imagine you living together."

Me neither, but here we are, living and sleeping together, sharing a life.

A door swings open, and Ethan emerges, white as a ghost. He stumbles toward us, his hands stuffed in his pockets, his jaw clenched tight, his throat working hard.

"Oh, shit. You okay, big guy?" I reach for him, careful not to disturb Cal. "Come here."

"I'm fine," Ethan mutters, but his voice lacks its usual confidence. He collapses into the chair beside me, and his head falls to my bare stomach. With a grimace, he extracts his hands from his pockets and holds them gingerly in his lap.

Eager and impatient, I demand, "Let me see."

"It's nothing," he insists, eyes squeezed shut. "Later."

"Bullshit." I run my fingers through his newly trimmed hair. "Show me."

He slowly lifts his left hand. His ring finger is wrapped in clear plastic, two bold black bands encircling it.

My throat tightens. "You got a wedding ring tattoo?"

"Two of them," he groans, his breathing shallow, his skin clammy. "One for each of you."

The sentiment hits me like a check into the boards—unexpected and breathtaking. I blink rapidly, trying to contain the emotion welling up. I've never seen him this way—vulnerable, open, raw. "Fuck, are you dying? Anything I should know?"

He places his hand on my chest. "Maybe a heart attack. Let's not do this again."

I can't stop smiling. "You only get tattoo-married once, Coach. You're good."

Reece jerks upright, the ice pack slipping from his skull, and gives us that smug grin. "So, by your own logic, Aurora and I are tattoo-married." It's not even framed as a question.

"Congratulations." I smirk. "You're officially part of the harem. Welcome to the club. We go to bed at eleven p.m. and shower at nine—"

"Nope." He shakes his head adamantly. "I'm not showering with you."

I ignore him. "Ethan enjoys two mouths wrapped arou—" The hand on my chest clamps over my lips, and I chuckle.

Best day ever.

Chapter 41
Aurora

"They're here," Sadie singsongs from her seat across from me. "Look at them. A bunch of damn heathens."

My guys enter the restaurant dressed impeccably, sporting fresh haircuts. Ethan is in his classic black suit and white button-down, a flashback to the night we met. Jax is wearing the tailored charcoal-gray suit he wore to his last game, since that's what he had packed.

Then, there's Reece in all black—jeans and combat boots, his usual tight-fitting T-shirt under his leather jacket. He's straight off the cover of an MC romance novel and so damn hot.

Still... "Did you want him in a tux tomorrow?" I ask his sister.

"No. Have you seen my fiancé? I don't care what my brother wears, just as long as he's here."

Her fiancé, who drove us to the restaurant while the guys were getting ready, is also covered in tattoos, with messy jet-black hair and a beard trimmed along his jaw line. When they stand together—her delicate features against his rugged ones, her pale skin against his deep olive complexion—they make a gorgeous couple, drawing every eye in the room.

I sigh dreamily, satisfied to leave Reece exactly the way he is. "Okay."

"I haven't got a clue how you like three guys." Harper adjusts Danny on her lap. He's being shy with all the people here, his face tucked into her neck. "I can't even stand one."

"Don't say that." Sadie gives her a scowl. "You will, Harp. You just have to meet the right man."

These two are night and day. Similar in appearance, opposites in personality.

Jax's gaze sweeps across the dimly lit room, scanning faces until he finds mine. I rise from my seat and smooth down the silk dress that hugs my curves and accentuates my baby bump.

His expression transforms instantly—eyes widening, lips parting, as if the sight of me short-circuited his brain. That hungry, adoring gaze, the one he's had since the day we met, never fails to make my heart flutter.

He breaks from his trance and strides toward me with purpose, weaving between tables and people. When he reaches me, he pulls me close and whispers, "I've never seen anything more beautiful." He presses a kiss to my neck. "Trying to make me bawl my eyes out in front of Reece's family?"

Before I can formulate an answer, Ethan appears behind him, grabbing his collar and playfully yanking him aside. "Move."

"Fuck it. Go ahead. I'm booking us a suite tonight," Jackson mumbles, already on his phone. "This is some romantic wet dream shit right here."

Ethan shakes his head in amusement then draws me in, his hand cradling my belly possessively. "You're stunning. How are you feeling?"

"You clean up well yourself." I lean in and kiss his cheek. "My feet hurt in these heels, but otherwise, I'm okay."

He brings my knuckles to his lips. "Sit and take them off."

I notice the clear wrapping on his ring finger, and my jaw drops. "You got a wedding ring tattoo?"

A flush creeps up his neck. "Later." He steps back and shoves his hands in his pockets.

"Fine," I relent. "I won't embarrass you, but I love it. Where's—" My words fade when my gaze connects with Reece.

He freezes mid-conversation with Cal on the other side of the table. His dark gaze travels from my face to the curve of my belly then up again. His jaw clenches, the muscles bulging, and my cheeks catch fire. He approaches, his expression intense, almost predatory, and I bite my lip. Maybe I should get out of leggings and sweatpants more often.

He towers over me, cups my chin, and tilts my face to his. "Princess."

"Viking." My gaze drops to his lips, and I gasp. "You got your lip pierced again."

Silver metal glints at the corner of his mouth, the skin around it red and angry. Drawn to him like a magnet, I rise to my toes and press my lips to the small hoop. A surge of excitement races through me. I want to bite and tug it.

He inhales sharply and deepens the kiss. His tongue brushes mine, and the restaurant chatter becomes distant background noise. Rarely is he unrestrained, and never in public. I like it—a lot.

"Excuse me." A deep voice cuts through the haze. "I believe you're in front of our seats."

Reece jerks away, as if electrocuted. His entire body stiffens, and his stoic mask snaps into place. The transformation is immediate and jarring, from loving to rigid in the blink of an eye.

An older couple stands behind him—the man with silver hair, wearing a decorated military uniform, and the woman in a long floral dress, her blonde hair in a perfect chignon. It's clear who they are, not only from Reece's reaction, but from his father's broad shoulders and tall stature.

They stare at our group with mild annoyance, his mother with a tight smile, not yet noticing their son among us. Jackson shuffles closer to Ethan, creating space for them to sit, and casts me a knowing glance.

Mr. Abercrombie pulls out a chair for his wife, and, on her way to her seat, Maryanne's gaze flickers between Reece and me.

Her hand flies to her mouth. "Reece?" Her expression shifts from disbelief to shock to utter confusion. "I didn't even recognize you. What happened?"

What happened? Huh?

He acknowledges his parents with a curt nod. "Mom, Dad." His voice is clipped, formal, devoid of warmth.

My hand finds his, our fingers intertwining, his grip on me almost painful.

His mother steps closer, her eyes widening. "I saw pictures, but… Is that—" She squints. "Is that a name on your head?" She clutches her pearls—literally.

Reece turns to me. I lean over, and sure enough, he has my name tattooed on his scalp, blending with the intricate designs that climb up his neck. I don't know how I missed it. Apparently, I was too preoccupied with kissing him.

I can't help but grin. "Te amo," I mouth.

His eyes soften, and he mouths it back. "Te amo."

The pastor stands ramrod straight, his hand gripping the chair, his military background evident in every inch of his posture. "That's…quite a statement, defacing your body."

Anxiety and awkwardness swirl in my gut. Reece's jaw tightens, but he remains silent.

There's no affection between any of them, and although his father frightens me and I'm nauseated, I extend my hand. "Hi. I'm Aurora. It's lovely to meet you."

His father doesn't so much as glance at me.

His mother clasps my hand between both of hers, her touch warm and gentle. "It's nice to meet you, dear. You look nothing like your pictures online."

I don't even know what to say. Thank you?

***

Jackson

Sadie claps her hands. "Everyone, sit! The first course is about to be served."

Ethan insists on sitting next to Aurora, who's beside the Viking. That leaves me on the other side of Ethan, the farthest from Reece's parents.

Which is good, because I'm spiraling a bit, my mind drifting. Reece having a mother is stirring up something inside me. She's alive and has no relationship with him. It's gut-wrenching.

His father is intentionally intimidating. He didn't shake Aurora's hand, refused to even acknowledge her. He wore that uniform knowing what Reece has been through. It's a slap in the face. He's screaming, "Hey, look at me! I made it to retirement and you didn't." I bet he wasn't whatever Reece was—a medic or special forces or some shit.

I understand now why it was natural for Reece to care for Aurora—he cares for his sisters. They parent each other. Harper chastises him, and he gives the girls the affection they don't receive from their mother and father. Sadie is accepting, accommodating, and cheerful, probably the one who kept the peace in the family. Maryanne seems clueless, but I think it's an act to avoid her husband's wrath.

I'm assuming this based on a few minutes of interaction, but I hate them—well, maybe hate is too strong a word, but I dislike them very much. They should be hugging their son, fawning all over him. Reece may have tattoos and piercings, but he's a hero, for fuck's sake. He's one of the good ones.

I lean into Ethan. "Do I have to be polite?"

"Yes." He keeps his gaze forward. "For now."

He smells delicious, and I want to lick him all over. I lay my hand on his thigh. He gives me a sidelong glance but doesn't push me away. I move higher, and he snatches my wrist.

His lips twitch with amusement. "Stop it."

Danny fusses, wanting food, but he refuses to eat the appetizers brought out. Aurora isn't eating the crab cakes and stuffed mushrooms either. She dislikes slimy fungus and won't risk eating seafood while pregnant. I end up devouring her portion, forgetting to wait for Mr. Abercrombie to say grace. I'm starving. I'm an athlete and a husband of two; I require a high-calorie intake.

Reece grabs a basket of rolls and places one on Aurora's plate, another on his. He reaches out to his sister. "Harp, let me hold him so you can eat."

"Where is Daniel?" his father asks Harper, his voice laced with exasperation. "Where is your husband?"

Mr. Abercrombie reminds me of those preachers you find on television at three a.m., red-faced and screaming about the Holy Ghost, spittle flying from his mouth. I had a coach like that once, and I couldn't stop laughing whenever he became enraged.

Harper doesn't answer. Instead, she glances at her brother across the table.

"Don't look at him. Look at me when I'm talking to you."

Tack on the word 'boy,' and Reece's father sounds exactly like Kyle. I'm sure I've said something similar to Aurora. Sometimes, the bastard comes through my mouth. No wonder Reece hated me.

My brain trips, imagining what it might've been like to have a sister growing up with Kyle. I quickly push the thought away—nothing could've been worse.

I know Reece's father isn't Kyle, because the Viking would've killed him—burned him alive, that's what I would've done if anyone touched my sister.

The pastor continues to badger Harper, just loud enough for our group to hear. "Don't expect your brother to take care of you the way he did Sadie. He won't have a job much longer with that metal in his face and that *name* on his head. Return home."

Aurora lowers her gaze, her hand on her stomach, her chest rising and falling rapidly. Ethan places his arm around the back of her chair, and she peers over at him appreciatively, eyes glassy.

Reece bites the piercing in his lip and tugs the hoop. "I'll make sure Harper has everything she needs. Leave her alone."

"You've done enough," his father mutters out of the corner of his mouth. He unfolds his napkin with a sharp snap and places it on his lap. "We drove several hours to be here. Your mother was so excited, and you show up with…"

Danny cries, drowning out his words, and my knee bounces. I clench my teeth to keep from saying something. Instead, I reach for my water and take a long swig.

"Daddy," Sadie pleads. "Not tonight. Can we have dinner together for once?"

Daddy? Is that a Southern thing? Gross. I once heard Emily call Killian 'Daddy,' and I threw up a bit in my mouth.

Maryanne leans over the table, shielding Harper from her

husband. "Harper had the most beautiful wedding at our church," she tells Aurora. "I can't wait for you to visit. We just started decorating the nursery. You'd love it."

What is happening right now? Is she legit crazy? Aurora will not be visiting. She's about to have a panic attack.

Ethan grips my leg to ease my agitation. "Go get Danny, please."

Thank fuck. I push back my chair, the legs scraping the floor with how fast I move. "Hey, Danny the Dinosaur," I call out to get his attention. "Wanna color?"

He reaches for me, and I lift him into my arms.

"Do you have his markers?" I ask Harper.

"That's unnecessary," Reece's father interjects. "If she wants to be a single mother, she should learn to take care of him on her own."

He has thick, gray caterpillar eyebrows that wiggle when he talks. I picture my fist slamming into one when I punch him. Creepy and prickly.

Harper's cheeks flush. "I do! I always have."

He leans in, crowding Maryanne. "Then he needs a father's discipline. He's already behind other children his age."

I lose my temper. I hold Danny tighter and press his head to my chest to block out the noise. "He's four," I snap. "He's hungry and tired. Leave them alone." I echo the Viking, though I'd much rather tell his father to fuck off.

Face contorted in fury, Mr. Abercrombie tosses his napkin on his plate and rises.

Reece bolts from his chair. "Dad—"

Ethan's hand slams onto the table, the sharp crack of his palm rattling silverware and glasses. "Sit down," he snarls.

Everyone freezes. Even Danny stops crying, his pupils wide as I bounce him gently. Reece drops to his seat. Aurora gawks at our boyfriend, stunned.

Ethan's stormy eyes fixate on Reece's father, his expression thunderous. "We're here to celebrate Sadie and Cal's wedding. If you can't show basic human decency, then perhaps you should leave."

Maryanne's hand flies to her throat. The waiter pauses with our meals, tray on his shoulder.

The pastor's face turns crimson. "Excuse me? Who do you think—"

"I don't think. I know." Ethan cuts him off, tone deadly. "I know a man doesn't berate his children. Reece is family. He protects those I love; there's no greater honor. I won't tolerate you belittling him, and I definitely won't tolerate whatever you thought you were doing when you stood from that chair." His steely gaze is unwavering.

Something swells in my chest at him standing up for me—and Reece, but mostly me—and I can't help the smug smile that tugs at my lips. He loves me, and it's so damn hot.

"Dad. Sit," Reece says, quiet but firm, "or leave."

"Daddy, please," Sadie begs.

With a scowl, he sinks into his chair, nostrils flaring with each heavy breath.

Ethan faces forward and straightens his suit. "Sadie. Cal," he gives a polite nod, "my apologies. Everyone, let's eat." He gestures to the waiter. "I'm starving." Those intense eyes find mine. "Come here." He juts his chin.

Is it wrong that I hope I'm in trouble?

Chapter 42
Aurora

I steady myself against the wall of the hotel suite as Ethan slips off my heels.

He massages the arch of one foot before removing the other shoe. "Sore?"

"A little." I sigh as his thumbs work their magic on my aching feet. "Thank you for tonight. For…you know. All you do for us."

Reece went straight to the bathroom when we entered the room. I don't want him to overhear and think we're gossiping about him. Jackson is hunting down snacks and candy for a movie night.

"Of course." Ethan remains focused on his task, his touch firm yet gentle.

I reach down and run my fingers through his thick hair. "I didn't know how to handle it." My voice breaks. I feel terrible for not saying something, for not being more assertive, but Reece's dad scares the shit out of me. I'm certain he despises me. I'm definitely not who he wants for his son.

Ethan glances up, his gray eyes dark underneath his

lowered brows. "You shouldn't have to." His hands slide up and rub my calves. "That's our job. You take care of Reece."

Throughout dinner, Reece remained quiet, even when his sisters surprised him with an early birthday cake and his mother called him a Christmas miracle for sharing Jesus' day. He stayed that way even after his parents left, giving only Sadie an awkward hug.

I haven't a clue what I was thinking, trying to ease into their family by donating to their church. His sister said it was what they cared for most—their church—and I took that to heart. Not that I regret it. I still have hopes for his mother, but I doubt his father will ever accept us.

I knock on the bathroom door. "Can I come in?"

"Yeah." Reece's tone is flat, neither annoyed nor pleased.

When I enter, he's standing at the sink, his hair damp, the tattoo on his scalp red and irritated. The room is massive, with a rainfall shower and a deep soaking tub I wouldn't mind using right about now.

"Hey," I say softly and close the door behind me. "You okay?"

He turns toward me, his gaze downcast. "I'm fine."

"Liar." I encircle his waist, careful of his arm. "I thought we weren't lying to one another."

He rests his cheek on top of my head. "There's nothing more to say. This is why I didn't want to come."

"I'm glad we came. I got to meet your sisters and Danny."

He leans on the counter and releases a heavy breath. "I need some time with them." His gaze connects with mine, a silent plea of vulnerability and regret. "I need to figure out what's going on with Harper."

He's feeling guilty and responsible. I don't have siblings, but I have Gram. I can empathize.

Plus, this is Reece. He'll forever be rescuing others, and I'm fine with that.

"Whatever you need. We don't always have to be in New York or LA or traveling with the other two." A moment of insecurity hits me, and I backtrack. "Or do you mean now? Alone? I'm sorry." I step back. "Of course you should go."

His brows furrow. "Do you want me to go?" he asks, as if he already knows the answer.

"No."

"Okay then." His hand slides up my neck, his fingers tangling in my hair. "I want you with me. We'll figure it out."

"What about Christmas?" We're supposed to leave tomorrow after the wedding. Ethan has plans in New York, which most likely include Jax. "I doubt Harper wants to stay at your parents'. Maybe she can stay with us while Sadie is on her honeymoon?"

"I'll mention it to her." He doesn't sound confident.

"She can't spend Christmas alone. I'll ask Ethan." I unbuckle the sling from his brace to prepare for bed. "And Jax will spoil Danny rotten. He'll have every dinosaur in New York City."

He smiles. Finally. "I'm sure Harper will love that," he says, full of sarcasm.

"It's settled then." I help him remove the brace and set it on the counter.

He rolls his shoulder and stretches his arm with a grimace. "Whatever you say, princess."

I rise on my tiptoes and press my lips to his. Unable to resist, I bite and tug his piercing.

He groans, low and long. "You and this dress. You're driving me crazy." He deepens the kiss, his tongue intertwining with mine as his large hands grip my ass. His erection grinds into my hip, and I reach for his belt. The buckle clinks as it opens, and I make quick work of his zipper.

I gather my gown and fall to my knees in front of him.

"Angel." He cups my face and ghosts his thumb over my cheekbone. "You don't have to—"

"I want to." I yank his pants down to just under his ass, enough to free his length from his boxer briefs. "I want you. Please. Can I?"

He threads his fingers through my hair. "God, yes."

His thick cock is adorned with a ring above his balls, four barbells, and another ring through the head, glinting in the bathroom light. I tease the hoop at his crown, flicking back and forth with my tongue then circling it slowly until precum beads at the tip.

My gaze locked on his, I trace my tongue along his shaft, paying close attention to the piercings. At the base, I tug gently on the small hoop with my teeth, and his cock jerks.

"Fuck," he hisses and rocks his hips.

"Is that okay?"

His Adam's apple bobs. "Everything you do makes me wanna come. Keep going."

The piercings. The tattoos. I suspect Reece enjoys a bit of pain. To test my theory, I trail kisses up his thigh while stroking his length then bite into the curve of his hip.

"Aurora," he growls before fisting my hair and guiding me back to his glistening tip. "You're playing with fire. Don't tease. Suck me."

Doesn't he know I like to play with fire?

I take him into my mouth, taste his precum, and moan. His piercings are unfamiliar but thrilling. I've never done this with him, and I need it to be phenomenal. I want him to forget about tonight, about his parents.

I draw him in deeper until he hits the back of my throat and swallow around him. He thrusts forward, and I relax my jaw.

"Just like that," he praises, his voice strained. "Take every fucking inch of me."

He's not small, and I gag. He withdraws, and I dig my nails into his waist, pulling him in again. I hollow my cheeks and suck harder as he clasps my nape and fucks my mouth.

We establish a rhythm, sounds of pleasure echoing off the tile.

His body tenses, his girth thickens, and he cradles the back of my head, encouraging me to take his entire cock. "You're gonna make me come, baby. Fuck."

A fist pounds on the door. "Don't you dare finish in there. You are not having your birthday orgasm in the bathroom. I swear to God, I will break this door down."

Chapter 43
Reece

"It's not my fucking birthday!" I throw open the bathroom door, my cock—unfortunately—put away and flaccid, my chest heaving with fury and pent-up sexual frustration.

I might actually kill Jax this time.

"We're not celebrating tonight?" He raises his hands in a placating gesture, a smirk on his smug mug. He can't even pretend to be oblivious. "You didn't blow your load?"

"While you were listening through the door and running your damn mouth?" I take a menacing step toward him. "You fucking stalker."

"Reece," Ethan warns, but the word is laced with amusement.

Jackson smiles, confident I won't touch him with his boyfriend five feet away.

I don't hesitate—I lunge, grabbing his T-shirt and putting him in a headlock before he can react.

His smile widens. "Calm down, Viking. Don't hurt yourself." His body shakes with laughter. "She's given me a pity blow job a time or two. It'll be okay."

Jessica Lyn

I tighten my hold to shut him up, gripping my wrist with my other hand to prevent him from escaping.

Aurora rushes out of the bathroom. "Jackson Vaughn!" she chastises. Her gaze connects with mine. "That's not what happened. Please don't hurt him."

The truth is in her eyes, but still...he deserves some tormenting.

I dip my head. "Yeah, I know she did. I had to listen to it, remember? What were your exact words? *Do you think a blow job will make me feel better?*" I mimic in a high-pitched, whiny voice.

He feigns a dramatic gasp. "You listened to us fuck, and you call *me* the stalker?"

"It was my job," we say in unison, Jax mockingly, his tone echoing my previous taunt.

He's an instigator, and I decide I'm not giving in to his attention-seeking—or whatever the fuck he's trying to do. "Next time, I'll snap your skinny neck."

I release him with a shove, and he stumbles forward.

The grin never leaves his face. "For the record, blow jobs do improve your mood. It's science."

I drop my ass onto the end of the bed, an ache throbbing between my shoulder blades. "You know what else is science? That my dick is bigger than yours."

Motherfucker only chuckles. "You need a good fuck or fight, Viking. Let go of that bottled-up rage."

Aurora stands in front of me, her hands on her hips. "Are you hurting?"

I roll my shoulders to ease the pain. My spine snaps, crackles, and pops like a Rice Krispies cereal commercial. "Maybe," I grumble.

"Relax." She gestures to the head of the bed. "We're having a movie night."

Ethan comes up behind her, clad in boxer briefs and an

undershirt, and unzips the dress. It pools at her feet. She's wearing a black lace bra and panty set, and my cock takes notice. He gives her his shirt, and she slides it on.

Gawking at them is creepy, so I stand, strip to my boxers, and settle against the headboard. Jackson follows suit, and now all of us are in bed, watching a romantic comedy with the lights off.

No big deal—this isn't awkward as fuck, four grown adults having a sleepover.

Maybe I'm stressed, my mind too heavy, my body too tense. Maybe the asshole is right and I need to relieve some aggression—preferably on him. Maybe that's what he was trying to do by taunting me.

Jax leans forward and tosses me a package of black licorice. "What about Coach?"

I toss it back harder than necessary because—gross. "What about him? I don't look at his dick," I reply, referring to my last statement about my dick being bigger.

He whips a Slim Jim at my face, narrowly missing Aurora, who's between us, snacking on chocolate-covered peanuts. "But you look at my dick?"

I keep the Slim Jim, rip it open, and bite a piece off the top. "No. How many times do I have to tell you, I'm not interested in your dick. What the fuck is wrong with you?"

"I'm kidding, Viking. Relax. I love it when you blush." He turns his attention to the movie. "I meant, were you listening to Ethan too?"

"Nope." Lucas might have been, but he reviews so much surveillance footage that sex is nothing but background noise. "No need. We didn't think he had anything on Kyle." I take another bite of processed, spicy meat.

Jax peers around Aurora. "Then how'd you know about his family? When we were arguing in Laguna?"

The temperature in the room spikes, and sweat prickles

my hairline. "Ah..." I set the Slim Jim on the nightstand to give me time to fabricate something believable that's not a complete lie.

Three pairs of eyes drill into me, Aurora's most of all, and my brain short-circuits. I've got nothing.

When they were discussing Ethan's family, they were too far from the house for the microphones to pick up anything, especially with the wind off the ocean. It was one person who clued us in, and when I peer down at her, she reads the answer in my expression.

Her brows knit together. "Me? How?"

Might as well confess and get it over with. "You searched 'Iron Eyes' on your phone."

"Oh, shit!" Jackson's eyes widen with delight. "You accessed her phone? You may be the biggest stalker of us all."

He's amused, but Aurora clearly isn't, her jaw clenched tight enough to crack a molar.

"Can you shut up for once?" I snap at Jax. "I don't need your running commentary."

Aurora stares at me, her gaze filled with betrayal. "You saw my Google searches? Everything?"

I take back my earlier awkwardness. I'd rather be having an orgy than have her look at me with disappointment and distrust.

There goes any chance of finishing that blow job. I'm going to need a damn wheelbarrow to carry around my blue balls.

I nod. "Yes."

"You knew my favorite restaurants. My favorite foods and coffee creamer—"

"That was organic." Sort of. I may have searched her location history for repeated café visits.

"You knew I liked to read—*what* I liked to read," she

emphasizes, eyes narrowed. "You knew what books to buy me." She swallows hard. "Knew…"

When she went from reading monster romance to bodyguard romance, then reverse harems.

I'm drowning in shit here, but my lips still curl upward with shameless satisfaction. "Yes." I suspected she was attracted to me—at least physically.

Take that, Jackson.

She covers her face with her hands. "Oh my God."

"What?" Jax pops a piece of popcorn in his mouth. "You can't leave us hanging like that."

"Do you ever pay attention to what she reads?" I ask him, now the one with the smirk. "Better yet, do you even know how to read?"

"Yes, dickhead, I do." He gestures with his hand. "But go on, player. What does she read?"

"Straight up smut. Probably thinks about sex more than you do."

He shakes his head. "That's impossible."

Ethan bends forward. "Explain. Why is that embarrassing?"

"Go ahead," Aurora groans, face contorted in anguish. "You might as well tell them."

Again, I can't hide my shit-eating grin. "In New York, she started reading bodyguard romance, and then she switched to books about multiple men."

Jackson cocks his head at her. "You read sex books about multiple men?"

"They're not sex books." She rolls her eyes. "They're romance novels."

"Erotica," I correct.

"Anyhow." Jax dismisses me with a flick of his wrist. "Did you read about any foursome positions we could use tonight? Because I've been thinking about it, and I'm unsure."

She ignores his question about a foursome, probably for my benefit, finishes her snack, and snuggles beside me. She's quiet, and I start to worry.

I dip my head and kiss her temple. "Per-dón-ame." I attempt to tell her to forgive me, but I butcher the word, and it comes out fractured. I've been trying to learn Spanish on my phone, mainly because it's seductive when she speaks it, but I'm pretty terrible.

She crosses her arms over her chest. "You know every dirty little thing I read about." She frowns. "That's so embarrassing."

I turn toward her and slide my arm under the pillow to get comfortable. "Not *everything*." I tuck a strand of hair behind her ear. My fingers linger on her soft skin, and just that slight touch stirs my arousal. "Nothing to be embarrassed about. I've watched the three of you together, remember? You saw me come in my hand. If there's anyone who should be embarrassed here, it's me."

"I liked it," she whispers, her eyes no longer filled with humiliation but something else entirely. "Do you prefer to watch?"

Heat simmers between us, the movie forgotten.

Right now, I don't want my hand. I want to be inside her. But I'm not accustomed to sharing my emotions and desires, especially in front of other men. "I prefer to be with you."

Jackson peers over Aurora's shoulder, always eavesdropping. "I've only been joking, trying to loosen you up. You don't have to be in this bed. No pressure."

There's a pullout couch in the living room, but the idea is unappealing, the mere thought cold and lonely. Aside from the night we returned from the hospital, I've been sleeping better with Aurora by my side. The first night I slept with her, I slept for twelve hours.

Am I going to sleep apart from her, make her choose

every time they're home, which, now that we're moving to New York, will be more often? Doesn't seem convenient or practical. "We need a bigger bed."

His brows nearly hit his hairline. "Wait, are you serious? Are we doing this? Because I'm one hundred percent on board."

Ethan fists Jackson's hair in one hand and his throat in another, tilting his head back until their gazes meet. "I'm not sharing." The message in Ethan's piercing stare is unmistakable—Jax belongs to him, and he only shares with Aurora.

Jackson's expression softens with adoration. Aurora mirrors him with an amused smile, unconcerned her baby daddy is so possessive of her husband.

My face flushes. Call me boring, but I'm not as sexually open as they are. I have my dream girl, and she's all I desire. "That's not happening. No," I draw out, shaking my head vehemently. "Us two." I point to myself and Aurora. "You two." I gesture to them. "If you wanna share Aurora, I'll take her mouth. I have no interest in Jax. He's all yours."

After a swift kiss on the lips, Ethan releases his boyfriend —or tattoo-husband, I don't know.

Jackson reaches under the covers and adjusts himself, his eyes sparkling with mirth. "Damn, Viking. That might be the most you've said at once." He chuckles, grabs the remote from the bed, and shuts off the TV. The room goes black. The bedding rustles. "Can I kiss and touch my wife while you're with her?" His tone is gentle, lacking his usual snark.

I swallow my nerves. I've done plenty of difficult shit in my life. Having sex with the woman I love should be easy. I'm already painfully hard. "Yeah."

"Baby girl?" Ethan's voice cuts through the darkness. "Is this what you want?"

She shifts toward Jax. "I want this."

I kiss her neck while my eyes adjust to the faint moonlight seeping through the blinds, casting everything in shadow. Jackson's face hovers over Aurora's, their lips meeting in a slow, passionate kiss.

His hand disappears beneath the hem of her shirt. She releases a soft whimper and presses into my erection. I bite back a groan but can't resist grinding against her ass.

The urge to watch him touch her is overwhelming, and the command escapes my lips before I can stop it. "Take it off."

Without hesitation, he helps Aurora out of her T-shirt, returning his mouth to hers. The dim light accentuates the swell of her breasts, and I curse the black lace covering them. I manage to unhook her bra, the straps slip down her shoulders, and Jackson pulls the garment off, tossing it aside. Okay, I guess he's pretty useful.

Her tits spill free, fuller with pregnancy, and I'm mesmerized.

Jax palms her breast, teasing one peaked nipple with his thumb while drawing the other into his mouth. I can't look away as she moans and writhes, my cock throbs, leaking precum in my boxer briefs.

He releases her nipple, grazing it with his teeth, and a sinful jolt shoots straight to my dick. I'm not just tolerating this—I'm into it. Whatever boundaries I thought I had are dissolving by the second. This is who I am now—a man who watches another man touch the woman he loves and finds it unbearably arousing.

The bed dips, and Ethan moves closer, his silhouette merging with Jackson's. Their exact movements are hidden from my view, but Jax's deep, throaty groan tells me everything I need to know.

I caress the curve of her belly and slip a hand beneath the waistband of her panties, finding her wet and ready. "Fuck.

Get rid of the underwear too." I guide them down her thighs, and Jax handles the rest.

After he ditches her panties, he hooks her knee over his thigh and slides his hand between her legs. "I got her clit, Viking."

I glide my fingers through her slick pussy and ease two inside. She's soaked, her walls clenching around me as I thrust in and out. My knuckles brush his, and touching him while intimate doesn't horrify me the way I expected.

"Oh God." Her head falls back onto my shoulder, and she rocks her hips. "Reece, please."

I've never heard a sweeter sound than my name on her lips, desperate and needy. My mind empties of everything but this moment. I withdraw my fingers and yank down my boxers, freeing my erection to align myself with her entrance. Easing forward, I sink into her from behind, burying myself to the hilt. She gasps, and I groan at the perfect, tight fit.

"You feel fucking incredible." I grit my teeth to stop from pounding into her, struggling to let her adjust to my size. Every clench of her cunt around my cock draws another guttural groan from my chest.

She reaches back to grip my hip, her nails biting into my skin. "More," she whimpers. "Fuck me."

Jackson continues working her clit. I pull out to the tip then drive deeper, deliberately slow, letting her feel every ridge and piercing, every pulse of my cock. Her moans rise in pitch, and I lose myself in her, in us.

Chapter 44
Ethan

I have no idea where this foursome is leading—the entire dynamic has escalated over the last few days. I never expected Reece in our bed, never expected Jackson to *let* him in our bed.

I'm still navigating this relationship with Jax, particularly what to do with his body. I'm certain he'll get bored with me, but I love him too much to allow that to happen.

And because I love him, I want to explore every part of him. Nothing feels off-limits, not to me. I hold back because I refuse to fuck this up. I refuse to trigger anything that'll hurt him and possibly cause me to lose him.

Now, we have another dick in the mix, and I'm no longer the other slice of bread in the Aurora sandwich. I'm pressed to Jackson, which I have no problem with. It's only awkward because…I don't know if we're at the *rub your cock through my ass crack* stage yet. Or ever will be.

Jax is circling Aurora's clit while Reece fucks her. Our girl's face is contorted in ecstasy—eyes half-lidded, mouth parted. I'm stroking Jackson's length, slick with lube as he thrusts into my fist and grinds his ass on my bare cock.

Do I stop? Do I add lube to my dick for a smoother glide? We haven't been in this position. What is the proper etiquette here?

He doesn't appear to want me to stop, and I don't want to. He has a beautiful, firm ass, and the way it flexes with each thrust has my mind racing with possibilities.

I release him to grab the lube, and he groans in disappointment. I apply a generous amount to my palm and fist my length, getting it nice and slick. I return my hand to him, cupping and massaging his balls. He pushes back, and I slide my wet cock between his cheeks.

He freezes, and I hesitate, unsure if I've crossed a line.

I don't want him to be repulsed by me. I also don't want him to believe I'm disgusted by anything about him—that's far from the truth—or that I'm avoiding any part of him.

He glances over his shoulder, his pupils blown wide, his breath ragged. "Don't stop."

My heart hammers, my voice dropping an octave. "Is that okay?"

"Hell yeah." That's all he says before returning his focus to Aurora.

We're pretty terrible at communicating—verbally.

I stroke him, twisting my wrist at the tip, and slide my length along his ass. He groans, and his cock jerks in my hand.

We establish a rhythm, grinding against each other. The tight, wet friction is exquisite torture, each rock of my hips a plea for release.

Reece and Jax work Aurora's body in tandem. Her cries grow louder, her pleasure fueling my own, and I thrust harder along Jackson's ass, dangerously close to the edge.

I can't help but wonder what it'd feel like to push inside him—to have that tight heat wrapped around me. The fantasy makes my dick throb.

Would it be any different from fucking Aurora?

The mental image of Jax taking my cock is maddening. I can almost feel his ass clenching around me as I claim him inch by inch until he's gasping my name like a prayer.

Fuck—if I keep thinking this way, I won't last much longer.

A shuddering moan tears from Aurora's throat, rising in pitch until she shatters. Reece growls something I can't make out and continues rutting into her, the headboard tapping the wall.

My balls tighten, and I slow my pace, not wanting to finish yet. I curl my fingers tighter around Jackson's cock and work him with quick, deliberate strokes while sucking and biting his neck.

His hips buck, and he turns his head, seeking my mouth. I capture his lips in an urgent kiss, swallowing his moans.

While our tongues entangle, I slide my free hand from under the pillow to grip his throat. I clutch him to me and thrust against his ass. We're so close, we're practically one.

"Ethan," he whimpers into my mouth. "I want you."

"You have me, baby boy." My brain fully processes his words, and my rhythm falters as wildfire dances over my skin. "What do you mean?"

"You know what I mean." He sinks his teeth into my bottom lip. "I want you inside me."

I lose my breath and nearly come right then and there. I might have—a little bit. "Fuck..." I was not prepared for this. I've had anal sex. It's not as if I'm clueless, but what do I do with him after? Do we take a bath? Is that weird?

Plus, I'm so close. It'd be embarrassing to nut before I'm even fully inside him.

He bites my lip again. "Stop thinking. Do you like my ass?"

The way he asks—half teasing, half desperate—sends a heady rush of blood straight to my dick.

I pull back and roll my hips, letting him feel my entire length. "I do. I fucking love it. You got me dreaming about fucking you."

His lips spread into a smug smile. "Do it."

"Not tonight." I kiss him, slow and languid. "I want to take my time with you." And maybe have an actual conversation.

He makes a pouty, whiny noise and pushes into me. The head of my cock brushes his entrance, and I'm so tempted. Just a rock of my hips, that's all it'd take—and copious amounts of lube and stretching. I'm not small.

"Stop it." I tighten my grip on his shaft, working him faster as I grind my length between his cheeks with renewed urgency. The friction is heavenly—slick and hot along that perfect ass. "You'll get my cock when I choose to give it to you."

Sounds of pleasure fill the room—Aurora's breathless whimpers, Reece's deep grunts, Jackson's needy moans—and my mind clouds with lust.

"God, Jax. Come for me." My voice is nothing but a rumble. "I'm about to paint your ass with my cum."

He trembles, muscles taut with restraint. He thrusts harder, his movements becoming more desperate. "I'm close." His cock pulses in my hand. "I'm so fucking—" His words cut off, his body going rigid. He cries out, and hot spurts of cum coat my fingers, his cheeks clenching my length.

My release hits me like a freight train. Ecstasy spikes in my veins, and my vision turns white. My fist tightens around his throat, his pulse slamming wildly beneath my palm. I come in thick ropes across his ass, a hoarse, guttural growl ripping from my chest.

Chapter 45
Jackson

It's a nice day for a wedding, with clear skies and a gentle breeze moving through the trees. The weather is mild, not hot or cold, with enough clouds to keep the outdoor ceremony comfortable.

I sit with Ethan and Reece in the front row, still buzzing from last night's sexcapade. Ethan and I are in black suits with deep-red ties to complement Aurora's velvet gown. Reece is wearing distressed jeans, a T-shirt, and a leather jacket. His parents haven't shown up yet, but I'm starting to believe he dresses this way on purpose to direct his father's attention away from his sisters—or *us*.

The tattoo on his head likely served as a firm warning to the pastor: Aurora is here to stay; don't provoke me. It's smart—cuts through all the bullshit.

I jokingly asked if he was feeling emo today, and he shot me daggers with his eyes, which is an improvement over the dull gaze he'd adopted during the rehearsal dinner. The foursome must have worked. It's hard to be sad after coming and cuddling with three other people.

The string quartet plays as guests settle into white chairs

on the pristine lawn of some well-known resort. It's a small, intimate affair. No best man or maid of honor, no wedding party. Just a few dozen of their closest friends and family.

Harper rushes toward us, Danny trailing behind her like a little penguin in his tux. God, I hope we have a bunch of kids—they're so pure at heart, untainted by the world. At dinner, I rolled up my sleeves, and he colored in my tattoos, drawing a few new ones, perfectly content doing something so simple.

"Have you seen Dad?" Harper leans in to ask Reece, her voice tight with worry.

Reece's jaw muscles twitch. "Not since last night. Why?"

"He's not answering his phone. Mom either." She glances nervously at the entranceway. "The ceremony starts in fifteen minutes. Sades is freaking out. Aurora is trying to keep her calm with stories about how you two met." Harper places her hands on her hips. "You went through her phone to find all her favorite foods and books? That's a little crazy, Reece."

He pinches the bridge of his nose with a heavy sigh. "Back to Dad... Did he stay in the city?"

She shrugs. "Supposedly."

"Is he officiating?" I don't see any problem with the asshole not showing.

"No." Reece shakes his head. "Cal isn't Baptist. Dad is walking Sadie down the aisle."

Oh, fuck. "You can." I gesture to him, palm up. "You're as good, if not better."

Harper's eyes light up, her shoulders slumping with relief. "Yes, that's perfect."

He runs his fingers through his tousled fohawk. "I don't have clothes. I can't walk her down the aisle in this."

"Take mine," I offer, already loosening my uncomfortable tie.

His critical gaze rakes over my tailored suit. "Absolutely not."

I spread my arms wide, taken aback. "Why?"

He scoffs. "Your pants are so tight, I can see the full outline of your phone in your pocket."

"No, they're not!" I glance down at my fitted slacks, the fabric stretching over my muscular quads. "I have hockey thighs. You're awfully judgmental for someone with nipple piercings, you know that?"

Harper snorts and lifts Danny into her arms. "TMI, Jackson."

Reece tips his head back and groans in frustration. "There's no way I'll fit into your clothes. I'm bigger and taller than you."

All eyes shift to Ethan.

His face twists in horror. "Fuck me," he says under his breath.

While they change, I sit alone and reflect on our time in Charleston. Did we make things worse for Reece? Did we ruin his sister's wedding as he'd predicted? I hope not. If anything, we came together as a family—Sadie, Harper, and Danny included.

This trip brought our foursome closer, that's for damn sure. I didn't understand Reece before, didn't understand how much his sisters' happiness meant to him or how intolerant his parents are.

Movement in my periphery grabs my attention. I blink and blink again. Ethan approaches, and if it wasn't for his confident stride, I wouldn't recognize him.

The worn leather jacket hangs open, the silver zipper and buttons catching the sunlight. The T-shirt underneath stretches tight across his broad chest, revealing the outline of his pecs. Distressed jeans sit low on his hips, strategically frayed at the knees, and combat boots add two inches to his already imposing height.

He's straight out of a dream—a wet dream where my world is rocked by a six-foot-seven ex-con who smells like cigarettes and motor oil.

He drops into the seat beside me, and hilarity bubbles up from my chest—not at the outfit but at his disgruntled expression.

"Holy fucking shit. Can I please take a picture?"

He doesn't even glance my way. "No."

My shoulders shake with silent laughter, and tears sting my eyes. "My God, you're a panty melter."

"Jackson," he warns, a flush creeping up his neck.

"I'm sorry." I press my palm to my chest and draw a steadying breath to calm my raging hormones. It doesn't work. "The beard, the leather jacket, those jeans on your hips… I'm so hard, I could cut glass. I'd lick the bottom of your boots for you to fuck me. Smash my forehead into the bathroom mirror while you ride my ass, please."

"Can you shut up?" he grits through his teeth, but there's a hint of a smile in his eyes.

"No, you're so fucking hot. I'd take a puck to the nuts to suck your dick right now. Tie my hands behind my back and fuck my face until my throat memorizes every vein. I wanna taste you on my tongue for we—"

His fingers grip my jaw, and his lips crash into mine, killing my filthy monologue. I groan into his mouth, and he breaks the kiss, leaving me wanting more.

"Be a good boy, and maybe I'll reward you on the plane."

"Yes, Coach." I adjust myself discreetly. "Or do you prefer Sir?" My grin is absolutely feral. "Daddy? Master? Do you have a road name, perhaps?"

Reece walks his sister down the aisle, and the bride and

groom exchange their vows beneath the oak trees draped in Spanish moss. It's a picturesque Southern backdrop.

I glance at Aurora beside me. Her caramel eyes are glassy, catching the late afternoon sunlight. The Viking puts his arm around her and whispers something in her ear. She stares up at him in awe, her red lips parting. He kisses those lips—the same ones I've kissed a thousand times.

I recall him saying he'd propose one day, and, judging by the longing in her eyes, she wants that—the heartfelt proposal, the dream wedding, the handwritten vows.

Depression or sadness hit me out of fucking nowhere. She settled for me. She gave me what I wanted and needed, signing papers in a sterile office when a man who'd fulfill her fairy-tale dreams was there all along.

I didn't get down on one knee. I didn't propose. I never wrote the vows. I didn't even take her to the courthouse. I took her to Rocco's office to avoid attention.

Over and over, she set aside her dreams for me.

She deserves better. She deserves the man who will get down on one knee, who'll write his own vows and have the courage to recite them in front of a courtyard of people.

My lungs seize, and I can't draw in air, can't look away, can't stop the thought that they're meant to be, that I'm losing my soulmate. My best friend.

Darkness claws at my mind.

The scream builds in my chest.

A firm grip collars the back of my neck, anchoring me just as everything threatens to shatter.

"You're okay." Ethan's thumb traces gentle circles over my thrashing pulse.

"They're..." I swallow hard, my own eyes filling with tears. "Perfect."

"Yes," he dips his head and whispers, "and so are you, so

are we. Fate works in mysterious ways, baby. You have nothing to fear."

Am I afraid? Afraid I fucked up and it's too late? Afraid of losing the best thing to ever happen to me? Afraid of being alone with my nightmares?

You're not there anymore. You're not alone.

They're not my words, not my voice.

I stare into those stormy gray eyes. He's right. He's always right. I'm far from alone and far from my past.

"What do you need?" His breath is hot against my ear, and goosebumps erupt along my skin.

He continues to caress the curve of my neck, and the tightness in my chest eases. His touch grounds me, pulls me back from the edge. I draw a full inhale, then another.

The ceremony progresses, and the officiant binds the couple's joined hands with a red ribbon. I focus on the steady pressure of Ethan's grip, the warmth of his body beside mine. The panicked thoughts slow then quiet.

I glance at Aurora and Reece again, but this time without the crushing weight of inadequacy and dread. They're perfect, yes, but that doesn't diminish what we have, what we've been through.

Aurora turns as if she senses my gaze, offers me a soft smile, and weaves our fingers together. I give her hand a squeeze and face the man who saves me every damn time.

"We could have a wedding," I say, circling back to his earlier question about what I need. It's more what Aurora needs, but her needs are my needs too, same with Ethan, with Reece, and I know he'd appreciate a wedding. He probably fucking dreams about it, probably has his vows already written.

"You could," Ethan agrees.

My heart rate spikes, but not because I'm having another episode. "Do you want to get married?"

His dark brows pinch in a scowl. "To?"

"Me. Us." I gesture to our foursome. "*We* could have a wedding."

His eyes search mine. "You want that?"

"Yes." The snark returns to my body with a wicked grin. "I'd marry you. I'd marry the shit out of you."

His mouth quirks up at one corner. "A commitment ceremony? With the four of us?"

"I guess." I give a half-assed shrug. "What else is there? You already have the rings." I glance down at the tattoo on his finger, uncovered today. He was quite a baby when I applied ointment to it this morning—until I removed my shirt to apply ointment to mine, and he couldn't take his eyes off his teeth marks.

He nods, a slow smile creeping across his lips. "After Eli—when Aurora is ready," he corrects. "Where would we go? Somewhere private? Tropical? You could surf."

"You could relax." I picture him stretched out on white sand, playing on his phone, because he never truly relaxes.

"I'd watch you."

"And worry," I add.

His smile widens—a genuine smile that shows off those dimples. "Most definitely."

Chapter 46
Aurora

Danny fusses throughout most of the two-hour flight. Not even Jax can console or entertain him, and Harper is overwhelmed.

She apologizes, her face flushed as she rocks him back and forth. "I'm really sorry. He's tired. He doesn't do well in new situations and has never been on a plane."

I wave her off. "He's fine. I wish I could help you." Unfortunately, I can't lift Danny. The one time he was on my lap, Ethan watched him like a hawk, and when he accidentally kneed me, he scooped him up and handed him to Jackson.

After an hour of crying, Harper gives Danny a pacifier, and he lays his head on her shoulder and falls asleep.

Reece unclenches his jaw and shoots her a side-eye from the other end of the white leather couch. "Why didn't you do that sooner?"

"You're supposed to wean off the pacifier by age four." She lowers her tone to a soft whisper. "Daniel thinks it's affecting his speech."

Frustration forgotten, Reece leans closer and brushes his

hand over Danny's blond hair. "What did the pediatrician say?"

She hangs her head, her distant gaze fixed on the floor. "That he needs to see a specialist for an evaluation."

"Okay." He gives a curt nod. "Let's find one and schedule an appointment."

Jax and I share a glance, a silent understanding passing between us. They've been discussing security at the loft and the arena. If Reece is responsible for our family's safety, we need to provide him with *something*, especially if he plans to help Harper and Danny. But knowing Reece, he won't accept any financial compensation. We'll have to spoil his sister and nephew instead.

We touch down in New York around nine in the evening. I'm achy, everything hurts, and although I managed a quick nap against Ethan's shoulder, I'm exhausted.

The plane comes to a halt on the tarmac. I push myself up from the seat to prepare to deplane, and my legs become liquid beneath me. Tiny pinpricks of light explode across my field of vision, and the cabin tilts sideways.

Strong hands encircle my hips and guide me back to my seat. After a few seconds, my sight returns.

Ethan is crouched in front of me, his eyes clouded with worry, crow's feet deepening at the corners. "What's wrong? Are you okay?"

I realize I'm clutching the hard curve of his biceps and force myself to relax my grip. "I think I stood up too fast." The words scrape past my dry throat, my lungs working overtime, as if I'd sprinted up a flight of stairs. I let my head fall back onto the headrest and squeeze my eyes shut to stave off the lightheadedness.

"What else, angel? Are you dizzy? Weak? In pain?" Reece's voice cuts in, sharp with concern.

"Yes to all the above. Everything hurts." A self-deprecating laugh escapes me. "I'm pregnant and bone-tired." I've been in heels the past few days, my feet are swollen, and sleeping with three large men, even in a king-sized bed, is not exactly comfortable.

Ethan traces his thumb over my cheekbone. "Let's get you home, baby girl. I'll draw you a bath. It's been a long week—"

"It's been a long fucking month," Jax snarls, panic and guilt fueling his anger. "She needs to rest. She's been through too much."

"She will. She'll be locked in the loft."

Ethan's words are flippant, but I doubt they're a lie.

It's Rocco who picks us up. It's snowing and slippery, and Jax and Ethan lead me down the stairs as if I'm made of glass and might shatter at any moment.

Reece is between me and Harper, who's struggling to carry Danny and his canvas tote stuffed with toy dinosaurs, art supplies, and snacks. She didn't want to disturb him by passing him off to one of the guys.

But in only a thin jacket and a hoodie, the cold shocks him awake. He gasps, drops his pacifier, and then belts out a scream, flopping sideways. Rocco's cheerful demeanor becomes murderous. I've never seen him so much as irritated before now. He rushes up the stairs just as Jackson, Ethan, and I hit the bottom, and Reece turns to help his sister.

"Give him to me." Rocco lifts the crying child into his arms with ease then snatches the bag from Harper and tosses it over his other shoulder. "Do you have another soother?"

Harper stares wide-eyed at Ethan's uncle before catching herself and nodding. She digs in a pocket of the tote and hands Danny—who appears just as stunned by Rocco's salt-and-pepper beard—the pacifier.

Reece takes Harper's elbow to steady her on the wet stairs, and Rocco glares at the touch as if personally offended.

"She's my sister," the Viking grumbles, "and she's married."

Rocco glances between the two, and his expression softens. You can't mistake the resemblance. They share the same striking blue eyes and dirty-blond hair, though Harper's features are less angular than Reece's, her eyes more almond-shaped. She's also a foot shorter.

"Let's get in the car." Ethan's hand presses firmly on the small of my back. "Aurora is freezing."

"I'm fine," I insist, wanting to watch the show, but my teeth are chattering and my legs are wobbly.

We make our way to the waiting SUV, the snow falling gently and catching on my eyelashes. Rocco has somehow calmed Danny completely, the boy fascinated with the man's beard, tiny fingers reaching out to touch it with cautious wonder.

We all pile in. The vehicle is warm, and I sink into the leather.

Jackson slides in next to me and pulls me close. "I'll make you something to eat once we get to the loft."

Ethan's uncle secures Danny in a Spider-Man car seat, Harper beside him. "I hope this is okay," he says to her. "The twins picked it out. They have a nephew the same age." He fastens the buckle then tests the straps by tugging on them. "We'll need to get you both some proper winter clothes if you're staying in New York."

"I didn't know it'd be this cold," she explains, fingers fidgeting in her lap. "I've never been to New York."

"We're having a colder Christmas than normal." Rocco flashes her a reassuring smile. "We'll get you taken care of. No worries."

If they *take care* of Harper the way they've *taken care* of us, she's about to have an entirely different life.

I glance at Reece. His face might appear stoic, but the

slight narrowing of his gaze as he watches the middle Rossi brother tells me everything I need to know. The Viking isn't pleased.

The SUV pulls away from the tarmac, and my eyelids grow heavy, the vehicle's gentle motion lulling me toward sleep.

"Don't fall asleep yet." Jackson's green eyes brighten, but there's still a hint of worry etched between his brows. "You'll wanna be fully awake to see the loft."

Chapter 47
Ethan

During a recent conversation with Rocco, he said to me, "Let's not lose a thousand to save one."

He was taking aim at my obsession with Jackson, and I knew right then that Rocco had never been in love. The business was his mistress.

"Is that what you told my father?" I kept my voice level, but the question was a knife I wouldn't hesitate to twist if necessary.

The phone line went silent.

"Your father's situation was different," he finally answered. "He had an empire to protect, a family depending on him. It wasn't a straightforward decision."

Since Aurora came into my life, I've often wondered what I might've done in my father's shoes. I can't claim to understand the bond between brothers, but I know I would've emptied every bank account and fired every bullet before surrendering. I used to judge my father for taking six lives, but now? Six seems merciful. Hell, the twins racked up a higher body count at our beach house alone.

Dimitri raised his boys differently. There's a new generation of Rossi men, and we're even more ruthless.

"I hear you," I told Rocco, "but understand this—nothing comes before them. *Nothing.* If this empire crumbles tomorrow, they'll still stand by me. If I said we needed to disappear, they would—no questions asked. That loyalty goes both ways. If they're not happy, I'm not happy. If they're not safe, *no one* is safe. I'll burn this fucking world to the ground. Don't test me."

Now, I watch Rocco's calculating eyes follow Harper across the parking garage, his expression tense with the same protective instincts I recognize all too well.

I clasp his shoulder, unable to hide my smirk. "Welcome to the club. Try not to lose a thousand to save one."

Chapter 48
Aurora

"Jackson," I choke out, tears transforming the Christmas lights before me into glittering stars.

The loft has been remodeled beyond recognition. Where the old galley kitchen once stood now sits a security room to the left, a mudroom to the right. Past the entrance, the space opens into a chef's kitchen that belongs in a magazine—white, glass-fronted cabinets, a sprawling island with nestled stools, and marble countertops threaded with silver. Pendants and chandeliers hang from the ceiling.

A candy-cane arch adorned with fairy lights and actual candy canes—which I know was all Jackson—separates the open kitchen and living room. Thousands of twinkling lights are draped over the exposed wooden beams and brick archways, casting a golden glow that reflects off the hardwood floors and gleaming surfaces. There's even a lit stone fireplace.

The centerpiece of it all is the massive Christmas tree standing before the panoramic window, decorated with pink bows and ornaments, surrounded by Jax's beloved collection of mismatched furniture. Outside, fat snowflakes drift downward, turning our world into a perfect snowglobe.

"It wasn't me, babe." Jackson flashes that crooked grin I love. "This was all Ethan and Rocco. I arranged the Christmas decorations and gifts." He lowers his voice to a feigned whisper. "Coach spent all our money on a hockey team—I'll build you a house once the other one sells."

"No, I did not!" Ethan yells from the doorway.

I don't even care about a house. My gaze finds his, and I stare at him, dumbfounded. "You did this?" I glance around again, unable to believe what I'm seeing.

His face flushes from his cheeks to the tips of his ears. "Rocco supervised. He had a crew working day and night to finish before Christmas." Ethan steps closer and hugs me from behind, his hand cupping my belly protectively. "All I did was give them your Pinterest and approve or deny."

I relax into his chest, exhausted and overwhelmed but so damn happy. "I think I saved this exact kitchen."

"You did, but Jackson upgraded the appliances. He had to have a specific gas stove. Reece requested a surveillance room, Lucas needed some fiber-optic network and server, the twins couldn't live without a gym, and I'm pretty sure Dante snuck in an armory." He chuckles. "It was a combined effort."

Weaving my fingers through his, I tighten his arms around me. "And what did you require?"

"You, Jax, and our baby—Reece keeping everyone safe. That's it."

Danny's tiny feet drum on the hardwood, and he bolts past us, heading for the tree. The Viking is right behind him, scooping him up and spinning him in a circle. The room fills with the child's squeals, bright as the Christmas lights.

"Reece!" Harper chides, though amusement dances in her tone. "Don't get him sick."

"King," Danny insists, his small palm smacking his uncle's chest.

"You got it, buddy." Reece nods then gestures toward me. "What's her name?"

"Roar-a," the boy says with a growl.

Reece's eyes crinkle at the corners. "Good job. And who's the big guy behind her?"

Danny's voice drops to an awestruck whisper, "Baaaatmaaaan." He stretches each syllable.

Everyone bursts into laughter, Harper included, her eyes welling with tears.

Ethan's chest rumbles against my back. "Batman, huh? Hopefully I can live up to the hype."

The familiar sound of the elevator whirs to life, and the floor vibrates beneath our feet. I guess one thing hasn't changed.

The twins stride in, their arms full of wrapped packages.

"Honey, we're home!" Desi singsongs, his dark hair dusted with snowflakes. "And we come bearing gifts, because *someone* insisted we go shopping at nine p.m.…on a Saturday…on Christmas Eve Eve." He shoots Ethan a blank look. "Apparently, we've been reassigned?"

Ethan's arms loosen and drop to his sides. "No you fucking haven't. Tell Rocco to get his own security detail."

"Good luck with that," Dante comments on his way to the tree.

"We can handle both," Lucas calls out from the mudroom. Unlike the twins, who trample in with their boots on, he always removes his. "We all live in the same building. How much trouble can two girls be?"

When he enters, I cringe. His left eye is a horror show—the white completely consumed by red, the lid puffed and deep purple. I believe the doctor said he had a tear in his retina. Nasty bruises cover his face: sickly yellow-green edge his marred cheekbones while his jawline bears imprints of blue and black.

"Oh my God," Harper breathes. "What happened?"

He takes off his beanie, unleashing a mass of unruly brown hair. "Work. It's all good. I'm fine." His voice is casual, but his shoulders are tense.

Reece sets his nephew on his feet and wraps his partner in a gentle one-arm hug. "Are you sure? You don't look fine."

Lucas nods. "We'll catch up later." Then, wincing in obvious pain, he bends down to fist-bump Danny.

Jackson hangs his head and turns toward the kitchen, Ethan following with a tight expression. It'll be difficult for Jax to see Lucas, but as his injuries heal, so will Jackson's guilt. We'll all heal together in our new life.

"God, I'm starving," I announce and pull out a stool.

Jax opens the enormous stainless-steel fridge and assembles ingredients with practiced efficiency—eggs, cheese, bacon, vegetables, and fruits—setting them on the counter. He clears his throat. "Who wants an omelet?"

"You cooking?" Dante asks in jest.

Desi places gifts under the Christmas tree. "Then hell yeah. We're in."

Reece introduces his sister and Danny to the twins, although by the sounds of it, Rocco has filled them in. Then, everyone gathers around the island, chatting excitedly about everything from Christmas to donuts to Jax joining the Stars.

My heart swells as I take it all in, this beautiful patchwork family of ours.

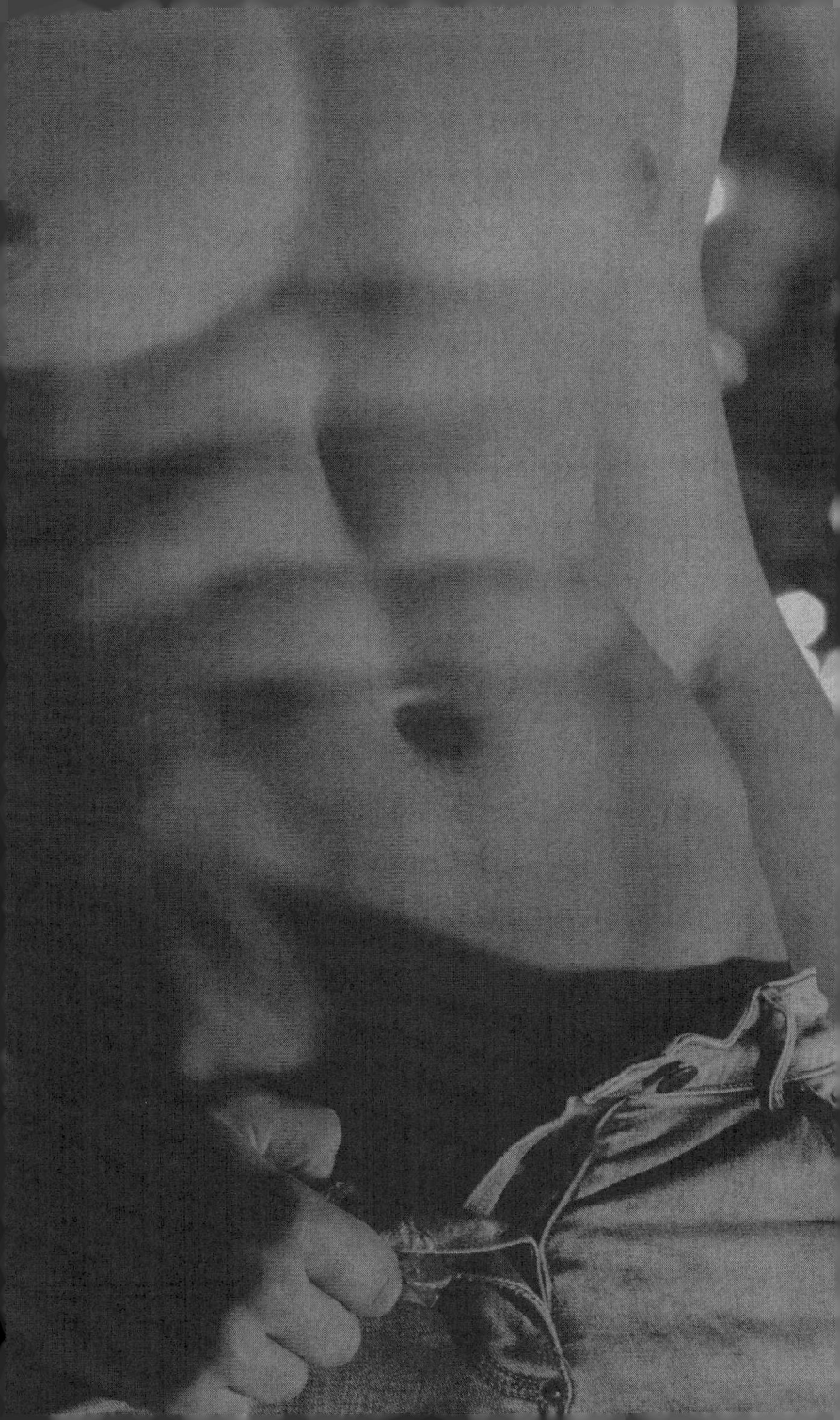

Chapter 49
Jackson

The scalding water scorches my skin, but no matter how hot I crank the lever, it doesn't burn away the guilt or distract me from the memories.

Aurora showered and fell asleep after dinner, exhausted from the long day, week, month. Reece is getting his sister and Danny settled into the guest suite. While Ethan went to the twins' apartment, likely to discuss mafia shit he didn't wish Harper to overhear, I stayed behind, avoiding Lucas like a fucking coward.

I want to support him, comfort him, but when I look at him, I relive my own trauma. The pain is visceral—a sharp blade slicing my skin, a kick in the ribs, hands where they don't belong... The flashbacks only last seconds, but they're torture.

And they keep coming.

My stomach twists, bile rises in my throat, and my chest constricts until I struggle to breathe. Tears prickle my eyes, and I press my forehead to the glass, my arms braced above me.

Will this horror ever end? We're safe in New York, but

the nightmare still follows me.

The shower door slams, but it barely registers through the mental fog. I'm too numb to react, too spaced out.

"Jesus Christ, Jax." Ethan reaches past me and twists the knob, cooling the punishing spray. "You're hurting yourself."

"Mm." I emit a sound that's half acknowledgment, half apathy, but I don't turn around. I can't. I've lost every bit of energy.

Soft lips press to the back of my neck. "I've got you." His tone is gentle but speaks volumes.

Whatever I need, he always provides. He'll drag me out of this darkness by my hair if he has to.

Kisses trail down my spine, each one a spark of life that ignites my soul and loosens the fist gripping my heart. He grabs the bodywash from the recessed shelf, slicks his hands, and massages my shoulders. The firm pressure of his fingers eases my tense muscles, and I release a shaky sigh.

"That's it, baby." He digs his thumbs into my tight knots. "Come back to me."

I don't hesitate. I lean into him, craving our connection. He holds me close, his arms around me, the water cascading over us.

His touch, coupled with the emotional drain, cracks something open within me. "Lucas—" My heart races, and a wave of dizziness washes over me.

Ethan traces the defined lines of my abs. "Lucas is well taken care of, I promise. He has the twins and Reece. He's focused on vengeance. He wants to fight these fuckers in his own way. He'll be okay. I'll make sure of it."

"Thank you." I inhale deeply and force myself to let it out. "I keep seeing it." My body trembles, and I take another breath of steamy air. "Every time I look at him, I see myself. I see that cell…"

Ethan's hands pause their exploration of my stomach but don't abandon me. "Do you want me to stop?"

"No." I shake my head. "I need you."

Even now, with my soul in tatters, I crave him—maybe even more so—and I know he craves me too. His arousal is pressed to my ass.

He resumes his caress. "What do you need?"

I swallow hard, my throat tight, and push back against him. "Love me."

He stills. "I do love you. I love you so much, it's insane."

"Show me." I spell it out for him. "Fuck me."

He grips my hips to stop me from grinding on him. "I want you to want me, not use me as a distraction."

I turn to him and encircle my arms around his neck. His wet hair is the color of midnight, and I can't resist burying my fingers in his thick waves. "I want you every fucking day —you know that." How could he not? I'm annoyingly clingy and begging for it. "I've wanted you since the first time the three of us slept together. I needed you long before then. You're the reason I'm breathing, the reason I have Aurora. You're far from a distraction." My eyes well up again. "You're the pulse in my chest, and not a day will go by that I don't need you. If that's the problem—"

"It's not." His lips find mine, desperate and hungry. "I was just checking," he mumbles between kisses. "I'll always give you what you need."

He deepens the kiss, and I melt into him. His hands slide down my back, cup my ass, and pull me closer until our erections brush.

I reach between us and fist his length. "Then give me this." I stroke him slowly. "Please. Take the edge off. Make me feel good." *Make me forget.*

His eyes darken, as if he can read my thoughts. He grabs my chin and backs me against the shower wall. "I want you to remember one thing." His fingertips dig into my jaw. "You're mine. Stop drifting off to places I can't follow. Every time you do, I want you to think about how pissed I'd be. Control what's going on up here." He taps my temple. "Flip the script. Picture me murdering every motherfucker who touches you." He leans in, holding my gaze, speaking directly to my memories. "No man is allowed to touch you but me." He kisses my lips gently. "Now turn around."

I obey, my heart pounding a frantic rhythm, and rest my forearms on the glass wall.

"Good boy."

Behind me, he flicks open the cap of the body oil. His praise, combined with anticipation, sends a shiver down my spine, and I shudder despite the heat.

His slick fingers trace the cleft of my ass. "Spread your legs wider."

My feet move at his command. He circles my entrance, and my breath hitches. He slides a finger inside me, and ecstasy shoots straight to my dick.

I rock my hips and beg for more. "Please, Ethan."

"So responsive." He adds a second finger while sinking his teeth into the curve of my neck.

The bite. The stretch. Adrenaline surges through my veins, and I groan, "More."

"I love how desperate you are for me."

His words carry a dark, satisfied smile, and my chest swells. All I truly want is to satisfy him—wholly—until he's as obsessed as I am.

He crooks his fingers, finding a spot that has me seeing stars.

My eyes roll back, and my forehead falls to the glass. "Fuck, right there."

"You're so fucking beautiful. Every part of you." He works

his fingers deeper, stretching me open while his free hand grips my hip to hold me steady.

The sensation borders between pleasure and pain, and I lose myself completely. "Please," I whimper, my cock throbbing and leaking between my legs. "I need you inside me."

***

Ethan

Steam curls around us, creating our own world where nothing exists but the two of us.

"You ready for me?" My voice is rough with need, and I swallow hard.

"Yes," he breathes.

I remove my fingers, slick my cock with more oil, then line up at his entrance. "Look at me."

He twists to meet my gaze over his shoulder, and the longing in his eyes has desire swooping low in my stomach, the air catching in my lungs.

"I want to see you." I thrust forward. "Don't look away."

His pupils dilate, and his lips part on a sharp gasp. I breach that tight ring of muscle and pause, letting him adjust. His ass pulses around me, and I hiss, tensing my thighs to keep from plunging into him.

"Don't stop," he whimpers, brows pinched. "Please don't stop."

He pushes back, I slide in another inch, and we both groan. His eyelids flutter, but he doesn't break eye contact. It's intense, the connection between us intoxicating, transcending the physical.

"I love you." The words slip out before I can stop them. "I love everything about you."

"Love you too," he whispers, breath ragged. "I love being yours."

I love being yours. Fuck, if that doesn't tear me apart.

He's mine. Mine to care for and love. Mine to protect and adore. All mine.

I widen my stance and weave our fingers together above his head. "Go ahead." I place a kiss below his ear. "You're in control. Take my cock."

He rocks his hips and draws me deeper. He trembles, muscles taut, and bites his bottom lip.

"That's it, baby." I squeeze his hands, digging my fingertips into his palms to anchor him to me. "You can take me. Show me how much you want my cock."

He sinks back until I'm fully seated inside him, his ass flush against me.

"God, Jax." My chest heaves, and I fight to remain still. "Your ass feels so fucking good."

Unable to resist, I roll my hips, and a choked moan escapes his throat.

"Please, Ethan."

His tight heat clenches, and my knees nearly buckle.

"Fuck me," he begs. "Give it to me."

Releasing one of his hands to grip his hip, I withdraw until only the tip remains then punch forward slowly, making sure he feels every inch.

"Holy fucking shit," he groans, his glazed eyes locked on mine, pleasure contorting his features. "You're huge."

I can't hide my smug smile. "Is it okay? Are you okay?"

He mirrors my grin. "Fuck, yeah. Give me that big cock, Coach."

"You're ridiculous."

I thrust again, watching his face for any sign of discomfort. There's none—just pure, unadulterated ecstasy.

"Harder." He arches his back, all cut muscle and smooth

skin. "You won't break me, Ethan. I can handle you." He grinds against me, taking me deeper. "I want all of you. Every dirty part. Give it to me. Use me. Fuck me."

His admission unleashes something primal within me, and I drive into him, wanting to imprint myself on his soul.

We establish a rhythm. His body jolts with each slap of my hips, his hand clutching mine. He turns his head, seeking my mouth. My lips find his in a rough, messy kiss, our tongues tangling as we swallow each other's desperate moans.

I angle my hips, searching for that spot that will make him—

"Fuck—right there." His forehead falls to the glass.

I hammer into him relentlessly, hitting his prostate with each stroke—or at least, I think I am. His moans echo off the tiles, more needy with each thrust.

His ass becomes a vise grip, and I reach around to palm his erection, finding him slick and leaking at the tip.

"You gonna come for me?" I alternate between massaging his balls and stroking him.

His free hand reaches back to thread through my hair. "Y-yes."

I nip at his neck. "Tell me where you want my cum, baby boy."

"Inside me."

His rushed answer pushes me closer to the edge, and my balls hug my shaft.

We become feral for one another. He fists my hair, and I stroke him hard and fast. We meet each other thrust for punishing thrust, our bodies colliding.

"I'm going to fill your ass with my cum, Jax." I increase my pace, pounding into him, my control slipping. "You take me so fucking well."

He clenches my length and lets out a strangled cry. His

dick jerks, and his hot release coats my fingers. His ass pulses around me as if he's milking the cum straight from my balls, and my entire body twitches.

I bury myself deep, emptying with a guttural growl, my cock jolting with aftershocks.

"Jax... God..." My forehead drops between his shoulder blades, and I gasp for air. "My legs are numb. I can't move."

He laughs, fucking laughs. "That was awesome," he pants. "I can't wait to do it again—like tomorrow."

I'm reluctant to pull out, and my spent cock softens inside him. "No."

"Why? I'll fuck Aurora while you fuck me...and Reece can fuck her too. It's perfect."

Jesus Christ, he's going to be the death of me. "Save that for the destination wedding you're planning."

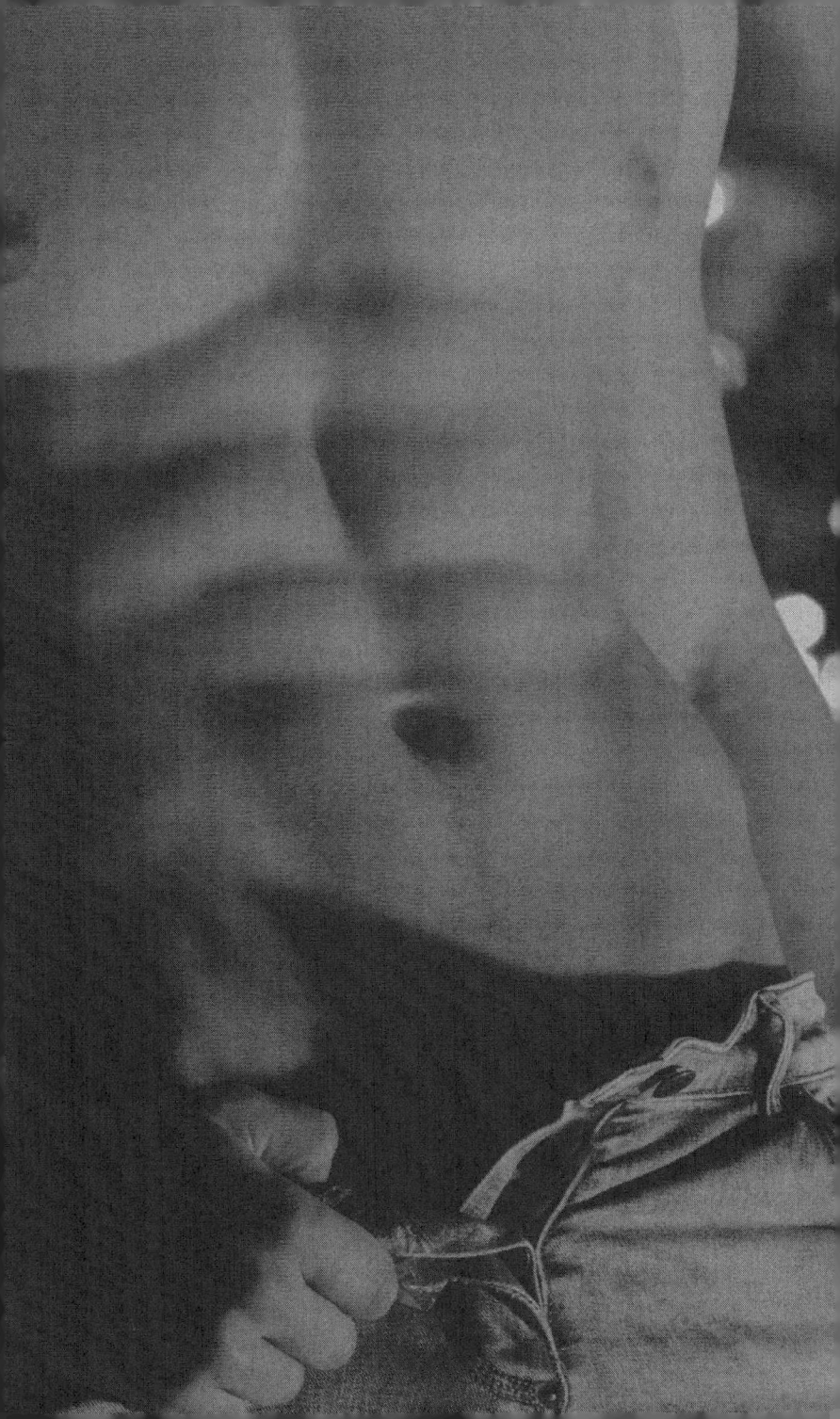

Chapter 50
Jackson

The sizzle of bacon hitting the hot griddle is the most satisfying sound at seven in the morning. Well, the second most satisfying. Aurora's sleepy 'I love yous' as I slipped out of bed hold first place. After her dizzy spell yesterday, I'm committed to ensuring she receives proper rest and nutrition. I'm home—*we're* home. I can finally make her my priority.

Danny's eyes go wide. "Ba-con. Hot," he says around his pacifier. His blond hair sticks up in all directions, and he's clutching his dinosaur plushie as if it might escape.

I woke this morning to the sounds of whispers and tiny feet running across the loft, Reece's side of the bed empty. I couldn't help but smile. This is our future—all of us together, the pitter-patter of little feet—and it's absolutely beautiful.

"Yup. That's why you have to stay on the other side of the island. But..." I hand Danny a wooden spoon, "you get to stir the pancake batter. Not too many chocolate chips this time, okay?"

Reece leans against the counter, his good arm stretched

over the back of Danny's chair protectively. "Why don't you give me the binky and dinosaur? I'll put them in your bed."

"With Mama?"

"With Mama," the Viking agrees. "We'll let her sleep, since you got her up so early." He ruffles the boy's hair.

Danny hands the pacifier and stuffed animal to his uncle then gets to his knees on the stool. He stirs the batter, adding handfuls of chocolate chips with the intensity of a scientist conducting an experiment, his tongue poking out slightly.

"Be right back. Don't move." Reece rushes down the hall toward the guest suite.

I flip the bacon and watch Danny closely. At the sound of familiar footsteps, I glance up.

Strong arms wrap around me from behind. "Mornin', baby." Ethan presses his lips to the side of my neck. "Feeling alright?"

He's asked me the same question only a million times since we showered last night, and he gently washed every inch of my body.

"Morning. Coffee's ready." I lean back into his touch, turning my head for a quick kiss. "I'm perfect. You sleep okay?"

"Like a rock. Didn't even hear you sneak out." He gives me another kiss just below my ear then reaches around to steal a piece of bacon before heading for the coffeemaker. "Mm, this is good. You'd better be careful. I might start expecting breakfast every morning."

I scoff. "You're spoiled, you know that?"

He grabs a mug and sets it on the counter. "One hundred percent, and I love each and every minute of it."

Reece returns and takes a seat next to Danny. "Harper will be out soon. I told her to take her time." He grabs a strip of crispy bacon and shoves it in his mouth.

"You're both animals." I shake my head. "Get a plate. Don't be a bad influence."

Ethan hands out plates, and I serve them each a few slices, pushing the rest aside to start on pancakes and eggs. Reece blows on a piece to cool it down for his nephew, and Danny gobbles it up before reaching for another.

The floor vibrates with the rumble of the elevator—no security system necessary to signal visitors. Plus, there's a keypad inside to operate the lift.

"That'll be the twins." I pile more bacon onto the growing stack and take a deep breath, bracing myself for Lucas. I refuse to allow my past trauma to ruin our family's first Christmas Eve. It's ruined enough of my life.

Desi and Dante stroll in with two pink boxes, followed by Rocco, who's struggling to carry the largest Lego set I've ever seen, along with another dinosaur plushie. I may need to build a house sooner than I thought. Our baby will be here in a few months, and I'm sure we'll all be spoiling him, too.

Danny's eyes go round as saucers, the wooden spoon forgotten in the batter. "Legos!" he shrieks and nearly topples off his stool.

Reece catches him with one arm before he face-plants on the floor. "Easy, little man."

Danny races to Rocco, jumping up and down with excitement. "For me?"

"For you. Would you like to put it together?"

"Uh-huh." He nods vigorously. "Now?"

"Of course." Rocco lays the Lego box down on the coffee table and takes a seat on the couch. "Is that okay with your mom?" He glances around for Harper.

"Jesus Christ." Dante slides in next to the Viking and plucks a piece of bacon off the stack. "He's so fucking whipped. Had us up at six a.m. to find that damn T-Rex set."

"Hey, killer." Reece elbows him in the ribs. "Where's my partner? Still in bed?"

"You know it," he mumbles with a mouthful of food. "He'll be up after his third shot of espresso. He was awake all night *researching*," he says with air quotes.

"Morning, sunshine. Did you miss me?" Desi sets the donut boxes on the counter and gives me a one-armed hug around the neck. "We came with sustenance, but I see you got started without us."

"Watch it," Ethan snarls from his spot at the breakfast table, where he sips his coffee. "Blood only goes so far. Don't be touching what's mine."

I flash him a cheesy grin while pouring the pancake batter.

Desi raises his hands in a placating gesture. "Jackson is not my type; I'm not into hot jocks."

Dante snorts. "You fooled around with half our high school football team."

"I did not! It was only…" His twin stares at the ceiling as he counts on his fingers. "Only three people. The quarterback doesn't count; he was barely an athlete. Anyway, I have a fiancé now, so—"

"He is not your fiancé." Reece cocks his head in exasperation. "You're as bad as Jax, who claims to be married."

Before Desi or I can argue, footsteps pad down the hall, and Aurora enters the kitchen, wearing adorable pink and green plaid pajamas. Her dark hair is tousled from sleep, her eyes still heavy-lidded.

Harper follows her, also dressed in pajamas. She takes one glance at Rocco and our company and turns back to the bedrooms.

Aurora makes a beeline for me and wraps her arms around my waist. "Mmm, pancakes." She buries her face in my chest. "My hero."

"And here, I was going to make you hot chocolate," Reece grumbles, but jumps up to fill the kettle anyhow.

I kiss the top of her head, inhaling her jasmine and vanilla scent. "Good morning, my beautiful wife," I add for the Viking's benefit.

The sweet domesticity of this moment is something I've only dreamed of, something I never believed would happen. Yet, here I am, making breakfast in our new home for nine other people, surrounded by Christmas lights and love.

Before I finish the eggs, the elevator clanks, and Lucas appears in the doorway. He raises his hand in an awkward wave. "Morning, everyone." His gaze meets mine briefly before skittering away.

My throat tightens with emotion, and I swallow it down. "Hey. Breakfast is almost ready." I crack an egg on the griddle, grateful for something to focus on. "Coffee's fresh."

"Thanks." He scans the room. "Oh shit! Is that Legos?" He races toward the living room despite his injuries.

With a grin, I turn my attention to the eggs, carefully flipping them while trying to keep the yolks intact. Aurora is still pressed against me, her baby bump nudging my side when she reaches for a strip of bacon.

"Ah!" I playfully swat her hand away. "Sit down. I'm serving you."

She swats me right back. "The baby is hungry, and he wants bacon."

Chapter 51
Aurora

"You did this all for me?" I run my hand across the luxurious fabrics—silks, cottons, embroidery, cashmere, wool, and my favorite: pink tulle. "Where did you even find these?"

The studio is bathed in natural light from the panoramic windows. A large workstation sits in the center, left over from the original factory and stretching nearly the length of the room. Mannequins of various sizes—including one with a baby bump—take up a corner. Vintage gold floor mirrors are arranged along one wall, an adjustable drafting table and a professional sewing machine on the opposite side. It's everything I ever wanted and more. I can picture myself in here making all sorts of dresses. What I'll do with them, I have no idea.

Ethan's proud smile grows wider, revealing those irresistible dimples. "Rocco's tailor hooked us up with a fabric supplier."

"This is incredible. Thank you." I glance around once more, taking it all in. "I don't even know—"

Before I can finish, he steps closer. His large hands grip

my hips and, in one fluid motion, he lifts me and sets me on the edge of the workstation.

He settles between my legs, his palms braced on either side of me, caging me in. "I'd do anything for you." His eyes lock with mine. "Anything."

The heat of his body radiates against my thighs, and the intensity of the moment hangs heavy in the air.

He clears his throat. "The last time we were in New York, I got ahead of myself and made you promises I wasn't ready to keep." A flush creeps up his neck onto his cheeks. "This is me proving I've changed, proving I'm prepared to handle whatever comes at us."

My eyes well up—damn pregnancy hormones—and I cup his face in my hands. "I never doubted you."

"Shh. I'm not finished." He places a soft kiss on my lips. "You have your studio, your bodyguard, and all my love and attention. I'll move Gram here, keep Jax healthy and happy, and ensure our family is safe. That's my vow to you."

"It's more than I ever dreamed of." I trace the trimmed beard along his jawline and return his kiss. "I love you."

"I love you." His hand moves to my belly, caressing our baby. "Thank you for putting up with my moods and temper."

I offer him a gentle smile. "I've seen worse."

His brows pinch slightly. "I know you have, but I don't want that to be us."

I glide my fingers up the back of his neck into his thick hair. "What *do* you want, Blackwood?"

This is Ethan. Everything is a power dynamic. If he's making promises, he expects something in exchange, and I know precisely what it is. He wants me locked in this loft.

"Your submission." He leans in closer, his breath hot against my neck. "Complete and total. In and out of the bedroom."

Despite knowing where this was leading, my pulse still races, and my words come out breathless. "You already have that."

"Do I?" he asks between kisses along my throat. "Did I give you permission to contact Bennett? Did you even run it by me? What about when Lucas went missing? How long did you wait before calling me? What about your plans with Emily?"

"You haven't let that go?" I shift on the workstation, my body responding to his proximity and touch. "You were busy with Jax, which I'm grateful for. Did you do all this for my submission?"

"No." His thumb brushes across my bottom lip. "I did this to keep you safe. Jackson too. I have you both right where I want you."

I don't disagree, but I at least have to give him some sass. "Will Jax be locked in this loft?"

"Jax is locked into a contract with my team, which I own. Everywhere he goes will be under my control. Do you dislike this loft?"

"No." I shake my head, my brows furrowed. "I love it."

"Okay then. If there's anything you need, all you have to do is ask."

He pushes his thumb into my mouth, and my lips automatically close around it.

"Now, no more talking."

His voice deepens to that dominating tone, setting off butterflies in my stomach.

"Rule one." His free hand slides up my thigh and under the hem of my sleep shorts. "You don't make decisions affecting your safety without consulting me. I don't care if I'm busy. I don't care if the arena is on fire. If something happens, I wanna be the first to find out."

Happily willing to play his game, I draw my tongue over the pad of his thumb and nod.

"Rule two." He traces the edge of my panties. "I need to know your whereabouts at all times. You don't leave this loft without my knowledge, not even to go downstairs. Understood?"

I agree, but I can't help but wonder what he'll do if I disobey. Give me another spanking? Torture me with rough sex?

"Rule three." He slips under the gusset of my lace thong, teases my slit, and slides two fingers inside me. "You don't go anywhere unless Reece and the twins are with you."

I whimper my answer and rock my hips. He curls his fingers, hitting that perfect spot, and circles my clit with his thumb. My thighs twitch as heat pools low in my belly, and I feel myself grow wetter.

"Rule four. You forget about the case and LA. You focus on caring for yourself and the baby. You're mine. I take care of what's mine. If you and my son aren't spoiled, I'm doing something wrong."

He quickens his pace. The sound of him working my sex is obscene. I must be soaking his hand, but in this moment, I can't muster an ounce of embarrassment. Pleasure overrides all else. I flex my hips and bite down on his thumb.

"One more rule, and then you can come." His heated gaze burns into mine. "At first, I'll be at the arena a lot. When I need you, you drop everything to see me, and when you need me, I'll do the same. When possible, you travel with me. Understood?"

I nod. I'd do it anyway.

"Good girl." He withdraws his fingers and his thumb. "Lie back for me."

I don't hesitate, wanting nothing more than his reward. He grabs the waistband of my shorts and underwear and tears them off. The cool air hits my bare, slick core, and I shiver.

He leans forward and kisses my inner knee. "Wider. Let me see what's mine."

I part my legs, my heels on the edge of the surface.

He pushes two fingers inside me, watching as he slides them in and out. "I'm so tempted to fuck you, but I want to taste this pretty pussy. It's been too long."

He grips my thighs, spreads me open, and devours me, sucking and licking. He flicks my clit with the tip of his tongue, and my hips buck. His beard scratches my sensitive skin, adding another layer of friction, and I thread my fingers through his hair to hold him in place.

"Ethan." My moan echoes off the studio walls. "Please. I'm so close."

He glances up, lips glistening, his gray eyes dark with desire. "Quiet. I don't want to share you right now. If Jax hears that siren call, he'll be kicking the door in."

He dips his head and sucks my clit between his teeth, and my back arches. He curls his fingers, and stars explode behind my eyelids. I bite down hard on my bottom lip to stifle my cries. My body tenses, waves of pleasure crashing through me. I gasp for air, the climax ripping through me with such force, my shoulders rack with shudders.

He doesn't let up. He sucks and licks and fingerfucks me, prolonging my orgasm until I'm boneless and begging him to stop.

"That's my good girl." He wipes his mouth with the back of his hand, his eyes never leaving mine. "So fucking beautiful when you come for me."

Epilogue
Jackson

I work harder, play faster. I don't allow myself to feel disappointment. Not about saying goodbye to my teammates and friends. Not about leaving the sun and the ocean. I don't even give Carmichael shit when he's a grumbling dick —because Ethan sacrificed his dreams for our family.

They retired his jersey—number forty-nine—at the arena with a packed house and a cheering crowd. I broke down, collapsing to one knee on the ice and bawling my eyes out, thinking about all he gave up. For me. For us. He will forever be the greatest man I know, and I'll do anything to make him proud.

It's been almost two months since I joined the Stars, and we've only lost one game. We clinched a playoff spot. I doubt a win is in the cards this season, but I'll make it happen in the coming years. Someday, Ethan and I will hold that trophy up together.

Reece, Lucas, and the twins continue to investigate my father's circle of sick fucks. I liquidated all of Kyle's investments and gave the money to a secret shelter for trafficking victims, a place the Viking was familiar with.

Jessica Lyn

Our life is beautiful, more than I ever imagined. I'm home more, travel less. I hold Ethan's hand as we stroll down the sidewalk and pop into his office whenever I wish. No shame. No panic...except for now, when Dr. Hill says, "Looks like we're having a baby today!"

It was a routine appointment, one we've been attending every week since Aurora was put on bed rest a month ago. Once she told them she was throwing up again, we went directly from the obstetrician's office to the maternity unit for observation and tests.

Ethan grips the back of the chair beside the hospital bed, the blood drained from his face. "But he's early?"

"Yes, a bit early, but thirty-five weeks is not unusual—especially when the mother has preeclampsia." She offers a reassuring smile.

Aurora sits upright, her hair in a messy bun, her eyelids drooping despite having slept most of the day and night. Reece adjusts the pillows behind her. He hasn't left her side in days. He's been warning us this would happen, saying her blood pressure was far too high.

I take Ethan's hand, finding it cold and clammy. "But everything's okay, right? Aurora and the baby will be okay?"

Dr. Hill nods. "Baby's vitals are strong. He's a good size. I would recommend a C-section, though. The baby's movements have slowed, and I'd like to avoid any further risk."

We just saw our son on the ultrasound; the technician pointed out his full head of hair. No one said there was a problem.

"Let's do it," Aurora cuts in, voice trembling. "When?"

The doctor checks her phone. "I'd say within the hour."

I swallow to wet my dry throat. My cheeks tingle, and I realize I've forgotten to breathe.

Holy fuck. We're having a baby.

Ethan sways on his feet and blinks repeatedly. "I...we don't have the nursery finished. The crib isn't assembled. We haven't even packed a hospital bag. I've been busy. I-I had a plan."

Of course he did. Coach always has a strategy.

The doctor leaves, and the room becomes a whirlwind of activity. Nurses bustle in and out, hooking Aurora up to more monitors and tubes. They explain the procedure, rattling off risks and protocols while Reece hovers, absorbing every word. Ethan paces beside the bed, texting frantically, his jaw clenched so tight, I worry he'll crack a molar.

I'm trying to focus, but my mind keeps screaming, "Today! Our son is coming TODAY!"

"Jax," Aurora calls out, reaching for me, her eyes shimmering. "I'm scared."

My own eyes well up. "It's okay to be scared." I take her hand in mine, careful of her IV. "I love you more than life itself. Everything will be alright." It has to be. I won't survive otherwise.

Her tears spill over, her words nothing but a whisper, her lips quivering. "I just want the baby to be okay."

"He's going to be perfect." I wipe her tears away, barely hanging on myself. *"You're* going to be perfect. You've given us the greatest gift. Thank you." The painful lump in my throat prevents me from pouring my heart out any further.

I've taken blows that broke bones, been driven into the boards so hard, I saw stars. I watched Reece almost die. But nothing, absolutely nothing, has ever terrified me as much as when the doctor walks in wearing scrubs.

"It's time," she announces, leaving no room for argument. "The surgical team is ready."

My heart hammers erratically against my ribs. My legs nearly buckle. Two nurses shift Aurora from the bed onto a gurney, and I can't release her hand. It's physically impossible. She's my lifeline.

"Can they all be there?" she asks, small and frightened.

A nurse grabs the IV pole and detangles the lines. "Only one support person in the operating room, I'm afraid. It's hospital policy."

Panic flashes across Ethan's face. Jesus, he's going to pass out.

"Go," I tell him, though it kills me. "Go meet your son."

His wide eyes search mine. "He's your son too. Are you sure?"

"Yeah." I nod, even as my chest constricts. I want to be with Aurora. I want to be there when our son enters the world. "I'll get the next baby." I force a smile I don't feel and release our girl's hand for him to take.

I lean down and kiss her one last time. "I love you—so fucking much." I press my forehead to hers. "I'll be waiting right here."

They wheel her away, Ethan alongside her, whispering reassurances I can't hear. The door swings shut, and it's only me and the Viking, the room silent.

My body shakes and my knees grow weak. My vision blurs.

Reece wraps his arms around me from behind, catching me before I hit the floor. "Easy. They'll be okay. Just breathe."

***

Ethan

I follow Aurora and the gurney down the hallway, the world narrowing to the squeak of the wheels and the thud of my shoes on the linoleum. We turn a corner, where a nurse hands me a pile of blue paper scrubs and a mask and points me to a closet-sized bathroom to change.

My fingers tremble so hard, I can't undo my belt. I bite the inside of my cheek until I taste blood and force myself to breathe in, hold, breathe out. Aurora needs me. My son needs me.

I have no clue how long it takes, but I get the scrubs on. I'm too flustered to figure out the mask, so I tie it around my neck and leave it dangling.

I exit the changing room, and she's gone. "Where is she?" I snap at the nurse.

Despite my pissy mood, he smiles, covers my head with a mesh cap, fixes my mask, and leads me to the surgical suite.

The cramped operating room is bright white. I'm dazed, as if I'm walking through a strange dream. She's already on the table, draped, masked, big brown eyes wide with terror.

The anesthesiologist is talking—something about a spinal, a sedative, don't touch anything blue, but everything is blue, and Aurora's arms are strapped down. Why are her arms strapped down? How will she hold the baby?

Oh my God, they're going to give *me* the baby.

I almost laugh deliriously, but then the OB is speaking, fast and sharp.

"We're starting. You'll feel a lot of pressure, Aurora."

I see the tip of the scalpel over the curtain, my stomach turns, and I glance away. Aurora's eyes are fixed on me, and I know I'm supposed to be her rock, but my teeth are rattling.

"You doing okay, love?" I manage.

"I-I'm going to have a scar to go along with the stretch marks. Battle wounds," she chuckles, but it's nervous and self-deprecating, her shoulders shaking uncontrollably.

I bend down, but I'm unsure if I'm allowed to touch her, to comfort her. "They're cutting my son out of you. I'll worship you 'til my death. Don't worry about a scar or a few stretch marks."

The doctor urgently calls out orders. I peer over the curtain and gag. It doesn't seem real. The lights are too bright. Christ, is there supposed to be that much blood?

They tug on Aurora's abdomen, and my head spins. How do women live through this? Fuck, we shouldn't do this again. One child is enough. *This* is enough. I'm about to have a fucking stroke or throw up. Most likely both.

A nurse holds up a slippery, bluish being who somehow came out of Aurora's body. He's motionless, and I start to panic—my heart pounds in my throat, my fingertips tingle. I swear, I'm going to faint, but then a wet, garbled cry splits the silence, and my legs nearly give out in relief.

The medical team exchanges times, numbers, and scores. None of it matters, though, because he's wailing, fists clenched and furious, a shock of dark hair slimy with blood and goo.

Aurora sobs, "Is he okay?"

They release one of her wrists, and I grip her hand in mine. "He's beautiful," I choke out. "Baby, he's perfect."

A nurse wipes him down, suctions his mouth and nose, and wraps him tight like a burrito. Then, my son is in my arms. His small face is scrunched, eyes squinted shut against the harsh hospital lights, and I pull him tighter into my chest.

"Hey, little man," I whisper, my throat constricted with emotion. "I'm your dad—well, one of them. You have so many people who love you."

His head fits perfectly in the palm of my hand. He has Aurora's upturned nose, and his lips are a miniature bow, puckered like his mother's. A dimple in his left cheek appears and disappears with each mewling protest he makes.

All the oxygen leaves my lungs. I can't breathe, can't

think. I can only stare at this tiny human who contains pieces of us, and for the third time in my existence, I fall so hard in love, it physically hurts.

"Let me see him, Ethan. Please," Aurora cries, tears streaming down her temples into her hair.

A nurse adjusts her gown to allow for skin-to-skin contact, and I bring our baby to her, bracing his tiny body in both hands so nothing can go wrong.

Sobbing, she kisses his head, and my son calms in an instant.

Still working on the other side of the curtain, the OB congratulates us. There's beeping, and the anesthesiologist checks something on the monitor and inserts a syringe into Aurora's IV. The neonatal team waits to whisk Eli away, but Aurora and I are in a bubble. The world can fuck right off.

She stares at our son through tear-soaked lashes, searching his face. "He looks like you." Her tone is slightly slurred and weak.

"He has your nose and lips. He's beautiful. You did it, baby." My chest swells with pride. "You fucking did it." I kiss her temple, her hair, her forehead.

A different doctor—the pediatrician, I believe—clears his throat, hovering with the gentlest persistence. "Dad, we need to take him to the NICU now."

I press my lips to the baby's soft cheek. I don't want to let him go. I don't think he should leave my arms. They take him from me anyhow, and suffocation builds in my lungs. My gaze remains fixed on Eli as they lay him in the bassinet.

"Go with him, Ethan." Aurora's voice fades, and her eyelids slip closed.

I'm torn. I wish one of the other guys were here to stay with her.

The anesthesiologist reassures me she's fine—her blood

pressure spiked, and they've given her some medication. They're finishing the surgery, and I'll see her soon.

With a heavy heart, I listen to Aurora and follow the pediatric team through the swinging doors and down the corridor.

***

Reece

Jax stares at the door, his elbows on his knees, his fingers steepled at his lips. He sits so close on the couch, his thigh is pressed to mine. He even rested his head on my shoulder a few times. Months ago, no one could touch him except Aurora. Now, he soaks up affection as if he's starving.

I can empathize. Jax and I possess similar qualities. I hadn't realized how alike we are until I came face-to-face with my fucked up family.

Meeting Lucas taught me to accept people I was conditioned to hate. Jackson showed me how to embrace my flaws and move forward. He never once gave me shit about my parents. He welcomed Harper and Danny without question. He could've been a dick to them to spite me, but he genuinely cares.

I put an arm around him and squeeze his shoulder. "Not much longer."

We were safety-checked, tagged with bracelets to match the baby's, and moved to a locked area near the NICU. That was over an hour ago, and Jackson has been coming out of his skin, alternating between pacing, questioning the nurses, and tearing up.

All we were told was Aurora was in recovery and the baby was in the NICU. If cleared by the doctor, he'd be able to stay with us in the specialized postpartum suite.

The door swings open, and a nurse wheels in a clear bassinet, Ethan close behind. He's still in scrubs, his hair damp and tousled, his face tight with worry.

Jax leaps to his feet. I follow slowly, tilting my head to peer past them, searching for our girl. My stomach sinks. She's still not here.

Ethan doesn't wait for the bassinet to stop before he scoops up the fussing infant and cradles him to his chest. "Do either of you know if Aurora plans to bottle or breastfeed?"

"Both," I answer. "So we can all bond with Eli."

Jax leans into Ethan and gazes at the baby, his eyes glassy. He brushes a knuckle across the infant's cheek. "He's so tiny," he whispers, his voice thick with emotion, a shaky breath escaping him.

Ethan's nostrils flare. "Five pounds and eight ounces. His blood sugar is a tad low, but they won't allow me to feed him without Aurora's permission." He shoots a harsh glare at the nurse, his jaw clenched.

Oh shit. Daddy mode has kicked in. Ethan is not about to let his son go hungry while Aurora recovers, and she'd want us to feed the baby.

"She plans to supplement with formula." I slip my phone from my pocket. "She picked out a brand if needed. I have a picture."

The nurse smiles politely. "That won't be necessary." After checking our bracelets, she retrieves a pre-made bottle.

Jax gives his boyfriend pleading eyes. "Can I feed him?"

"Of course." Ethan's expression softens. "Remove your shirt. The doctor said preemie babies benefit from skin-to-skin contact."

Jackson yanks his shirt off, tosses it on the couch, and sinks into the recliner. Ethan carefully hands the infant over, and I help adjust the blanket. Eli releases a cute little cry and shoves his fist in his mouth. He's so small; he looks barely bigger than my hand.

The moment the baby settles against Jackson's bare chest, his face just...crumples. He drops his head and nuzzles Eli as silent sobs rack his body.

Ethan cups Jax's nape and traces his thumb over his jawline. "He's beautiful, isn't he?"

He really is, with dark hair and perfect, delicate features.

Jackson nods and sucks in a deep breath to collect himself. Ethan gives him the bottle, his fingers trembling. He's running on pure adrenaline.

The infant's face scrunches in protest when the nipple touches his lips. "Come on, little guy," Jax coos, gently trying again. "You gotta eat, bud."

Eli takes to the bottle on his third try. Jackson exhales in relief and kisses the baby's forehead.

The nurse hovers close by. "He won't eat much, but he'll want to eat often."

"We got it," Ethan grumbles, one hand on Jax's neck, the other brushing Eli's hair.

She steps away, giving us space and making herself busy stocking the bottom of the bassinet.

I get Ethan a chair then lean against the other side of the recliner. "You okay?"

His eyes meet mine, a scowl between his brows. "They pricked his heel and all kinds of other stuff. He was *screaming*, and they wouldn't let me hold him. Felt like I was going to murder someone."

I can't help but smile. Wait until he finds out about circumcision.

"He shouldn't go anywhere without one of us," Ethan continues. "And watching them cut open Aurora... Jesus fuck, that was horrible. We don't spoil her enough for this shit."

"Where is she?" Something doesn't feel right, and my stomach twists. "She should be here by now."

He runs a hand through his hair, his shoulders tight with tension. "Her blood pressure spiked after delivery before it bottomed out. She lost more blood than they expected. Nothing dangerous," he adds when my posture stiffens and Jackson's head snaps up. "They're monitoring her closely, giving her medication." He swallows hard, his throat clicking. "They won't release her until she's stabilized."

Panic splinters in my chest. "I'm going to find her."

I ignore the nurse calling after me and push through the door. The maternity ward is a maze of hallways and rooms, but all I'm focused on is finding the woman I've sworn to protect and care for.

A stern-faced security guard sits at a small desk, blocking my path to the surgical suite and recovery room. He points to a sign. "Immediate family only."

My patience snaps, and I flash my bracelet. "I am fucking family. I should've been with her the entire time."

The guard stands. "Sir, you need to calm down."

Urgency surges through my veins. What I *need* is to lay eyes on her. "We can do this the easy way or the hard way. If you don't open that door, I'm going to do it myself."

He scans me from head to toe, seeming to weigh his options against my six-foot-six frame.

"I'll escort him," a familiar voice says behind me. "He's on her approved list."

Dr. Hill swipes her badge, and I follow her down the hall.

"The preeclampsia caused some complications during delivery," she explains. "We're administering medication to prevent seizures and hemorrhaging."

I make a noise of acknowledgment, my throat too tight to speak.

The recovery area is dimly lit, with partitioned sections

and the steady beep of monitors. She pulls back the curtain, and my heart stops. Aurora lies curled in a ball, pale against the stark white pillow, her thick lashes fanning her cheeks.

She shouldn't be alone like this, and I reach her in two strides. Carefully avoiding the IV lines and wires, I climb into bed beside her, just like she did for me when I was shot. "Te amo," I whisper.

Her eyes blink open. "Reece," she rasps. "I was waiting for you."

"Oh yeah?"

"Yeah." Her eyelids droop, her chest rises and falls. "My baby?"

"The most beautiful thing I've ever seen—after you, of course." I brush a strand of hair from her brow. "He's taking a bottle from Jax right now."

Her lips curve in a weak smile, and her eyes flutter shut.

I press a kiss to her temple. "You gotta get better. Ethan is a mess, growling at all the nurses. Jax is barely hanging on."

"I'm sorry," she mumbles. "I don't feel very well."

"I know, angel. Rest. I got you."

Her icy fingers find mine. "Viking?"

"Yes, princess?"

"You're never gonna let me have coffee again, are you?"

I scoff. "Never. Your blood pressure is too wonky."

***

Aurora

I wake to the sound of tiny cries and soft snoring.

"Shh, little man. Let your mommy and daddy sleep. They're exhausted, and the more tired your dad is, the louder he snores."

I open my eyes to find Jackson pacing and rocking the

baby. Ethan is asleep in the recliner, and Reece is passed out on the couch, sitting up. The hospital room is dim, with just a faint yellow glow from the baseboard lights.

"Jax, bring him here. I'll feed him." I grimace as I shift in bed. Each movement sends a jolt of pain through my abdomen, and my incision throbs under the bandages. The pain meds are wearing off, but I push past the discomfort, eager to hold and nurse my baby.

"Sorry we woke you." He gives me that crooked smile. "He only started fussing a minute ago." Jax settles beside me against the pillows, Eli cradled against his bare chest. His hat is on backward, hair sticking out the front, his eyes heavy, but he's beaming with happiness. "You need to be careful with those stitches."

"I'm fine." I pull back the blanket to see my son's sweet face—I can't get enough of him—then untie my gown. "What time is it?"

"Around midnight. We held off visitation until the morning, since you came out of recovery late." He carefully transfers Eli into my arms, helping me support the baby's weight. "Rocco arranged a catered dinner for the entire unit as thanks for dealing with us—well, for dealing with Ethan and Reece. I've been an absolute angel."

"For once," I joke, resting my head on his shoulder.

It takes a few attempts for Eli to latch. The doctor says it's normal, especially for a preemie, but eventually, he connects and starts to suckle.

I gaze at our baby, his tiny mouth working intently, his dark lashes lying on his dimpled cheeks, and every ache and pain is worth it.

"He's actually here," I whisper, afraid to break the spell of this moment.

Jackson gently strokes Eli's soft hair. "I can't believe he's real. I refuse to sleep; I'm worried if I do, I'll wake, and this will all be a dream."

His tone is raw. I glance up, and his bright green eyes swim with tears.

"It's real." I press my lips to his, letting the kiss linger. "We're not going anywhere."

He rests his forehead to mine. "Ethan says I'm not allowed to pressure you into having another baby, and if you don't want another one, I completely understand. Eli is enough. But if you ever do, I want you to know, it'll be different." His voice breaks, his Adam's apple bobs, and his breath shudders. "I won't fuck it up, I promise. I won't relapse. I won't be an asshole. I…I won't do this to you. I'm so fucking sorry." His last words are barely audible, his body trembling.

My heart clenches. "Hey, stop." I cup his face with my free hand and brush away the tears that escape down his cheek. "This is not your fault, Jax. These things happen. I'm okay. Eli is okay. You have so much love to give. You're going to be a great dad—to Eli, to any kids we have. We'll figure it out. We always do."

After a while of us staring at our little miracle, he asks, "If you could get married any place in the world, all four of us, where would it be?"

Wedding Bells and Baby Making
Summer 2026

About the Author

Jessica Lyn is a dark romance author who loves hockey, the mountains, and snow. She lives on the Oregon Coast with her family and a never-ending list of pets.

Her stories, initially chart-topping Kindle Vella serials, are influenced by a decade-long career in psych triage.

Outside of writing, she's into reading, traveling, crime docs, and a strong cup of tea.

Printed in Dunstable, United Kingdom